Snowballs, Fluff, and Murder

A Cozy Magic Midlife Mystery

Silver Circle Cat Rescue Mysteries
Book 5

Leanne Leeds

Snowballs, Fluff, and Murder
Silver Circle Cat Rescue Mysteries #5
ISBN: 978-1-950505-96-8

Published by Badchen Publishing
2709 N Hayden Island Dr.
STE 103131
Portland, Oregon, 97217

For permissions contact: info@badchenpublishing.com

Never try to outstubborn a cat.
— Robert A. Heinlein

Contents

Chapter One

My shoes squealed against the glossy tile floor as I bustled around the café, hastily gathering up abandoned mugs and crumb-strewn plates. I scooped up the messy dishes in my arms, the remaining dregs of coffee sloshing within their white ceramic confines. Weaving around the wooden chairs, I made my way behind the counter and unceremoniously dumped the dishes into the large plastic bin.

It felt like the end of the day.

But it wasn't.

It was only ten on a Tuesday morning.

Despite the hour, there were no customers tucked into the mismatched armchairs, no line at the counter, and no eager hands were outstretched to pet the resident shelter cats—who were no doubt devastated by the lack of attention. The chalkboard menu touted coffee and scones for a crowd that wasn't coming. Outside, the sky hung heavy and gray, like a soggy wet blanket stretched to the horizon.

Tablerock seemed to batten down the hatches, bracing for the cold front. Its impending attack was like the clock striking midnight on Cinderella's ball, except everyone was rushing home before turning into popsicles rather than pumpkins.

"That's the last of the dishes, Mom," Evie said as she closed and turned on the dishwasher behind the café counter.

"Great. I think we've got everything put away, so let's focus on the shelter side next," I said, trying to sound upbeat despite the nervous flutter in my stomach.

I looked out the front windows, taking in the ominous battleship gray sky. The clouds looked fit to burst, heavy with the promise of an impending once-in-a-lifetime Texas snowstorm. To add to the impending threat, an aggressive wind whipped through the bare tree branches outside like skeletal fingers clawing at the glass.

I shivered, and not just from the cold seeping through the windowpane.

This was shaping up to be the worst winter storm in decades, if not ever, to hit our small Texas town—well, not just our small Texas town. The entire state appeared to be on the verge of freezing over. We rarely got more than a dusting of snow down here, if at all, but the panicked forecasts were calling for up to a foot of snow, as well as drizzle that threatened to turn roads into sheets of ice because of below freezing temperatures that could last for several days.

We Texans could jump out of the way of a striking rattlesnake without even spilling our sweet tea, but snow and ice? A few flurries could do us in without even trying. We were about as well-equipped for blizzard conditions as a guppy in the arctic.

The jingle of the front bell drew my attention, and I looked up, expecting to see a customer—but instead it was Landon entering with all the flair of an action hero stepping onto the stage. His salt-and-pepper hair was damp from the icy mist and it gave him a sparkly, mythical look. In his gloved hands, he carried a plastic tote filled with split firewood.

All he needed was some epic background music and he'd look ready to slay a dragon or build a log cabin with his bare hands. Guess the storm wasn't keeping my knight in plaid flannel away after all.

"Hey, babe, how's it going?" Landon asked cheerfully, stomping the ice from his boots. "I've got my place all locked up and the heater set, faucet's dripping. Okay if I wait out the storm here with you?"

He smiled innocently as if I was doing him a huge favor instead of the other way around.

"Of course—welcome to the arctic apocalypse. We're just getting things cleaned up and prepped on this side," I said. "The shelter area is next. I want to take all the cats upstairs to the third floor—since heat rises, I think that's going to be the most comfortable place for them."

"Great. As you can see, I loaded up on extra firewood so we can keep the wood stove burning if we lose power. I have a few generators in my van, too," Landon said as he headed in to unload the tote. "Joe—the guy I hired to upgrade the electrical on this old house—did a good job with the wires underground, though, so I think we'll be okay."

The café door jingled open once more, bringing cold air in with Evie's boyfriend, Matt. He stumbled through the doorway, his lanky frame bent by the howling wind outside. He ran a hand through his disheveled hair as he pushed the door shut against the icy gale.

"Aye, it's getting nasty out there!" Matt exclaimed as he stomped the snow off his boots, flecks of slush spattering across the welcome mat. Shivering, he unwound the navy scarf from around his neck, his cheeks flushed red from the biting wind. Grasped in his leather-clad palms he carried coils of orange extension cords, an array of flashlights, and what looked like an overnight bag. "I brought some more of these in case the power goes out."

I reached for the supplies in Matt's arms. "Thanks. I'll put them upstairs—that's where we're going to keep the cats and probably ourselves. Are you riding out the storm here with us?" I frowned. "What about your grandmother?"

Matt's laugh lines crinkled as he grinned like a kid on Christmas. "Abuela's soaking up the sun in Mexico right now while we're all stuck in this tundra."

I raised an eyebrow.

"She's visiting my great-aunt. Not gonna lie, I'm a little jealous she might be lounging on a beach in paradise, sipping margaritas, but I'm glad she's safe. She hates the cold." He rubbed the back of his neck, glancing around the empty café. "But yes, I was hoping I could stay here. I thought you might need the help, too."

"Well, of course, Matt. Consider our home your home. You're welcome to stay as long as needed."

"Gracias, Ms. Rockwell. I'll help move the cats."

Matt trudged up the stairs, two plastic cat carriers balanced carefully in his hands. As he reached the landing, he exchanged familiar nods with Landon, their heads bobbing in greeting.

Having worked alongside each other on many café and shelter projects, an easy camaraderie existed between the two men. Their sturdy builds and casual rapport gave them the air of brothers, though Landon's salt-and-pepper hair betrayed their age difference starkly.

The next hour passed in a blur of activity as we prepared the shelter side, making sure the third-floor cat area was clean and stocked with blankets, the cat litter was brought in from the outside storage, the cats were fed, and the emergency supplies were stocked.

Laurie breezed in from the attached vet office, her cheeks flushed rosy red from the cold. As one of my closest friends and Tablerock's resident veterinarian, she was a welcome sight.

"This storm's shaping up to be a veritable beast,"

Laurie said, unwinding a chunky ivory scarf from around her neck. "My morning was a complete wasteland of cancellations. The brand new heater is sputtering like a dying jalopy and doing almost nothing for the exam rooms. They're so cold I can practically see my breath clouding in front of me."

She rolled her eyes in exasperation. "Why on earth did I think installing gigantic bay windows in the exam rooms was a good idea? Might as well have put in an ice rink!"

As I handed Laurie a steaming mug of coffee, Landon was stoking the fireplace, the warmth radiating outward. "You didn't want those energy efficient double-paned windows, remember?" he reminded her.

"I'm sure I did not say that."

"Oh, I'm sure you did."

"Fine. I admit it. I was cheap—and now I changed my mind. Do they make triple paned windows?" she deadpanned, warming her hands on the mug.

"They have quadruple paned windows," Landon told her. He was like a walking Home Depot ad. "But since you only wanted to pay for single-paned and weren't particularly happy with that, you won't like the price."

"I don't care. I'll take those," Laurie nodded. "Just as soon as I can chisel my checkbook out of my frozen drawer. Can you get them installed by noon?" She took a sip. "And in case you were wondering, I absolutely did mean noon today."

Landon chuckled sympathetically.

"Do you want to bring the patients you have up to the third floor?" I asked her, pointing upward. The news droned on about the winter storm in the background, warning of dangerously icy roads, power outages, and frigid temperatures not seen in decades. "We have more than enough room. I'm bringing all the cats upstairs. I think it's going to be the warmest place in the house."

Laurie considered it for a moment. "I don't actually have patients right now, just boarders. Two dogs and one cat—from the same home—are here while their owners are out of town. It might not be a bad idea to move them, just in case we lose power on the clinic side. That, and we can concentrate on heating just one space."

"You staying here?"

"Mia and Oliver took Shep and Sherlock with them to Gary's, so I'm good," Laurie said, referencing her two teen children and two Rough Collies. "They thought the dogs would cause too much of a ruckus if I brought them here." She smirked. "Did I mention that Gary just got a new velvet couch? I'm sure he's thrilled to have those shedding machines there."

Laurie appeared to have a rapport with her ex-husband, and I was occasionally envious of the ease with which they balanced annoyance at one another with support for the sake of the kids. She frequently coordinated school pickups and drop-offs for her two children, and they'd show up to their children's sports games together, politely chatting on the sidelines.

"At least we're all together here," Evie said, pulling her cardigan tighter around herself. She gave me a brave smile, but I could see the tension in her eyes. Storms and prolonged power outages were slightly concerning for her because of her heart condition. I reached over and gave her hand a comforting squeeze.

"Absolutely," I said firmly. "We'll hunker down and weather this thing. The most important thing is that we are prepared, and we're all safe."

The wind howled outside like an angry pack of wolves as the first flurries began swirling past the windows like tiny butterflies. Our cozy little cat shelter suddenly felt about as sturdy as a house of cards against the snowy wrath Hurricane Frosty was bearing down on our small town.

The café door suddenly flew open with a bang like a gunshot, letting in a blast of frigid air and shouted voices that hit me like a shockwave. I jumped about a foot in the air, nearly tossing the mug in my hand up to the ceiling like a catapult. Frozen fingers of air crept down my collar, making me shiver.

"You should have just stayed at the station, but noooo, you had to insist on driving over here in this mess!" Josephine exclaimed, her voice loud enough to cause an avalanche.

"Are you serious? You're somehow blaming me that

you don't know how to drive in snow without careening all over the road?" Mario volleyed back, their bickering at full volume.

My eyebrows shot up in surprise as Josephine and Mario barreled inside.

Josephine shimmied out of her stylish wool coat like a glamorous snow princess, tiny ice crystals scattering to the floor. Beside her, Mario shrugged off his police department jacket and placed it near the heater grille. His cheeks appeared flushed from cold… or possibly likely annoyance at Josephine.

The two hadn't been getting along very well of late.

"Um, hi guys," I said tentatively. "Is everything okay?"

Josephine huffed and turned. "No, it's not! Officer Know-It-All here drove over even though the roads are horrendous. And then I slid into a tree trying to avoid him, and even though it's his fault, he won't stop lecturing me about it!"

"You crashed because you don't know how to drive in winter conditions," Mario countered. "Just because your Cadillac has all-wheel drive doesn't mean it's the same thing as four-wheel drive. There's a difference! You never should have been on the road with—"

"Oh please. It has four wheels, and it's all-wheel drive. Obviously that means it's four-wheel drive," Josephine shot back, her angry, know-it-all attitude on full display.

"So, Josephine, that's not actually how—" Landon started in his usual patient peacemaker tone.

I quickly reached out a hand to stop him. "I wouldn't."

Landon raised an eyebrow. "But she's wrong, I should just explain—"

"Trust me. Do not go down that road," I advised. Trying to correct Josephine when she was in a mood like this was like poking a hibernating bear—you'd only end up getting mauled.

Landon looked back helplessly, clearly wanting to set her straight but also valuing his safety.

Mario and Josephine continued their heated debate, unleashing creative insults at each other as they unwound their snow-flecked scarves and gloves. Josephine's usual immaculate style was disheveled from the wind, her sleek black hair mussed and damp. Mario's dark hair stuck up every which way, making him look like he'd stuck his finger in an electrical outlet.

Clearly their short drive over had been eventful.

Suddenly, Mario turned to me, looking chagrined. "Sorry for just busting in like this, Ellie. After Josephine bumped into that tree, your place was the closest spot I could get to safely. I would have called, but the cell signal seems to be a problem right now."

Evie looked at her phone. "We still have internet."

"For now," Laurie said.

"You make it sound like I crashed into that tree!" Josephine harped on Mario's earlier comment. "I just gently brushed against it when the car slid a teensy bit. And it was completely your fault for being in my way, anyway!"

Mario rolled his eyes so hard I thought they might get stuck pointing at the back of his head. "There's still bits of tree bark embedded in your front fender from 'brushing' that tree," he muttered.

I could see them getting ready to argue again, so I stepped in between them. "Don't worry! I'm glad you're both safe, and the tree and car will be dealt with after the storm. Come on, everything is being moved to the third floor. That's the most comfortable warmth-wise."

Josephine grumbled under her breath but followed me toward the stairs, dragging her feet like a pouty toddler.

"I better get back out there and make sure no one else is plowing into trees," Mario said, unable to resist one last jab. He looked pointedly after Josephine. "You're welcome for getting us here safely, by the way! I'm sure you just forgot to say thank you."

Josephine whipped around, mouth open for a fiery retort, but I looped my arm through hers and steered her away from Mario. "Let it go," I whispered.

The two of them—the feisty attorney and the by the book (mostly) cop—had always had something of a fractious relationship, but things had really deteriorated after Alice Grey's murder around Christmas. The case had driven a wedge of mistrust between Josephine and

Mario, their clashes growing more frequent and more caustic.

Nowadays, it was rare that Josephine and Mario didn't snap at each other. Every interaction between them teetered on the brink of utter disaster, like a dynamite shed surrounded by lit fireworks. One wrong word could turn their combative spats from mere squabbles into a full-fledged, no-holds-barred war of words with explosive verbal attacks that made me wince.

Just as Mario turned to leave, his police radio suddenly crackled to life, a burst of static words breaking the silence. He paused mid-step, forehead creasing in a deep frown as he leaned in to listen intently.

"Copy that," he responded tersely into the radio after a few seconds, his grave tone sending a prickle down my spine. Mario returned to us, fatigue etching new lines around his eyes.

"What is it?" Landon asked.

"Just got word that all roads are now considered impassable due to ice build-up," he announced, raking a hand through his tousled hair. "The department wants all police personnel to shelter in place until it's safe to travel again."

Mario's shoulders slumped slightly as he delivered the news, and Josephine let out a sharp huff of breath, her eyes widening. Their reactions said it all—we were now well and truly snowed in, severed from the outside world.

The storm had claimed the roads, and us along with them.

My eyes widened in surprise. "I thought the storm wasn't due for a couple of more hours. If it's this bad now..."

"It's already below freezing, so it's already bad." Mario nodded grimly. "A few cars have already slid off the roads. An ambulance got stuck trying to get to a crash scene. It's too dangerous for any vehicles to be out there right now."

"In other words, it wasn't my fault," Josephine snapped.

Mario glared at her.

"Wow," Matt murmured. "Okay, then."

"You two are more than welcome to stay here with us," I said to Mario and Josephine. "Safety first."

Josephine and Mario's eyes met, mirrored reluctance in their tense expressions. More time together was clearly the last thing they wanted in their fraying state. Josephine's mouth pressed into a thin line, fingers drumming impatiently on her arm. Mario's shoulders slumped as he gave a resigned shrug, acquiescing to necessity over personal feelings.

"I guess we don't have much choice. Thanks, Ellie," he said politely—if not enthusiastically.

Josephine sniffed, avoiding looking at him. "Yes, thanks ever so much," she added in a tone dripping with sarcasm. The tense silence that followed was thick with unspoken aggravations, crowding even this large space.

I resisted the urge to knock their stubborn heads together like coconuts.

"It's no problem at all for you both to stay," I said briskly, forcing cheer into my tone. I clasped my hands together. "Now, who wants more coffee? Hot chocolate?"

Josephine arched one sculpted eyebrow. "No bourbon?" she asked.

Sure.

That's what this situation needed.

Booze.

Chapter Two

I MADE MY WAY UPSTAIRS TO THE ISOLATION ROOM while balancing two saucers full of tuna chunks—one for Belladonna and one for Ginger. As I pushed open the door, I was met by two pairs of golden eyes peering out from the shadows.

"Good morning, you two," I said cheerfully, setting the food down. "I brought a treat for breakfast." I hoped my chipper tone masked the slight frustration I felt at needing to bribe the imperious Belladonna into cooperating with... well, anything.

Ginger bolted straight into the food with gusto, purring eagerly as he buried his face in his own dish, but Belladonna emerged regally from her cat tree, leaping down to the floor slowly. She sauntered over with deliberate movements to inspect the offering, flicking her tail with a queenly indifference.

She delicately picked up a morsel of tuna with her teeth.

"Only the finest tuna for you, your highness," I said, laying the flattery on thick. Belladonna spared me the briefest of withering looks, as if to say I was dangerously close to crossing the line between humoring her and humiliating myself.

Admittedly, there were days I did not see the difference.

Once the sleek black cat finished, she hopped back into the cubby with the crystal talking plate and turned her intense gaze on me, eyes narrowing. "I sense a disturbance in the atmosphere today, human," she declared ominously. "The skies grow heavy with ill portent. I am sure you humans can't sense it, but a great calamity approaches."

"We have things called radars, so we know about it. There's a big winter storm headed our way," I explained. "They're saying it could be historic for this area. We're expecting a lot of snow and ice over the next few days."

"You need to see an image of what's coming on a screen?" Belladonna licked a paw indifferently. "We felines detected the shift in the atmosphere days ago. Your human contraptions for predicting such things are terribly primitive."

I made a mental note to curb my embarrassing impulse to treat Belladonna like feline royalty when I needed something from her.

She already had a big enough ego.

"I was thinking you and Ginger should join us upstairs on the third floor. We're moving all the animals there, and we're going to hunker down upstairs for the duration. It should stay warmest up there."

Belladonna's ears flattened. "And why, pray tell, would we leave our perfectly comfortable quarters down here?"

Didn't I just explain that?

"Heat rises. It will be warmest on the third floor. I just want to keep everyone together in one space so we can keep the heat concentrated," I explained. "We have blankets, food, litter—everything you need. Come on, Bella. It will be like a fun sleepover."

Belladonna gave me another withering look. "A sleepover implies voluntary participation for amusement," she scoffed. "This is clearly an evacuation under duress."

"Well, maybe so," I conceded. "But it's for the best."

Belladonna heaved a great sigh, as though I had asked her to trek through the wilderness rather than go up a flight of stairs. "Very well. If we must suffer this indignity, then suffer it, we shall. Come, Ginger!"

With that, she swept imperiously out of the room, tail held aloft like a flag leading a procession. Ginger scrambled after her obediently, nearly tripping over himself in his eagerness to keep up.

Upstairs, the third floor was abuzz with activity as we prepared it for its new occupants. The resident cats eyed us bustling humans curiously from their perches atop the cat trees and tunnel maze lining the walls.

I set Belladonna and Ginger's bowls on a small table near the others. The two newcomers sniffed cautiously at their new environment.

Suddenly, the door burst open and in marched Laurie, followed by a parade of furry companions. Two excitable Maltese dogs yapped and pranced about, while a stately white cat glided alongside, walking in synchronized steps with Laurie.

The resident cats peered down in bewilderment at this canine invasion.

"Riley, Sadie, Princess—come on in and make yourselves at home," Laurie said warmly to the three animals.

Princess the cat immediately hopped up on a cat tree and began meticulously grooming herself, apparently nonplussed by her new surroundings. The two Maltese dogs, Riley and Sadie, yapped eagerly, tails wagging, as they inspected every corner and tried to sniff the wary cats peering down suspiciously from their perches, eyes wide and ears flattened.

Belladonna took one look at the frolicking dogs and her eyes went wide with horror, as if Laurie had unleashed a pack of rabid wolves. With a hiss, she hightailed it out of there as fast as her furry legs could carry her, heading straight back downstairs to her isolation room sanctuary.

Ginger scrambled after just as swiftly, nearly wiping out on the hardwood in his haste to follow her.

"Oh, come on, you two. The dogs will leave you alone," I called after them reassuringly, but my words didn't slow their indignant exodus.

Laurie raised an eyebrow as she watched Belladonna's exit. "She still isn't a fan of dogs, huh?"

"Nope. But we knew that considering how she reacted when you started using the talking plate drink tray thing with canine patients," I said. "Nothing's changed. I guess this is a bit much for them."

As the day wore on, fat snowflakes began swirling outside the windows, tossed about in the building wind. The forecasted storm had arrived.

I busied my restless hands entertaining cats with strings and laser pointers, tidying shelves, reorganizing supplies—anything to keep my nerves at bay.

Matt and Landon kneeled before the stone fireplace, feeding crackling logs into the flames. Warmth emanated from the hearth, driving back the icy chill that tried to creep in through every crack and crevice. I shivered and rubbed my arms briskly.

Josephine sat hunched on the sofa, scowling down at her laptop screen. Her manicured nails clicked aggressively across the keys as she typed. I glimpsed phrases like "unacceptable behavior" and "reevaluation of your role" peeking through the gaps between her fingers.

I didn't envy the recipient of that message. Josephine in a temper was a force to be reckoned with.

It was mid-afternoon when the blizzard began in earnest, and the temperature outside plunged.

Mario stared out the window, looking down every so often as updates crackled through his police radio. His brow furrowed as each new report came in.

"Two-car collision over on Oak Road. No injuries reported. Drivers advised to find shelter or drive home if able," the radio squawked.

"Tree down blocking access to Briar Lane..."

"Widespread power outages being reported..."

The radio dispatches painted a vivid picture: calls coming in one after another, the situation outside deteriorating by the minute, and Mario's expression grew more agitated with each update. Being cooped up here while people needed help out there was a little like torture for him.

As dusk fell, the snow swirled ever thicker and heavier. The world outside the frosted windows faded bit by bit. Bright streetlights across the road became hazy halos, then mere shadows behind the icy veil. The lined rooftops of houses blurred, indistinct shapes disappearing into the white void.

"I have never seen anything like this," I murmured.

In reality, no one had.

This was a winter storm for the ages.

Laurie and I prepared quick meals—a hearty venison chili made with the meat Landon had hunted, some crusty bread from the café, and a salad rounded out the simple dinner. It wasn't fancy, but it warmed our bellies on this frigid night.

Night fell as we ate, darkness swallowing the world outside.

Though it wasn't like we'd been able to see much, anyway.

Mario scraped the last bits of chili from his bowl, then set it down with a ceramic clink. "At least we still have electricity," he commented. His gaze flicked pointedly to Josephine. "I guess we should be thankful you hit a tree and not an electrical pole."

Josephine's spoon halted midair, chili dripping back into her bowl. Her eyes narrowed to icy slits. Shoulders tensing, she slowly lowered the spoon. The clank of it hitting the ceramic bowl reverberated in the silent room.

Then, with a resounding bang that made us all jump, she slammed both palms down onto the tabletop. Her bowl of chili teetered, thick red liquid sloshing over the sides, dripping down to splatter the plastic picnic tablecloth I'd brought up.

Uh oh.

Her meticulously outlined lips peeled back into a snarl. "I have had just about enough of your sanctimonious needling of me," she seethed through gritted teeth. Josephine jabbed an accusing finger at Mario. "We need to either have this out, or you need to shut up. Which is it going to be?"

Mario held up his hands defensively. "Whoa, let's just take it down a notch here," he said. "No need to get all worked up. It was a joke."

"It was not a joke. Don't tell me not to get worked up when you've been needling me nonstop since you got here," the lawyer shot back. Her fury rippled through the room like flames licking along a lit fuse, and the situation felt poised to explode.

"I haven't been needling you," Mario insisted. "I just made a joke about you hitting a tree, that's all. Lighten up."

A red flush mottled Josephine's complexion. "Lighten up? Lighten up? Oh, please—that is not even close to all. You've made snide comments and given me attitude every time you've been within three feet of me for months." She leveled a bitter, glacial glare in his direction. "So let's have it out right here and now. What exactly is your problem with me?"

Mario shifted uncomfortably, avoiding her gaze. "I don't have a problem—"

"Horse pucky," Josephine interrupted sharply. "Spit it out."

Mario met Josephine's icy glare with a smoldering one of his own. "You really want to know?" he bit out.

"Spit it out."

He leaned forward, broad shoulders tensing. "My problem is how you have no qualms demanding *I* break every rule to help you, but then the second things get tough for you, you disappear."

Josephine's lip curled derisively. With a flip of her glossy hair, she waved a dismissive hand, but before she could say anything, Mario snapped at her.

"You asked! Don't ask and then wave your hand like you're a judge dismissing a lawsuit!" He slammed a fist down on the table, making the dishes rattle. "I'm expected to show loyalty to this group. Keep the talking cat nonsense and the information they spit out under wraps." His lip curled derisively. "But where's the loyalty from you, huh? Where's the reciprocity?"

Josephine scoffed, tossing her hair. "That's completely different and you know it. I have professional and ethical obligations guiding what I can disclose related to client privileged information."

"Oh please, client privilege?" Mario rolled his eyes. "I think you get off on playing games with people. I put my career on the line for this group and this cat stuff. But you?" He let out a harsh bark of laughter. "You high-tailed it out of here the second it served you, leaving the rest of us to fend for ourselves."

"Nonsense! I have a duty to uphold the law and the legal protections, same as you," Josephine shot back.

"Yeah, and I have a duty to fully disclose details related to any criminal investigation. Withholding information could cost me my job," Mario argued. He loomed across the table, eyes boring into hers. His voice dropped to a gravelly whisper. "So you tell me, Josephine—everyone can risk but you?"

"You'd get another job easily enough somewhere else. Me?" She jabbed a finger into her chest. "I'd be disbarred. Never allowed to practice law again." Her eyes locked onto him, frigid and severe. "So show me where in your precious police manual it says you have to tell all and sundry about talking cats and magic plates. Go on, I'll wait." Josephine stared back, unflinching, jaw clenched tight.

"You just don't get it, do you?" Mario clenched his jaw. "It's about integrity. I can't just pick and choose which facts to disclose based on personal preference. I have a code of conduct, and I break it every time I hear a tidbit of information from a cat that I wind up chasing down."

"For goodnes's sake, Mario, we all have codes of conduct," Josephine shot back. "Mine requires privilege and discretion in the representation of clients. Yours has plenty of gray areas. More than mine, by the way." She leaned forward, eyes flashing. "Again—if I violate client confidentiality, my entire career goes up in flames. So don't talk to me about loyalty and integrity when you don't face the same stakes."

Mario's mouth opened, a heated retort already forming. But before he could unleash it, I quickly stepped between the two sparring adversaries.

"Okay, let's all just take a breath here," I implored, holding my hands up in a calming gesture. I made eye contact with each of them. "This storm has everyone stressed and on edge. Tempers are flaring." I kept my voice low and soothing. "Let's step back a second."

I watched the corded muscles in Mario's forearms relax marginally as my words sank in. Behind me, I heard Josephine let out an irritated huff of air. But she thankfully held her tongue.

Keeping my placating stance between them, I continued, "How about I make some tea and we can all just… relax a little?" I suggested, trying to further defuse the tension.

Josephine gave a curt nod, not looking at Mario. "Fine by me."

"Yeah, okay," Mario agreed begrudgingly.

I quickly busied myself preparing mugs of chamomile tea in an electric teapot we'd brought up while Mario and Josephine sat in prickly silence. Matt and Landon exchanged awkward glances but wisely kept their mouths shut.

Minutes later, I distributed the mugs, the aroma of soothing chamomile mingling with the lingering scent of chili. Josephine accepted hers wordlessly, immediately taking a long sip.

Mario blew on his before tasting it. "Thanks, Ellie," he breathed. I could tell he was still simmering about the argument, but was keeping a lid on it for now.

I waited a beat, ready to intervene again if needed—but for now, this temporary cease-fire would have to do.

I wasn't always so unconcerned about it. I, too, felt

upset and a little betrayed by Josephine's disappearance during the Alice Grey case. But Josephine and I had discussed it, both apologized, and promised to handle things differently if a similar situation arose again.

You know.

Like grownups.

Mario and Josephine didn't seem capable of that same reconciliation yet.

Josephine set her mug down with a soft clink. "I should not have lost my temper," she admitted begrudgingly. "That was unfair of me."

Mario's eyes widened slightly in surprise. "Yeah, well, I, uh, shouldn't have antagonized you, either," he responded after a pause. "I'm on edge from being stuck here... but that's no excuse."

Neither offered the other an apology.

But it was something, a form of progress—although shaky and fragile.

"I think we're all on edge. The storm has everyone wired up," I said.

Around us, the wind continued to howl, rattling the windows in their panes. But inside, the mood had lightened a fraction. There was still tension simmering below the surface, but the fire of anger had dimmed.

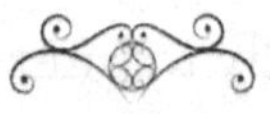

Evie set down her mug and looked around. "How about

we take our minds off the storm for a bit? Does anyone have a good story to share?"

Josephine perked up at the suggestion. She swiveled to face me directly, cocking one sculpted eyebrow. Crossing her legs, she leaned in, giving me her full attention. "You know, I don't think you've ever told me the full story of how you and Evie ended up in the town of Tablerock. What made you leave Austin and start this place?"

I leaned back in my chair. "Well, it's kind of a long story..."

"We've got time, Mom," Evie said with an encouraging smile.

"All right then." I shifted to get comfortable, readying myself for the tale. "Back in Austin, I worked as Director of Customer Service for a small business called Tiny Tangy Solutions." A wistful smile tugged at my lips. "I loved that job—had been there over a decade. My team was like family."

I gazed off, momentarily lost in fond memories. "I took genuinc pride in providing good service and taking care of my employees." I gave a small self-conscious laugh. "I know. It sounds cheesy. But it meant something to me. I really believed we were doing good—providing good jobs, good service." I shook my head, a tinge of old sadness in my eyes. "Naive, I know."

"I feel a *but* coming on here," Josephine said.

Clearing my throat, I continued. "Anyway, about ten years ago, the owners sold the company to a big conglomerate..." I trailed off, seeing it all play out again: the forced reorganizations, the hostile takeovers, the hours long meetings, the way everything we'd built crumbled slowly until nothing was left. My shoulders slumped at the recollection. "Tiny Tangy Solutions got bought out by a huge corporation, Perseverance Worldwide Holdings, and everything changed."

Matt shook his head sympathetically. "That's usually how it goes with big buyouts."

I nodded. "At first it was small things—fewer perks, reduced budgets. Then they started laying people off and consolidating roles. They demanded we bring in less qualified people at lower salaries to replace people with experience."

"Mom was so stressed out," Evie said.

"I was. It was difficult. They altered our approach to customer service. It was no longer about actually helping people, but about squeezing the most productivity out of cheap labor to increase profits and providing the bare minimum of service to avoid losing customers. They disgusted me.

"I realized after a while it wasn't *them*. It was me. It was what they were asking of me, and what I had to do as a condition of my job. My goal there was no longer to look after my team or to provide good service to our customers. It was to wring every ounce of profit from the ground like water from a stone." My voice was filled with disgust. "When they made me fire hundreds of loyal employees as part of more 'streamlining,' that was the last straw."

I took a long sip of tea before continuing. "Of course, opening my mouth against that meant I would be next on the chopping block. Sure enough, a month later, my position was eliminated, and I was shown the door."

"That's... well, I was going to say awful, but honestly, Ellie, it's not an uncommon story," Josephine said. "I'm sorry it happened to you, though."

"No, you're correct. It's not unusual." My head shook. "I swore I would never again sacrifice people for corporate greed or be complicit in such ruthless behavior. I had a bit of a nest egg thanks to the severance, so I got as far away from that environment as possible. I wanted to start over somewhere new." I laughed. "With cats."

Evie reached over and squeezed my hand supportively.

I gave her a grateful smile. "And that's how I wound up here in Tablerock, using the severance to buy our original property and turn it into the shelter. No more putting profits over people."

"Good for you," Josephine said forcefully. "I've seen way too many companies pull those same awful moves. It takes courage to walk away instead of compromising yourself."

"It really is an inspiring story, Ellie," Matt added with an admiring grin. "Not everyone walks away from corporate America to do something selfless. You took a bad situation and turned it into something great."

It had been a tough road, but knowing I had made the right choice to leave a toxic environment buoyed my spirit.

"What happened to the company after you left?" Laurie asked curiously.

I shook my head. "It sold itself again. The rich got richer, while the people who made it what it was got screwed. I heard through the grapevine that customer complaints have skyrocketed, and employee turnover is now at an all-time high."

The old pain and anger I expected to resurface as I told the story never did. Instead, a sense of calm washed over me. The story wasn't as painful as it used to be. Looking around at my dear friends and our cozy shelter, I realized I was content with my current situation.

Tablerock had given me so much—purpose, community, love.

My past struggles faded considering all I had gained.

I couldn't regret the pain anymore, because it had brought me here, and as much as Perseverance had tried to dim my inner light, they hadn't succeeded.

They had given me the courage to shine even brighter.

Chapter Three

After I finished telling the story of how I came to start the cat shelter, a contemplative silence settled over our little group. The only sounds were the crackling fire and faint howl of wind outside.

"Well, I know a bunch of cats that are happy you wound up here, Ellie," Landon finally said, breaking the silence. "I'm sure it wasn't easy leaving your career behind, but you took a bad situation and created something wonderful here."

I gave him a grateful smile. "Yep, went from corporate cog to crazy cat lady in one fell swoop. At least the cats are honest about being self-centered divas—unlike certain executives I used to deal with. What about you, Landon?" I looked at him. "What made you decide to become a carpenter?"

"My daddy gave me Lincoln Logs before I could crawl." Landon leaned back in his chair, a thoughtful look crossing his rugged features. "And he's the one that got me into woodworking." A wistful, faraway look entered his eyes. "He was a master carpenter—had these huge, muscular hands that could make anything out of wood. And I mean anything. As a kid, I used to love visiting him in his workshop, watching him measure, saw, and sand pieces of wood until they turned into tables, bookshelves, chests..."

He trailed off, shaking his head with a rueful little smile. "Growing up, I was in awe of him. The way he could take simple materials and create these sturdy, beautiful, functional items—I know it's just a skill, but it seemed like magic to me."

I could picture a young, wide-eyed Landon full of admiration for his talented father. There was still a hint of that adoration in Landon's eyes now when he spoke of his dad, and it reminded me of how Evie used to look at her own dad when she was little. Before everything soured between us.

A lump formed in my throat as bittersweet memories of those innocent, trusting days flooded my mind, but I quickly shoved the recollections away before they could fully form.

Now wasn't the time to let old regrets claw their way to the surface.

"By the time I was about ten years old, I was desperate to be just like him," Landon continued. "So he started teaching me the basics—how to use the different tools properly, how to look at the wood grain and visualize what it could become. We worked side-by-side on projects, his big, calloused hands guiding my smaller ones."

Landon's voice took on a rough edge. "When I was fourteen, Dad was diagnosed with stage four lung cancer. It was already really advanced by the time they caught it." He cleared his throat. "He only lived another eight months after the diagnosis."

A heavy silence settled over the room. I reached out and gave Landon's arm a sympathetic squeeze. Losing a parent so young was a pain I couldn't imagine.

After a moment, he continued. "In those last months, Dad and I spent as much time together in his shop as we could. At first, he still took the lead, showing me the steps. But eventually, as he got weaker, I started taking on more of the work myself under his guidance. I think..." Landon's voice wavered slightly. "I think he wanted to pass on as much of his knowledge as he could before he ran out of time."

Despite the sheen in his eyes, a fond smile crossed Landon's face. "We worked on his final project together—a beautiful cherry wood crib for my baby sister, who was on the way. The day we finished, it was one of the proudest and saddest of my life. I think I knew, somehow, that my sister would never get to meet our amazing father."

My heart ached imagining what Landon's mother must have gone through—grieving the sudden loss of her beloved husband while preparing to bring a new life into the world. The emotional whiplash of it all was unfathomable. I couldn't even conceive of how she found the strength to go on.

"Dad died less than two weeks later. At the funeral, I promised him I'd keep pursuing woodworking, maybe apprentice with another carpenter someday. I owed it to him to carry on the legacy that gave me such pride as a kid."

His story gave me a new appreciation for Landon's inner strength and maturity. He had taken hardship and loss and crafted something meaningful from it.

"I'm so sorry, Landon," I murmured sympathetically. "It's clear how much your father meant to you. Losing him must have been incredibly painful."

Around the room, the others echoed similar words of condolence.

"Sorry for your loss," Matt and Mario offered sincerely.

"That's awful. I can't imagine," Evie added, her voice filled with compassion.

Even Josephine set aside her typical sarcasm, simply shaking her head and saying, "My condolences. No child should have to experience something so traumatic."

Landon lifted his head, meeting my gaze. "So that's why I became a carpenter. It connected me to my father and carried on his memory. Every time I work with wood, I feel closer to him."

Losing a parent was a nearly unbearable pain, but clearly Landon had gained so much from the time he shared with his father. I couldn't help feeling a swell of admiration for the man beside me.

"It was a beautiful story, Landon," I whispered. "I'm sure your father would be so proud of the talented carpenter you've become."

Landon gave me a small, sad smile. "I hope so." As if he wanted to lighten the somber mood that had fallen over the room, he turned to Josephine. "What about you? What led you to pursue the law?"

Josephine straightened, an impish grin spreading across her face. "Oh, that is quite the story!" She chuckled. "You see, I was something of a troublemaker as a child."

Matt's eyebrow arched upward skeptically. "Oh, really?" he drawled, his voice tinged with sarcasm. "I find that hard to believe."

"You watch that tone, young man," Josephine told him, but she wasn't seriously annoyed with him. "Yes, I was a bit of a teenage malcontent. I constantly had run-ins with authority figures for my little... well, let's call them indiscretions. Nothing too terrible, mind you, but I was quite the independent spirit." Her eyes twinkled with mirth. "I talked my way out of trouble so often that my mother predicted I'd become either a con artist or a lawyer."

Evie laughed. "Well, I'm glad you decided on a lawyer. I can't picture you as a con artist."

I could.

"Indeed," Josephine said primly. "Anyway, the

definitive moment came in middle school when a friend and I got caught sneaking into the teachers' lounge. Back then, it was a smoky and mysterious place that we were just sure held many secrets. Secrets, of course, we wanted to know."

Landon chuckled. "The smell of the smoke would have given you away."

She waved a hand airily. "You're probably right, but we didn't think about that. We just wanted to see what kind of gossip we could overhear, and we'd thought about doing it a dozen times but were sure we'd get caught."

"I'm pretty sure that eventually, you do it," Laurie said.

"I'm pretty sure she's going to get caught when she does," Evie told Laurie.

Landon shook his head. "I think she managed it."

"Hush, all of you. On this day, it was around Thanksgiving and when we peeked in, we saw a table covered with a tablecloth for the teacher's potluck. That was our chance, and we took it. We slid into the room and hid under the table listening to all sorts of entertaining stories not intended for our ears—not realizing, of course, they'd remove that tablecloth right after the turkey potluck."

"Which they did," Mario guessed.

"Indeed."

"They saw you?" Evie asked.

"Almost immediately." Josephine's eyes danced with

delight. "Naturally, I did what any quick-thinking almost-teenager would do—I immediately burst into obviously fake wailing, going on about 'the voices' and how I was just looking for a quiet place because the cafeteria was too noisy. My friend, catching on, said she knew something was wrong with me and she was just trying to help me to the nurse's office."

By this point, we were all chuckling at the image of a young Josephine boldly feeding teachers lies from under a table.

"So a teacher pulled us out, baffled," Josephine continued. "My friend was useless by that point, just staring wide-eyed like a deer in headlights. But I kept going on about auditory hallucinations and sensory issues, throwing out every psychobabble term I could think of."

She smirked triumphantly. "We didn't just get out of trouble—that teacher took me under her wing, suggesting all these accommodations for my 'issues' and even started a special class for kids with sensory problems before anyone knew kids had sensory problems. I milked it for the rest of the year, but my lie actually morphed into something pretty good for that school and students that truly needed extra help."

"Wow," I said. "Honestly, not where I thought that story was going."

"That was the moment I realized I could talk my way into or out of anything. I was destined to become a lawyer. I realized a good argument, even if not precisely true, has the power to change things for the better." She gave an exaggerated bow. "The rest, as they say, is history."

I chuckled.

Leave it to Josephine to bend a nosy childhood adventure involving a form of trespassing and disability appropriation into a school sensory accommodation program and a blossoming legal career.

Matt chimed in. "I think everyone here knows my career origin story since I just joined my uncle's P. I. firm." He gave a self-deprecating shrug. "Nothing as exciting as dodging teachers or making masterpieces with Dad."

"Right," Evie drawled, her eyes glinting playfully. "A magic plate that allows cats to talk is just such a boring catalyst for a career change."

At that, everyone burst into genuine laughter, the rich sounds reverberating around the room. Matt held up his hands in mock surrender to Evie's sarcasm.

"Okay, okay, you've got me there," he admitted with an affable grin. "What about you, Evie?"

Out of the corner of my eye, I saw Evie's smile falter ever so slightly. She fidgeted with the hem of her sweater, a nervous habit she'd had since childhood.

"Oh, you know..." Evie trailed off vaguely with an airy wave of her hand. She avoided meeting Matt's gaze.

"I don't know if I really knew or chose to do this with the cats, honestly," she mumbled. "Like, would I have if it had been my choice? I don't know. Maybe. With my situation, it's not like I had a lot of options."

My heart ached at her defeated tone.

I opened my mouth, but before I could respond, Landon leaned toward Evie and asked, "You don't think you would have helped your mom with the shelter? Was there something else you wanted to do?"

Neither of us enjoyed discussing the limitations her health issues placed on her life.

Evie finally lifted her head. "No, that's not what I mean," she said hurriedly. "I do want to help Mom and care for the cats. It's just..." she trailed off uncertainly.

I looked at my daughter. "You don't *have* to talk about this."

With a small sigh, she said, "No, it's okay. Sort of. It's just... my heart condition didn't really impact my life too much as a kid. I mean, it did. A lot. But I didn't realize it. Yeah, I had surgery when I was two to fix a congenital defect. And then more surgeries. I had activity restrictions and regular cardiology appointments." Evie absently traced the scar on her chest through her shirt. "But I didn't understand back then how limited my options would be. How early I'd have to think about my career and life path based on my health and need for health insurance."

Evie was disabled. Not having health insurance was dangerous (even life threatening) for her, and her frequent inability to work made losing health insurance treacherous. Her doctors recommended she get on disability to ensure she had medical insurance, and so she did as soon as she turned eighteen.

But being on disability was very difficult.

Evie met my eyes before continuing. "In school, other kids were dreaming about becoming astronauts or Olympic athletes or rock stars. But me?" She gave a sad little laugh. "By high school, I knew I'd never be able to scuba dive to see coral reefs up close, so marine biology was out. I couldn't join the cheer team or play sports, and my grades weren't great, so scholarships were out. I couldn't go skydiving like some of my classmates planned for their senior year."

Her shoulders slumped slightly. "While friends were getting excited about college and travel and adventures, I was trying to be pragmatic and... scale back my expectations for my life." She absently twisted a strand of hair around her finger. "Eventually, I accepted that my heart meant limiting my dreams, so... I guess I never developed this big life's passion that you all had. Helping Mom with the cats just seemed like the practical choice, given my reality."

As Evie finished her story, her eyes took on a faraway, melancholy look, and my throat tightened with emotion, but before I could find words, Landon spoke up.

"Evie, just because your ambitions had to be more practical and accommodate some issues doesn't make them any less meaningful," he said. "Life throws us all kinds of curves. What matters is what we do with the cards we're dealt." He smiled encouragingly. "And from what I've seen, you play your hand well. You have so much compassion and dedication, and you don't give up. Your mom and these cats are lucky to have you."

Evie offered him a tremulous but grateful smile. "Thanks, Landon. I'm lucky to have all of you, too."

She blinked rapidly then, as if holding back tears, then turned her gaze down to study her hands folded tightly in her lap once more. Her shoulders curved inward, making her seem smaller, more vulnerable.

Seeing Evie retreat into herself like that clutched at my heart. I wished I could protect her from the pain and self-consciousness her health challenges caused. But all I could do was be there for quiet support when she needed it.

I reached over to give her arm another gentle, reassuring squeeze.

At my touch, she looked up, managed a smile, then took a bracing breath before straightening her spine. The weight of memories seemed to roll off her as she centered herself once more.

As everyone finished up their chili, Mario and I started clearing the small tables scattered around the room. The cheerful clinking of bowls and utensils filled the air as we stacked them efficiently.

I caught Mario's eye and tilted my head toward the makeshift washing area in the corner. "I'll wash, you dry?"

He nodded agreeably and followed me over. The tiny sink was really meant for washing cat bowls and dishes, but it would work for our chili night necessities, too.

I reached over and cranked the hot water knob, expecting a rush of steamy liquid. Instead, a frigid burst of water shocked my fingertips. I adjusted the knob further, but not even a hint of warmth flowed out.

I sighed, watching the relentlessly cold water swirl down the drain.

Well, at least the pipes weren't frozen and the main line was still functioning. Small mercies. The hot water heater may have gone out—or it was so cold, the water cooled before reaching the faucet.

As if to mock me, the electricity flickered.

With the last bowl dried and put away, I turned to find the rest of the group settling into the spacious third floor.

Evie was curled up catlike on the plush couch, completely lost in the pages of a thick novel. She absently twirled a strand of her chestnut hair as her eyes rapidly scanned the lines, her face animated with intensity.

On the jute rug in front of the flickering fireplace,

Matt and Landon sat cross-legged, intently focused on their poker game. Matt's brows were furrowed in concentration as he peered at his cards, while Landon leaned back casually against a cat cabin, poker chips stacked high in front of him.

Laurie lounged next to Josephine on the adjacent loveseat, fully absorbed in scrolling through her phone. The lawyer had her laptop open on her thighs, but her attention was divided between answering emails and dodging the cats constantly trying to walk across her keyboard. I could hear her intermittent sighs and irritated mutters about "incompetent clients" and "annoying cats."

The shelter felines had indeed claimed every available surface and draped languidly across laps and arms, kneaded threadbare cushions, or groomed themselves near the fire. I was just debating whether I should try to lure Belladonna and Ginger back upstairs when Mario stood and cleared his throat tentatively.

"Hey, uh, since we were all sharing stories earlier, can I tell you guys why I became a police officer?" Mario asked.

Laurie glanced up from examining her nail beds. "Oh, I didn't share why I became a vet, either."

She paused for dramatic effect before hitting us with...

"I like animals."

Laurie punctuated this mind-blowing revelation with an oblivious shrug.

Riveting stuff.

Someone call Hollywood and get this woman a movie deal.

"That's it?" I asked. "No emotionally moving childhood memories of nursing an injured squirrel back to health? Just... you like animals?"

Laurie nodded. "Yep, I like animals. That's it!" She waved her hand toward Mario with the flair of a master showman. "Please, wow us with your noble motivations for becoming a cop after my jaw-dropping story arc. I'm sure it'll have us all on the edge of our seats."

Mario shifted his weight, suddenly looking like he wanted to sink into the floor. "Uh, you know what, maybe we'll wait—"

"Nonsense!" Josephine cut in, giving him a sharp look over her glasses. "You brought this up, Mario. No backing out now just because you have to follow an impossibly entertaining act."

Laurie just smiled while Mario fidgeted under our expectant gazes.

"It's just... not the typical reason you'd expect. But it shaped who I am." He raked a hand through his dark hair. "It involves an old classmate of mine who disappeared when I was in my twenties." His gaze dropped, pain flickering across his face. "Her name was Juna Brucker. I don't know if any of you remember the case."

The lighthearted mood in the room deflated faster than a balloon at a dartboard convention.

Chapter Four

Mario shifted his weight, rubbing the nape of his neck as he gathered his thoughts. "It's not the usual story you'd expect," he began slowly. A frown creased his brow, and he raked a hand through his dark hair. "Juna Brucker was a classmate of mine."

At the name, his gaze dropped to the floor, pain flashing across his face. He took a deep breath before continuing. "We went to high school together here in Tablerock. I'd known her for years." Mario lifted his eyes, meeting each of our gazes in turn. "Some of you may remember when she disappeared. It was all over the local news at the time."

Evie and Matt exchanged curious glances and shook their heads. Landon frowned, pondering it for a moment before shaking his head as well.

"You know, I think I do recall that name, actually," Josephine said slowly, tilting her head. "Wasn't she that young musician who went missing about... oh, maybe fifteen years ago?"

Mario nodded, looking mildly surprised that Josephine remembered his friend. "Yeah, that's right. I'm a few years younger than you, so it was back when I was in my early twenties." He leaned back against the sofa, crossing his arms over his chest. The firelight flickered across his face. "Juna was incredibly talented—she could play guitar, piano. And her voice..." He shook his head, looking off into the distance. "I'll never forget it. Clear as a bell with this aching sweetness."

Mario went quiet for a moment, seemingly lost in the melancholy memories. The only sounds were the crackling fire and howling wind outside.

"Were you two involved?" I asked him.

Mario's lips quirked in a bittersweet half-smile. He glanced away almost shyly. "No, we weren't a couple." A wistful look crossed his face. "I definitely tried to get her attention, but we were just friends." Mario's expression sobered, his smile fading. "No disrespect to my Cecelia, but I regret now not telling her how I really felt back then. Maybe things could have been different that night."

He shook his head as if to clear it and continued his account, the lingering heartache audible in his voice.

"Anyway," he said after a deep exhale, "she was a year older than me and used to perform down at Whiskey Bend—this little dive bar on the outskirts of town. The one at the crossing?" He gave a small, sad laugh. "She would never have gone there normally, but she wanted to perform so much. Juna drew in crowds."

I knew the Whiskey Bend.

The worn, weathered building sat right on the highway intersection before entering Tablerock, making it hard to miss. With its dingy windows, fading wood exterior, and neon signs advertising cheap beer, the dive bar had always given me an uneasy feeling thanks to the rough, intimidating patrons often gathered out front.

The firelight flickered in Mario's dark eyes as he went on. "I remember she was driving out to play a set one night when she just... vanished. Her best friend, Clara Adams, found her car parked on the shoulder of the road leading out to Whiskey Bend, still running, lights on. Like she'd stopped for some reason. But inside..." Mario's voice grew hoarse with emotion. "Inside was her three-month-old kitten, Fluff. No trace of Juna. It was like she'd evaporated into thin air."

"Poor baby," I murmured. Yes, okay, it was for the tiny kitten. But my heart ached for Juna just as much as her pet left alone in the car.

He paused and jerked his head, giving the impression he was trying to dislodge the painful memories. "They searched for weeks but never found a single trace of what happened to her. No leads. No clues. Nothing." His hands curled into fists at his sides. "And after a while, people just seemed to give up and move on. Even Clara."

Losing a friend in such a sudden, inexplicable way

had clearly left scars on Mario's psyche that still lingered.

"I'm so sorry, Mario," I murmured sympathetically. "That must have been incredibly painful and confusing for everyone who knew her."

He nodded, gazing into the fire. "It actually tore our friends' group apart. We were in our midtwenties, we felt invincible. We didn't know how to process something like that—the injustice of it. The lack of answers." Mario's jaw clenched, old anger and helplessness simmering under the surface. "Juna's manager Gordy accused Clara of not caring enough, of giving up too easily. Clara got—" He looked up. "You don't need to hear about this. Anyway, I joined up with the police academy as soon as I could."

"To find Juna?" Evie asked.

"To find anyone that might disappear. I felt the police didn't care about her, that they just shrugged off her disappearance. I wanted to make sure that never happened, that I would bring answers where there were none. Justice where there was none." He shook his head firmly, as if shaking off the last remnants of hard memories. "I wanted to be able to tell grieving families that the case was solved or give them closure they desperately needed."

"That's very admirable, Officer Lopez," Josephine told him.

Mario lifted his gaze from the fire, making meaningful eye contact with each of us in turn. "I don't know about admirable. But I became a cop to speak for those who weren't here to speak for themselves. For those like Juna."

"No, I agree with Josie. That's admirable, Mario," Landon said supportively. "You know, difference makers usually have powerful stories behind what drives them. Yours will help you stay centered on your purpose when things get difficult."

Mario gave a humble shrug. "I just want to live up to the ideals and ethics that drew me to law enforcement in the first place. Uphold the law, absolutely—but also care about people and outcomes over stats or political games." He sighed deeply, some of the stoic rigidness easing from his posture.

"I hope that old case gets solved someday. I know it's a long shot after all this time, but Juna—and all the other cold cases out there—deserve justice," Matt said.

I felt like I understood Mario better. His powerful account of losing someone close in such a traumatic, unresolved way explained so much about the man he had become. I could see now why he usually viewed law enforcement in such black-and-white terms—the rules created order in a world where terrible things could happen for no reason.

"Well," Josephine said, "I can't argue that seeking justice for those wronged or harmed is a worthy endeavor." She gave Mario an appraising look. "Perhaps you and I disagree at times on how precisely to bring about that justice. But it seems we share the same fundamental goal of protecting those who need it."

The prickly lawyer's statement of support wasn't exactly glowing. But, given how they'd been treating each other lately, this grudging acknowledgment of their shared values felt like a standing ovation.

Mario's eyebrow quirked upward in surprise. "Maybe."

This was the closest I'd seen Josephine and Mario get in a long time. Perhaps they were finally remembering that, despite their sharp words and opposing approaches, they were both trying to uphold justice in their own way.

Matt lifted his mug. "To seeking justice."

As I brought the chamomile tea to my lips, the rising steam washed over my face, soothing and warm. In that instant, inhaling the sweet aroma mingling with traces of our shared meal, I felt profoundly grateful for the connections circumstance had woven ties between this unlikely group of people.

"Is it just me, or is it getting even colder in here?" Laurie asked, rubbing her arms briskly.

I took a look around. The glowing fireplace provided warmth, but there was an icy undercurrent in the air that no amount of tea or firewood could dispel. Despite cupping the hot mug, my fingertips were chilled.

"You're right, it does feel like it dropped a few degrees," I agreed.

"I'll add another log," Landon offered, rising to stoke the fire once more.

Matt looked at his phone screen. "Whoa. The temperature is down to twelve degrees Fahrenheit now. No wonder it feels so much colder. That's... that's crazy cold."

Spending a childhood in Upstate New York had hardened me to frigid temperatures, but Texas winters rarely reached below freezing for more than a few hours at a time. This relentless, bone-deep cold was foreign to this land and most of these people.

"Well, we knew this storm was going to be one for the record books," Mario said.

Almost on cue, he glanced down as his police radio sputtered to life with another weather update. Ice accumulation on the roads was getting worse. An eighteen-wheeler had jackknifed trying to exit the highway. Emergency crews were struggling to respond.

Mario picked up his cell phone. "I should try calling Cecilia again to check in," he said. "The cell service has been sketchy with the storm and I haven't been able to reach her since dinner." Worry creased his brow as he scrolled to his wife's name.

It went to voicemail after several rings went unanswered.

Mario's brow furrowed even more.

"Hey babe, it's me again," he said after the tone.

"Still riding out the storm over at Ellie's shelter. Roads are completely iced over now, so I'll be here for a while longer. Call me when you get this. I hope you and the furry kids are staying warm. Love you." He ended the call and scrubbed a hand over his face. "Voicemail again. The cell towers must be overwhelmed. Or frozen."

"I'm sure she's fine," Evie tried to reassure him. "You guys got that new internet with the satellite things in the sky like us, right?"

He nodded.

"We still have internet—she probably does, too. Send her an email. Maybe you two can do a call on Scoot."

I shuddered at Evie's mention of Scoot, that awful video conferencing software that forced you to stare at a grid of faces from around the world. It was like a creepy cartoon come to life, with all those pixilated people gawking at you through the screen.

I hated Scoot.

Still, Mario's concern was understandable, and Evie's idea was a good one. Being separated from loved ones during a crisis put everyone on edge.

Across the room, Josephine pulled out her own cell phone. "I should try Charlie again, too. His conference was supposed to wrap up today, so he's likely trying to fly home by now—though I can't imagine planes are taking off in this weather."

She navigated to her husband's name and put the call on speakerphone. It rang five times before clicking over to a robotic voice mail message.

Josephine frowned. "Charlie, darling, it's Josie again. I'm still at the cat café riding out this dreadful storm. The roads are impassable now, so it appears I'll be stuck here for the foreseeable future. I do hope your flight wasn't delayed or cancelled, but I suspect it was. Do ring me back when you get this message. I'll keep trying you. Ciao for now."

She ended the call with an irritated huff. "Honestly, the cell service during this mess is utterly abysmal."

"You just made a call," I pointed out.

"But he didn't pick up."

"That's not the phone company's fault."

"You don't know that.

"The networks are probably overloaded between the weather and people trying to reach each other," Matt said with a nod. "It's possible neither of the calls rang on the other end."

"Traitor," I told Matt, then winked.

"People need to communicate in times like this." Josephine tucked her phone back into her handbag. "I shall have to lodge a strongly worded letter of complaint with the telecommunications commission once this tempest has passed. For now, I'll send Charlie an email. Maybe wherever he is, they've got those newfangled internet sky balls, too."

Josephine sounded confident, but somehow I doubted a strongly worded letter from one crabby customer would revolutionize cellular infrastructure during natural disasters.

But far be it from me to stomp on Josephine's indomitable spirit.

I stood, collecting the empty mugs scattered around the room. "Anyone want more tea or coffee to warm up?"

A chorus of no's and head shakes answered me.

At the utility sink, I gave the hot water knob an experimental turn. Just like before, only an icy gush poured out. I jerked my hand back with a gasp again, and felt silly.

"Still no hot water?" Landon asked, coming up behind me.

I shook my head in bafflement. "It's like ice. I figured it would have heated back up by now."

Landon frowned. "The hot water heater itself is likely fine. But with the brutally cold outdoor temperatures, the water is probably cooling off before it can travel up the pipes."

"Oh, that makes sense," I said. Though not super helpful in actually getting hot water again.

"Since the main line still works, once the indoor temperature rises, the water flowing through the pipes will stay warmer and we'll get hot water again." Landon gave me a reassuring smile. "This old house just has a lot of plumbing to heat. But don't worry—we've still got electricity heating the water heater."

I sighed, willing the laws of science to cooperate. "As long as we don't lose power, we should be okay, then."

As if on cue, the overhead light flickered ominously.

I held my breath, imagining the power shorting out and leaving us in total blackness. We'd be reduced to cowering around emergency candles like it was pioneer times.

Landon and I exchanged uneasy glances.

"I brought gas generators just in case," he said. "It's fine. We'll be all right."

Despite the brave front, I could hear the faintest waver of uncertainty in his voice. But I nodded confidently, trying to mirror his reassurance. "Absolutely. We're prepared."

But were we really?

For a storm of this scale in a house this old?

I didn't know the answer.

I also didn't want to find out if the answer was no.

I busied myself tidying the kitchenette, willing away my nerves. As I washed the mugs by hand in the icy water, I thought of Belladonna and Ginger, still sequestered away on the second floor. I should check on them and try once more to coax them upstairs where the group was gathered.

After putting the last mug away, I grabbed a jacket, put it on, and headed for the stairs.

"I'm going to go down a level and check on Bella and Ginger again," I announced. "Hopefully, I can convince them to come join the rest of us up here where it's warmer."

"Do you want me to come with you?" Matt asked, halfway rising.

I waved him off. "Thanks, but I've got it. You all stay and keep warm."

Evie gave me a knowing look. "If anyone can sweet talk those two into moving, it's you, Mom."

I doubted anyone could, but I crept down the shadowy second floor hallway toward the isolation room, keeping my footsteps light. If Belladonna sensed an entourage approaching, it would only make her balkier.

Wait—is balkier a word?

If it isn't, it should be.

Approaching the closed door, I stared in confusion. How on earth did these two cats manage to get the door completely shut? I supposed they could have jumped up and pushed it closed somehow, but it just seemed odd...

Though, frankly, it was no odder than them mysteriously escaping the isolation room day after day. I still had no explanation for that.

I rapped my knuckles lightly on the door. "Bella? Ginger? It's just me. I wanted to check in on you two." When no yowling protest met my greeting, I eased the door open.

Inside the cozy space, Ginger was curled up on a cushion near the small heated bed where Belladonna perched regally. Two sets of luminous eyes fixed on me as I entered.

"Evening," I said to the imperious black cat. "Are you and Ginger faring all right down here?"

Belladonna stared at me a moment longer, her vivid golden eyes unblinking. Then she rose gracefully and sauntered over to the cubby housing the magic talking cat platter. "We are adequate," she intoned in a cool, aloof manner as she settled herself delicately on the crystal surface.

"Good, I'm glad."

She began languidly grooming her front paw, feigning indifference with each slow lick.

I inched closer. "I know you two aren't thrilled with the crowd upstairs, but it's getting chilly." I rubbed my chilled arms for emphasis. "I really think you'd be more comfortable if you joined us on the third floor where the entire group is gathered. It's warmer with the fire going, everyone in there, and the heat rising."

I waited for a response, but Belladonna merely blinked those inscrutable golden eyes.

"We have food, cat trees, toys..." I told her. "Anything you need to be comfortable. I even broke out those flannel blankets you like."

The aloof cat stared back silently. Just when I thought she'd ignore everything I said, with a swish of her plumed tail, she spoke.

"While we remain content in our own domain, the declining temperatures do present a small cause for consideration," Belladonna said with a begrudging frustration. She turned her face toward me. "If you can ensure our comfort and dignity are not unduly compromised by this upheaval, then we shall permit our relocation."

It took all my willpower not to roll my eyes at

Belladonna's haughty declaration of "allowing" me to keep her furry butt from turning into a furry popsicle.

"Your generosity astounds me, Your Highness," I replied, unable to keep the sarcasm totally out of my voice. I moved slowly to scoop up the grumbling Belladonna and plop her into the hallway before she could change her mind. Ginger trailed after us eagerly as we headed for the stairs.

I grabbed Fiona's talking plate crystal drink tray thing.

No point in leaving it down here.

After returning to the third floor, Belladonna deposited herself on a plush cat tree in the corner. She surveyed the crowded room with obvious disdain, nose wrinkled as if detecting an unpleasant odor. But she made no move to leap back down the stairs.

I took that as acceptance.

Ginger, to my surprise, immediately flopped by the fireplace next to Hondo, purring contentedly.

Josephine sat on the plush sofa, her laptop open on the side table beside her. Digby, the one eyed tomcat, dozed contentedly in her lap as she idly stroked his velvety ears. Her eyes were fixed on the screen.

"Huh," she murmured absently after a while. Digby raised his head at the sound of her voice before settling back down with a snort through his one good nostril. Josephine kept reading, occasionally jotting notes.

Some time later, another soft "Huh" escaped her lips.

"What's that about?" Mario asked.

Josephine looked up from the screen to meet his eyes. "Mario, your friend Juna's search didn't end because everyone stopped caring," she said. "Your friend's search ended because her father asked that the missing person's report be closed."

Mario opened his mouth to respond, but no words came out.

Chapter Five

Josephine's information dropped like stones into the room, sending ripples of surprise outward. You could've heard a feather drop in the stunned silence that followed—even the cats seemed surprised.

Mario stared back at the lawyer, his brow furrowed deeply and his head tilted to the side, as if her statement were some foreign language he couldn't comprehend. "What do you mean, her father asked to close the case?" Mario finally said, his voice tinged with disbelief.

Josephine tilted her laptop screen so he could see. "Just what I said. According to the police reports, Paul Brucker formally requested that the investigation into Juna's disappearance be scaled back after six months of searching yielded no solid leads."

Mario moved closer, squinting at the glow of the computer screen. His eyes scanned back and forth rapidly as he read through the file Josephine had pulled up.

"Citizens can do that?" I asked in surprise.

"Citizens can ask whatever they want," Josephine replied matter-of-factly, not looking up from the screen. "Whether the police comply with a request like that is another matter. But in this case..." She pursed her lips, eyes still fixed on the report. "It certainly *seems* they scaled back their efforts shortly after Paul's request."

Mario shook his head as if he could shake off Josephine's words through sheer force of will. "No," he insisted. "That can't be right. Juna was Paul's only daughter. He wanted to know what happened to her."

Josephine's shoulder lifted as Digby padded across the back of the sofa behind her. "Maybe he felt it was time to move on, or that prolonging the investigation was futile."

"I don't believe it."

"You don't believe it?"

"No."

With a soft huff, Digby circled the sofa and resettled in Josephine's lap, kneading the lawyer's pants. In an idle manner, she pet the plush, velour ears of the cat while looking over the documents illuminated on her laptop screen. Her sharp gaze lifted and fixed on Mario. "Okay. You don't believe it. What I want to know is, how did you not know this until now? This is a police file. You never looked at it?"

He stood up and began pacing in front of the fireplace, looking deeply troubled. "No. Look, Paul was supportive when I joined the academy. He even took me out for a beer after graduation and told me to always stay true to myself, that I had what it took to be one of the good ones. That Juna would be proud." Mario shook his head, his steps quickening. "He never once mentioned asking to close the investigation. Never even hinted at it."

"I don't know why he'd mention it to you, though, honestly," Laurie said, her brow furrowing. "You were his kid's friend. Unless he specifically confided in you for some reason, I wouldn't call it suspicious that he didn't bring it up."

"It's the request itself that seems questionable," Matt countered. "Why would a grieving parent willingly ask police to scale back efforts to find their missing child?"

Laurie's eyes went wide. "Wait... are you suggesting the father could be involved somehow?" She looked genuinely shocked by the implication.

Matt held up his hands. "I'm not outright accusing anyone here. But you have to admit that it's an odd move that warrants some scrutiny." He turned to Josephine. "What exactly was his stated reason for the request? Did the report say?"

Josephine scanned the document again. "It just says 'lack of viable leads and need for closure.' Rather vague reasoning, if you ask me." She looked back up, peering over her glasses. "While I won't speculate on motives, I will say such a request from a parent is... unorthodox. A little odd. Unexpected. Make of that what you will." She glanced at Mario. "Though so is a friend not bothering to look at a murder file he has access to."

Mario froze mid-stride, his worn boots squeaking against the hardwood floor as he pivoted sharply to face our group once more. "Now, hold on a minute. The only reason I never looked at Juna's file myself was because Paul *and* my superiors at the academy advised against it. They said with my personal connection, it could be too emotionally difficult."

"Who told you that specifically?" Evie asked curiously.

"Both Paul and the officer in charge of training my cadet class—Lieutenant Everett." Mario sniffed derisively. "Of course, Everett also said I was 'too soft' for law enforcement and needed to develop a tougher edge, and that was crap. So, in hindsight, maybe I shouldn't have listened to his advice."

"I know him. That man always was rather heavy on questionable advice and light on compassion," Josephine remarked dryly.

Mario nodded in agreement. "No argument there. Even so, Paul was Juna's father and Lt. Everett was Juna's ex-boyfriend. Why would they deliberately keep me from looking into her case?"

Juna's ex-boyfriend?

Did he say his training officer was Juna's ex-boyfriend?

Josie's head tilted back in surprise, her lips parting

slightly as she removed her stylish computer glasses to let them dangle casually from the beaded chain looped around her neck. She fixed Mario with an intense, probing stare. "Officer Lopez, are you telling me the two people who advised you not to examine Juna's case file both had close personal ties to the victim?" Josephine asked, arching one brow.

"Stop. Just stop." Mario shifted uncomfortably under her scrutiny. "This is a small town," he said with an annoyed eye roll. "You sneeze here, three people say bless you. So yeah, of course, people connected to the case know each other. That means nothing."

Josephine held up an imperious finger. "Small town or bustling metropolis, it's irrelevant." Her expression grew somber, mouth pressing into a severe line. "There is only one plausible reason a grieving parent would actively impede an investigation into their own child's disappearance."

"And that is?"

"To conceal information," Josephine finished, letting the grave implication hang heavily in the air between them. "Possibly incriminating information."

A tense silence followed Josephine's blunt statement as Mario's eyes bulged like he'd jammed a fork into an electrical outlet.

"You can't be serious," he sputtered, looking at Josephine and seeming unable to wrap his mind around the disturbing possibility she had raised.

"I am simply pointing out the questionable nature of

Mr. Brucker's actions," she clarified in a measured tone. "You know the man. You have greater insight into his character that I lack, so I leave it to you to interpret the implications. But in my opinion? Your personal connection has made you overlook the obvious."

"All right, let's all take a moment here," I said, holding up my hands before this cold case could heat into a volcanic argument. Considering Mario and Josephine's prickly present problems, I figured a head-on collision was imminent if someone didn't get in there with a red flag. "Wildly hypothesizing about motives and reasons regarding a fifteen-year-old case won't get us anywhere productive."

Josephine angled her laptop back toward the empty spot on the sofa beside her. "This is not mere speculation on my part," she countered. "I have Juna Brucker's full case file pulled up right here." She tapped the screen for emphasis. "Paul Brucker's request to cease actively investigating is clearly documented. By all means, feel free to review the file yourself if you doubt my interpretation." She looked at Mario. "Read it. You know, for the first—"

"Stop needling him," I told her. I did not have the emotional bandwidth for mediating another epic battle tonight. "Have some compassion."

Josie rolled her eyes, but remained quiet.

Mario's dark brows had drawn together in a perplexed frown. "I don't understand. How do you have access to Juna's complete case file?" he asked Josephine, a note of accusation entering his tone.

The lawyer turned her shrewd gaze on him. "Do you recall when your department digitized and merged all those dusty old paper files about three years ago?" she asked. "Access to the new database was opened up for approved applicants. I applied and was granted access—and I pay quite a hefty monthly fee for it. All aboveboard and by the book."

"You may have more access than I do," Mario mumbled.

"You should apply for this, then." Josephine gave him a curt, businesslike nod and returned her attention to the laptop screen. Her manicured finger scrolled through the digital report.

Mario sat beside her, the sofa cushions letting out a muffled whomp. He leaned in, his gaze fixed on the scrolling digital files, his brows knitted, deep creases running across his forehead as he scrutinized each pixelated word.

While Mario poured over the case file with Josephine, the rest of us busied ourselves with minor tasks around the room—stirring the fading fire, neatly refolding blankets, refreshing the cats' water bowls. Anything to avoid crowding Mario as he scrutinized the police reports, his brow furrowed in intense concentration.

As I watched Josephine and Mario work together to examine the case file, I couldn't help but feel relieved. For the first time in a long time, their antagonistic dynamic gave way to focused collaboration, both driven by the common goal of discovering the truth about Juna's investigation. I hoped that this would help to mend the frayed bond between these two strong-willed friends.

Nearly an hour later, Mario finally sat back against the sofa cushions with a heavy, drained sigh. He raked both hands through his dark hair in frustration. "This file is a complete mess," he declared irritably.

"How so?" Landon asked.

"It's full of cryptic gaps—interview notes with no context, vague allusions to evidence with zero actual details." Mario tossed the laptop onto the sofa as if to physically separate himself from the unsatisfying report. "None of this makes any damn sense," he muttered, scowling down at the screen as if it had offended him.

Evie furrowed her brow. "Fifteen years ago, Tablerock was still a pretty small town," she mused aloud. "Spotty police record-keeping in a major case like this wouldn't be too surprising back then, I would think." After a moment, Evie turned to Mario. "Hey, did the county sheriff's department get involved in the investigation at all?" she asked.

It was a legitimate question.

An unconventional relationship existed between our eccentric settlement and county police for as long as anyone could remember. They came in whenever they thought Tablerock PD was slacking or couldn't handle things on their own, and it's possible that the gaps in this case file were simply information that ended up in the county's case file instead.

"You know, I think they did assist initially in the search efforts. I'm not sure if they ever took an active role in the actual investigation or just provided manpower for canvassing the area initially." Mario frowned. "If there was friction over jurisdiction or records being withheld from county investigators, though, that might explain some of these weird gaps."

Landon leaned forward, forearms braced on his worn jeans. "You know, we're all going to be stuck up here together for at least a few days until this storm passes," he pointed out, and gestured to the small printer on the side table. "We've got a printer here. There are whiteboards and a projector downstairs we could grab. Working on figuring out what really happened to Juna could give us something productive to do.

"Only if you want to go down that road, of course," he added, his salt-and-pepper beard catching the firelight, glinting silver as he looked at Mario. He took a slow breath, his broad shoulders rising and falling beneath his plaid flannel shirt. "This woman was your friend, and we may uncover things you'd rather not know. Maybe you'd rather just play cards. Nothing wrong with that. No shame in wanting to let sleeping dogs stay out—"

The two snowy Maltese erupted in a fit of excited yipping, their petite bodies quivering with enthusiasm. Tiny paws skittered and scrambled across the floor as they zipped around in hyper circles, clouds of silk-soft fur bouncing with their movements.

"He didn't mean dogs would go out!" Laurie shouted. "I don't know what ridiculous country saying he was planning on using here, but it had nothing to do with you two!"

The Maltese duo's frenzied yipping and prancing gradually slowed, their fluffy bodies losing momentum and hope for a romp in the backyard. Their perky ears drooped, and soon the pair plopped down, rump hitting the floor with a soft thud. Before long, plaintive whines emanated from both pooches.

"I know. None of us are happy about it, kids," Laurie told them.

Beady eyes blinked heavily as the adrenaline rush passed. Tiny pink tongues lolled out as they panted, winded from their bout of euphoria.

"Sorry," Landon said with a chuckle. He turned and looked at Mario. "Well?"

Mario considered Landon's proposal, then gave a firm nod. "Yeah, let's do it. If there's any chance we can uncover the truth after all these years, I want to take it. I owe Juna that much."

"I don't want to dissuade anyone," Laurie said,

looking uncertain. "But don't dismiss Landon's point about not doing it. Do you think you'll be able to maintain enough emotional distance to really analyze this?" she asked Mario. "With your personal connection, it could be easy for your viewpoint to get clouded by what you already know and how you feel."

"I appreciate the concern, but yes," he stated with calm confidence. "My priority here is the truth wherever that leads. Besides, we're locked in a cat shelter. How much information are we really going to be able to uncover here?"

Laurie considered him for a moment, then nodded. "All right then. I'm in, too. Let's set up a murder board and see what we can figure out."

Landon and Matt headed downstairs together to gather office supplies for our impromptu cold case review session while I tidied up the room once again.

This was the third round of cleaning I'd done that evening, and I was amazed by how swiftly a confined group of cats and humans could clutter up a space. Crumpled napkins, stray pens, and candy wrappers seemed drawn to every surface as if by magnets. No sooner had I dusted a bookshelf than an extra layer of cat hair, crumbs, and general detritus appeared.

This cycle was never ending.

Well, at least the cats were enjoying themselves

tonight, even if my cleaning efforts felt like putting beads on a string someone forgot to knot.

As I straightened scattered cushions and neatly folded blankets, I noticed Belladonna sauntering lazily over to the magic talking cat platter. With a graceful leap, she settled atop the polished crystal surface, casually grooming a paw as she observed our activities.

"I couldn't help overhearing your troubles regarding this missing musician from years past," she said, eyeing Mario with cool indifference.

"I'm almost afraid to ask why you're bringing this up," he said.

Belladonna flicked her tail. "I can be of some small help in unraveling this little mystery of yours," she stated matter-of-factly. "I have to be better than you. You humans seem to have taken an entire lifetime to get nowhere thus far."

Mario stared at her and said nothing.

"This disappearance occurred fifteen years ago, you say?" she mused aloud, golden eyes narrowing as she tilted her head.

"It'll be fifteen years this winter since Juna went missing," he confirmed. "Why?"

Belladonna lazily smoothed her whiskers. "Idle curiosity," she replied, but her inscrutable gaze remained fixed on Mario, hinting at possible knowledge unspoken. "Your friend was going to a bar?"

Around us, the others slowed their tasks, exchanging uncertain looks. Whatever insight Belladonna thought she had, she wasn't sharing it quickly and none of us could decipher the motivations for her questions.

"Yes," Mario answered.

"Hmm..." She began purposefully grooming her front leg. "Was this bar, by chance, near a railroad crossing?"

Mario's eyebrow shot up at that. "As a matter of fact, it's right near the old railway junction outside town." He looked at me. "I didn't say anything about that earlier. How did she know that?"

"Why are you asking her?" Bella paused her grooming to fix him with an exasperated stare. "I am a feline. I am formerly the companion of an elderly woman who possessed a mystical platter. My lifespan surpasses the norm. So does my knowledge. Knowing all that, you want to know how I'm aware there's a railroad track by a bar?" Belladonna responded, her tone layered with frosty irony and haughty indignation. "That's what surprises you?"

"Okay, no need to get snotty, cat," Mario muttered, looking slightly abashed.

Satisfied she had reestablished her mystique and superiority, Belladonna resumed delicately grooming her sleek fur. "This tavern rests beside the rails... interesting," she murmured. More slow, deliberate licks of her paw. "The locale is rather isolated, isn't it? Not the bar—where Juna's car was found. No other businesses or homes nearby?"

"That's right," Mario confirmed, leaning forward

intently. "It's pretty remote out there. Just the bar, the railroad crossing, and open countryside for miles. Juna's car was found a few miles from the bar."

"How perfectly dreadful," Belladonna remarked with exaggerated dismay.

Belladonna arched her back in a luxurious feline stretch before raising one dainty leg straight up to continue her meticulous toe bath. Her rough pink tongue slid between each delicate bean with painstaking attention.

Mario fidgeted on the sofa, fingers drumming against his knees. His eyes remained glued to the unhurried cat, intense as lasers. I could almost hear the ticking of a bomb inside his skull, countdown seconds from detonation.

Just when it seemed Mario would explode from the unbearable suspense, Belladonna finally paused her bathing ritual. Holding her leg in midair, she swiveled her head to meet the cop's stare. "Tell me... was there not some mention of a pendant among this musician's possessions in the police report?" she asked casually. "A little bauble with a rose motif?"

Laurie and I looked at each other as Mario's eyes lit with surprise.

"There was! Juna's friend Clara was interviewed about a custom rose pendant Juna often wore. It was found in the car." He stared hard at Belladonna. "How could you possibly know about the pendant?"

That's what I wanted to know.

No one had mentioned anything of the sort.

Belladonna blinked her luminous eyes coyly. "We cats have our ways of gathering intelligence." She tilted her head. "Though I admit some details elude me at the moment. Refresh my memory—what was this woman's name again?"

"Juna. Juna Brucker," Mario told her.

"This young lady departed her apartment, attempted to travel to this lonely rural tavern beside the railroad, but she never made it there. She simply disappeared without a trace, leaving only her car and a kitten?"

"That's right," Mario confirmed. "It's like she just evaporated into thin air."

Belladonna tsked in exaggerated dismay, delicately washing a paw. "This is quite a perplexing puzzle. However shall it be solved?"

"Since you apparently know details the rest of us don't, how about sharing some wisdom? Any cryptic clues or prophetic visions you want to pass along, oh wise one?" I asked, unable to mask the impatient edge to my tone.

If she actually had insight into this cold case, I wished she'd just spit it out instead of dragging it out for dramatic effect.

Belladonna paused her fastidious grooming to peer at me. "Well, I hardly have all the details. I only know as much as you've told me, naturally. Because how could I know more than that? How? How could I know more?"

Mario looked ready to burst.

Laurie coughed to disguise a laugh.

Oblivious to our collective frustration, Belladonna resumed her deliberately extensive grooming ritual. We all waited in tense silence as she dragged out each languid lick of her paws and legs.

"Although... I suppose if you're searching for answers from that night, there is one obvious solution staring you in the face that no one has looked into yet." She lifted her gaze expectantly. "A solution you people should have stumbled upon already."

"And what might that be?" Mario bit out.

"Why, speak to the witness who was in the automobile, naturally," Belladonna replied mater-of-factly, as if it were the most obvious solution imaginable. "The woman's young kitten was present during the incident. She surely retains some memories from that night." Belladonna licked a paw casually. "You should ask her what she saw and heard."

She blinked innocently as we all stared.

"Are you saying Juna's cat Fluff is still around after all these years?" I asked slowly. "That she's still here in Tablerock?"

Belladonna yawned languidly, displaying her small pink tongue. "I am saying more than that. And yet, in truth, I am saying far less," she replied with typically feline opacity.

I frowned, straining in vain to extract any real meaning from Belladonna's evasive words. Around me, the others exchanged equally bewildered looks, at a loss. "Belladonna, we don't understand—what exactly are you saying?"

The sleek black cat responded by languidly arching her back in a leisurely feline stretch, signaling an end to her audience.

Oh, you've got to be kidding.

But nope.

She wasn't.

Bella stepped gracefully down from the magic platter, then sauntered away, pointedly oblivious to the stunned silence still permeating the room.

"That cat has always been an infuriatingly smug little witch," Josephine muttered irritably, voicing what we were all thinking.

"Getting a straight answer out of her is like trying to nail jelly to a wall," Mario said. "How do you deal with this?"

"Well, I guess that's all the mystical insight we'll be getting from Her Royal Highness for now," I said dryly. "We're just going to have to muddle through with logic and investigative work like mere mortals."

"Maybe not," said a voice I didn't recognize.

Chapter Six

We all turned to stare at the magical meow mechanism saucer gizmo.

On the plate was an older silvery-gray cat who had come to Silver Circle after her elderly owner passed away. The gray American Shorthair could be mistaken for a Russian Blue because of her coat, but she was a big cat, weighing more than the Blue's top weight of twelve-ish pounds. Laurie had estimated her age to be around fifteen years old, give or take.

Many of the cats in the shelter chose not to speak through the magic plate, and in all her time here, she'd never chosen to utter a single word through the crystal dish.

Apparently, that had changed.

"Ursula?" Evie asked.

"Yes. But I was once called Fluff," the elderly cat told us. "I knew Juna—briefly—as a young child. A very young child." Ursula's tone reminded me of Belladonna. Regal. Sure of herself. "I don't know how much help I will be to you."

The cat's luminous emerald green eyes stared unblinkingly. Not a whisker quivered as she sat like a feline sphinx. The only movement came from the tip of her long, slender tail, twitching ever so slightly against the silvery metal of the magic plate's edge.

"Do you remember Juna?" Mario asked, his voice tinged with both hope and skepticism.

"Vaguely. I was very young, and I didn't stay with her long," Ursula said. "She adopted me when I was three months old. That's roughly the equivalent to a human four-year-old."

Mario leaned forward intently. "What do you remember?"

The elderly cat's vivid jade-colored eyes grew distant, as if peering through the veil of years. "I remember the night in the car," she began slowly. "The girl was nervous. I could smell her fear, though she tried to hide it. We drove for some time in the dark. There was tension and silence between us. I was afraid to speak."

A twinge of anguish pierced my heart as I pictured the young cat curled up and trembling in the car, silenced. It took a tremendous amount of fear or trauma for a kitten to be rendered too afraid to speak.

"As we neared an old railroad crossing, flashing red lights appeared. I heard the rumble of a train. The girl stopped and turned off the car. We sat waiting. I suppose we were waiting for the train to pass."

The cat's gaze focused once more, meeting Mario's intense stare. "When the sound faded, the girl tried to start the engine again but it wouldn't turn over. I remember her cursing and repeatedly cranking the key as the car just made a whining noise. She began to panic. I began to panic."

"Why were you panicking?" I asked.

"Because she was."

"What happened then?" Mario asked.

Ursula tilted her head thoughtfully. "She kept trying the ignition and I could sense her fear rising. She reached for something under her seat and got out of the car. I watched her walk to the front and lift the hood, leaning over the engine with a flashlight. After a few minutes, I saw her shoulders slump, and she slammed the hood down hard. She paced around the car, chewing her nails and muttering to herself for some time."

The cat's eyes narrowed. "At one point, Juna froze and stared into the dark distance beside the tracks. I could see her through the side of my crate. She stood utterly still, like a statue, barely breathing. Her face had gone white. She looked terrified." Ursula blinked slowly. "Yet when I peered out into the night, I saw nothing. I did not know what frightened her, but I was sure her fear spiked sharply. She scrambled to lock the car doors after she climbed back inside and huddled low in the seat."

I could picture the scene, imagining how frightening it must have felt for a young woman alone on a remote road at night. A chill crept down my spine.

"She tried the engine again and again, to no avail," Ursula continued. "Finally, she just sat there in the dark, arms wrapped around herself, rocking slightly. At one point she took her phone out, but it didn't seem to work. We must have sat there for over an hour."

Ursula smoothed her whiskers with one paw. "Finally, she turned to me and talked to me. Then she opened the car door and stepped outside. I watched her walk steadily along the side of the road into the darkness until she disappeared from sight. And that was the last I ever saw of her."

A haunted silence filled the room as we absorbed the cat's chilling account. Mario's face had gone ashen.

"What did she say to you?" Matt asked.

"I was a kitten. I was learning to understand your mouth sounds, but I didn't know them then. I don't know what Juna said to me. I do know she meant it to be soothing."

"She just walked away into the night alone?" he asked hoarsely. "Are you absolutely sure she wasn't taken or chased?"

Ursula gave a solemn nod. "She left of her own accord. I detected no other humans nearby until a bit later." Her eyes softened with sympathy. "I know not what strange force compelled her into that darkness. But I do know the choice to walk into it was hers alone."

Mario wiped a tear away with a trembling hand, and Laurie stepped over to squeeze his shoulder comfortingly.

"Thank you for sharing your memories, Ursula. I know that couldn't have been easy." Mario managed a weak but grateful smile. "You've given us the first objective eyewitness account we've ever had of that night. It's... helpful."

I watched Mario closely, noting the conflicted emotions playing across his face. Clearly, Ursula's cryptic words had stirred up more questions than answers inside him. He likely wasn't sure yet whether her contribution would prove useful, but he wanted her to understand his gratitude.

She seemed to.

Ursula dipped her head in acknowledgment. Then the elderly cat drew herself upright, shoulders back, head held high. With effortless dignity, she stepped gracefully down from the magic plate, leaped up onto the nearest cat tree, and settled calmly on the highest perch after curling herself into a neat circle.

"As much as I'd love to launch into a three hour discussion of what that cat just shared, I'm exhausted," Josephine said, unleashing a jaw-cracking yawn.

At least three of us echoed with our own cavernous yawns.

Between the blizzard, the ice storm, and cryptic cat plate revelations, I think all of us realized we could use some rest.

The power was still on, but with the relentless blizzard raging outside like a snow cone machine gone berserk, that could change at any moment. The ferocious winds had finally died down as evening fell, yet the bitter cold front sweeping through had plunged the temperature to a frosty low that would keep even polar bears inside watching StreamFlix.

I eyed the illuminated ceiling fixtures warily, wondering how much longer the electricity would last against the tempest hammering our small town. If the power failed during the night ahead, this cozy loft would maintain its heat for a time, but eventually the icy grasp of the storm would creep in.

I pulled my quilt tighter around my shoulders and added another log to the crackling fire, willing the electricity and the flames to continue.

We'd lugged a motley assortment of mattresses, blankets and sleeping bags upstairs to the loft area earlier that evening. Now an array of improvised beds dotted the open space around the central fireplace like strange mushroom patches sprouting up haphazardly.

I looked around, finding it interesting how personalities shone through in the makeshift sleeping areas like an interpretive art exhibit. Mismatched sheets and quilts added bursts of color to the cozy nests we'd each assembled according to our own particular aesthetic.

Josephine's elegant black satin pillows contrasted wildly with the pink flannel My Little Pony blanket tucked around Laurie's feet next to her. Mario had crafted a downy pallet out of old shelter towels and moving blankets from Landon's truck. And somehow, Matt and Evie had transformed a pile of cushions into a perfectly proportioned nest they could snuggle into together with room for a dozen or more cats.

Landon's space for us was—of course—meticulously organized, with blankets folded to crisp hospital corners and pillows in pristine white cases lining up neatly like soldiers awaiting inspection.

Despite the randomness of bedding materials, everyone seemed content with the little cocoons they'd crafted. Cats had already claimed several of the quilted hollows, their purrs harmonizing with the crackle of burning logs. Sleepy murmurs and yawns echoed around the room as we all settled in for the night ahead.

As I snuggled into my cozy nest next to Landon, Callie sauntered over. The calico cat sniffed delicately at my pillow, then turned a few tight circles and kneaded the cushioned surface before settling down with a soft purr.

"Here you go, kids," I heard Laurie murmur. Glancing over, I saw her tucking the two Maltese into a fuzzy dog bed wedged between her mattress and the wall. The pampered pups circled enthusiastically before burrowing under her blankets instead in a frenzy of wiggling fluff.

Before long, the only sounds were the gentle crackling of flames in the fireplace and the soft sighs of slumber from human and beast alike.

I awoke to dazzling morning sunlight streaming through the bay window, bathing the loft in a warm golden glow. Bleary-eyed, I glanced around the just-stirring space. Laurie was already up and dressed, kneeling quietly by a pile of folded blankets. She meticulously matched up corners and smoothed out wrinkles, pausing now and then to stifle a yawn.

Across the room, Mario remained dead to the world amid a fluffy cloud of purring cats draped lazily across his slumbering form. Many shelter felines claimed him as substitute space heaters during the night. Landon lay splayed out next to me, while Josephine burrowed like a hibernating mole under a mound of blankets.

Scanning the rest of the loft, I noticed two empty spaces where Evie and Matt's temporary beds had been. The pair of early risers were nowhere to be seen—likely they had already risen to start breakfast downstairs. The rich aroma of brewing coffee soon wafted up from the stairs to confirm my hunch.

"Electricity stayed on all night," Laurie announced cheerfully when she saw I was awake. "I gotta say, I was surprised when I woke up and saw the lights still shining. This storm's knocked the power out all over, so I figured our number would be up at some point."

She dumped an armful of quilts onto a chair. "But we lucked out. And we've got enough food to last a few more days if we end up stuck here." Her eyes crinkled with good humor. "Of course, if Matt keeps eating all the chocolate chip cookies himself, those might not make it."

I awoke slowly, stretching out the kinks that had set into my back from my first night on the hard loft floor. My joints creaked in protest as I shuffled across the room toward the large third-floor windows and looked out.

I gasped aloud at the dazzling sight.

A blinding sea of white engulfed everything outside. Overnight, a few feet of snow had piled into glittering drifts, transforming our world into a pristine winter wonderland. There was no sign of a footprint in the smooth expanse of gleaming white that now surrounded the shelter. Sparkling mounds buried our cars up to their doors. In this frozen, silent scene, nothing moved.

"Beautiful, isn't it?"

I turned to see the miraculously conscious form of Landon regarding the wintery vista with quiet awe, his salt-and-pepper beard catching the morning light like a fuzzy, electrified beacon.

"Morning, sunshine," I greeted him. "Love what you've done with your hair. The whole 'escaped yeti' look really works for you. But as to your question? Yes—it's absolutely breathtaking. Like we woke up in Narnia or some magical snow kingdom. I've never seen Tablerock look so picturesque."

Landon chuckled, running a hand self-consciously through his impressive bedhead. "Mother Nature sure outdid herself with this storm." He smiled over at me. "Hard to believe. Seems almost too perfect."

"Pretty as it is, it's a problem. It's not supposed to get above freezing for at least another two days," Laurie said, stepping up beside us to peer out at the sparkling winter vista.

"Which means," Josephine added as she strode over, oddly messy in my borrowed sweatpants and sweatshirt, "we're all stuck here together for that long at a minimum."

"With that much accumulation and the ongoing freeze, I'd bank on us being snowed in here a good three to four days," Mario called from his bedroll. "Once it melts, it's going to be a mess."

Laurie's shoulders slumped slightly. "I was hoping the worst was past, and we'd be dug out by tomorrow. But I suppose a few more days hunkered down together won't be so bad." She managed a wry smile. "At least the power and heat are holding steady for now."

"Don't jinx us!" Josephine snapped, glaring at Laurie like she'd just cursed the wood-paneled walls around us. "What are you trying to do, summon snow demons?" Josephine theatrically rapped her knuckles on the nearest wooden surface, then turned slowly to stare up at the ceiling lights as if daring them to blink out. "I swear, it's like you've never seen a horror movie in your life."

"I haven't."

"Well, good, then you'll probably die first when the serial killer shows up."

"No, that would be Evie, since she's the youngest and a vir—" I abruptly clamped my mouth shut, but the inappropriate words had already mostly tumbled out.

Smooth, Ellie.

Real smooth. At least she didn't—

"Coffee, anyone?" Evie chirped with obviously forced cheerfulness. The words came out through gritted teeth as she regarded me with narrowed eyes, Matt trying to look distracted behind her. In her hands she balanced a tray laden with steaming mugs, the rich aroma of fresh coffee filling the room.

She stared at me unblinkingly, her gaze like daggers shooting from her eyes. If looks could somehow magically transform people into frozen statues, I'd surely be a human ice cube by now, frozen in place under the blistering fury of her glare.

I mouthed "I'm sorry."

My daughter just stared.

I squirmed under the palpable waves of irritation radiating from her tense posture, practically wilting under the heat of her wordless reprimand—fully aware I deserved it after putting my foot in my mouth so awkwardly.

"Indeed," Josephine remarked briskly while grabbing a mug of coffee. "Now that we know what to expect, we can settle in and make the most of this extra time."

"Speaking of extra time," Landon said, turning from the snowy vista outside, "let's get set up to work on Juna's case while we're stuck here."

Landon and Matt got to work setting up the whiteboards and projector that had already been brought up the day before.

With a grunt, Landon rearranged the whiteboards around the room, maneuvering the unwieldy rectangles into makeshift workstations. Meanwhile, Matt busied himself untangling the projector's cords and cables, making sure everything was hooked up properly.

I watched in amusement as our loft headquarters transformed into a conspiracy theorist's situation room before my eyes. Dry erase markers, pens, and stacks of paper soon joined the whiteboards as Landon stepped back to survey his handiwork with satisfaction.

"Is it just me, or is anyone else starving?" Josephine asked as the alluring aroma wafting up from the kitchen below reached us.

Mario's stomach let out a loud gurgle. He chuckled sheepishly. "I could definitely eat. Breakfast time?"

"Everything should be done," Evie said.

"I'll head down and plate it all," I volunteered.

Evie's eyes narrowed slightly. "I'll come with you," she said, a bit too casually.

As we descended the stairs together, I felt Evie's

gaze boring into the back of my skull. I winced, fully expecting the blistering reprimand I deserved for my thoughtless joke earlier.

The second we stepped into the café, I spun to face her. "Evie, I am so incredibly sorry for what I said up there," I blurted out in a rush. "I don't know what I was thinking, letting something so personal and inappropriate slip out like that. I never should have said it. Please forgive my complete lack of filter. I feel awful."

Evie held up a hand. "Mom, stop. It's okay. I know you didn't mean anything by it."

I shook my head vehemently. "Doesn't matter. I never should have shared something so private. I don't know what's wrong with me sometimes." I smacked my palm against my forehead in frustration.

"Nothing's wrong with you," Evie said. "Really, I'm not upset. It was just an awkward moment."

I grimaced. "Okay, if you say so. I still think it was so wrong of me."

Evie quirked an eyebrow. "Wrong of you to assume, sure."

I blinked in surprise. Wait... was she implying...

No.

Surely not.

She would have told me.

"Evie, have you—" I hastily derailed that wildly inappropriate train of thought. "—um, checked on the bacon in the oven?"

None of my business whatsoever.

None.

Not at all.

"Anyway!" I said brightly, clapping my hands together before Evie could check on the bacon or answer my question. "Let's get some breakfast platters whipped up for the crew, shall we?"

Evie chuckled. "Good plan. I'm starving, too. And you're going to need a healthy breakfast to give your brain the energy it will need today. After all, you'll have a lot to obsess over." She shot me a playful wink as she headed for the fridge.

She's just teasing me.

Right?

Of course she is.

Chapter Seven

With full bellies after a hearty breakfast, our group gathered around the whiteboards Landon had set up in the living room. The smell of coffee permeated the air as steaming mugs were topped off. Multicolored markers and pens lay ready beside stacks of blank paper on the sofa end tables.

Landon stepped up to the whiteboard, uncapping a red marker with a flourish. "Let's get started compiling everything we know about Juna's disappearance," he said, poised to write.

I grabbed a pen and notepad, flipped to a fresh page, and wrote "Juna Case Notes" in my messy scrawl. Across the coffee table, Josephine had already opened her sleek laptop. Her manicured nails clicked briskly over the keys as she pulled up a spreadsheet template.

"I'll enter details digitally as we go," she announced

without glancing up. "That way, we have digital records of our spitball session."

Mario scanned the room, taking in our preparedness, and I noticed his gaze lingered on Josephine. Though tension still simmered beneath the surface, I sensed a temporary truce in their locked eyes and terse nods. United in determination, if not yet understanding.

"Good thinking, Josie," Mario told her. "Okay, let's do this. Where do we want to start?"

Matt leaned forward, brow furrowed in concentration. "It seems to me that we need to start by recapping everything Ursula told us last night," he suggested. "Her eyewitness account seems to be the most objective information we have to work from in this whole mystery. It's also the only new information."

On the lowest perch of a tall cat tree near us, Ursula sat straight and dignified, intently following our every movement with her vivid green eyes. Her silvery-blue coat lay neat and smooth, contrasting with the casual sprawl and messy fur of Ginger on the middle shelf. Above them both, imperious, Belladonna gazed down like a queen observing her subjects, sleek black fur gleaming.

Matt swept his gaze over each of us. "It's new information. No one else has given that kind of detailed, minute-by-minute breakdown from the perspective of an observer who was physically present. Not even Mario has that, as close as he and Juna were."

Mario nodded firmly, jaw set with conviction. "We

need to start with her account as a baseline. It's the closest thing we have to ground truth."

I wasn't sure I agreed with Mario and Matt.

Yes, Ursula's story was new, but the cat was still a baby at the time. She hadn't spent enough time with Juna to truly bond or know her, and it had been fifteen years. If Ursula had been a four-year-old human eyewitness, we'd definitely doubt her reliability after so many years—and fifteen years is a lifetime for a cat.

I twirled my pen, conflicted.

But then again, cats are not human. They have uncanny memories and perception skills according to all the research. Maybe her account was more accurate than a person's after all this time. I frowned. How would the scientists know, though, really? They couldn't talk to them the way we could.

Glancing at Ursula, I tried to read her inscrutable stare. She inclined her head, giving the impression she was listening to my silent query, considering me as I considered her.

"Agreed," said Landon, snapping me out of my thoughts. He wrote *Ursula's Account* at the top of the whiteboard in large block letters and underlined it. "Okay, what are the key details she mentioned?"

Josephine knitted her brows together as she tapped her stylus pensively against her chin. "To me, the first really relevant point we need to highlight is that Juna seemed overtly afraid during that drive. According to

Ursula, her fear levels spiked sharply at one moment in particular, but we don't know why."

Landon wrote *Juna seemed afraid* and *Fear spiked suddenly* on the board.

The lawyer leaned forward, gesturing with the stylus as she spoke. "I find that significant. It sounded to me like Juna was clearly anxious and on high alert well before reaching the railroad tracks or having problems with the car. Was she really just going to play a gig, or was something else going on?"

"I think we should write down Juna having car trouble at the railroad crossing, then getting out to check under the hood," Evie added. "The police said nothing about the car having a problem. Did someone fix it to cover that they sabotaged it, or did the police not check? That seems off to me."

Landon quickly added those facts below the first two.

"After the car wouldn't start, Juna just sat there trying to use her phone, but it didn't work," Matt recounted. "Was the phone sabotaged?"

Again, Landon neatly recorded each detail on the board.

"She said something to Ursula in a soothing tone before stepping out into the night alone, but because the cat was young, we don't know what that was," I finished.

Landon wrote the last point and stepped back, surveying the information.

"So what do we make of all this?" he asked, turning to the group.

"Ursula's account gives us some vital clue about her mental and emotional state leading up to those last moments," I said. "Whatever happened to her on that night, it didn't start that night."

"I agree with Ellie." Josephine tapped a perfectly manicured nail against her chin. "It seems clear she was unnerved by something or someone that night," she mused. "The question is—what?"

"Or who," Matt added darkly.

Evie tilted her head as she scanned the whiteboard. "Ursula said she stared into the distance like she saw something, but there was nothing there. I don't want to offend anybody, but could it have been a hallucination or paranoia? Some kind of psychotic break?"

I scribbled "hallucination/paranoia?" on my notepad as a possibility, but it seemed unlikely to me. A hallucination didn't seem to fit with what I knew so far about Juna's behavior. I reasoned that paranoia was more plausible. Maybe she had a stalker she was afraid of that night?

Frustrated, I scratched out the words with my pen.

For now, it was just conjecture. Until we had more facts, the source of Juna's fear remained a mystery—and I didn't see how we were supposed to uncover facts stuck up here on the third floor. But, I sighed, the possibilities swirling in my head were useless until we uncovered more real clues.

Josephine shook her head decisively. "I don't think Juna had a psychotic break. If she were mentally ill, her father would have told the police. Two, I think Ursula would have noticed. One thing we've learned since that plate showed up—cats have excellent instincts and observational abilities. If Juna was truly experiencing a mental break, I think the animal likely would have sensed it. She sensed the girl's anxiety."

"I agree with Josie," Laurie chimed in. "Animals, especially cats and dogs, are hyper-attuned to that kind of thing in humans because they're domesticated."

"Okay, so not a hallucination or psychotic episode," I concluded.

"It really does sound like she was definitely afraid of something specific that night," Mario insisted. "I just wish we knew what."

Matt started pacing, brow creased in concentration. "Her fear spikes, she stares into the empty distance... then she leaves on foot on a road hardly anyone travels on and disappears. Was she just trying to get a signal on her cell phone? Was she heading to the gas station a few miles away?"

Josephine cut in. "Okay, Mateo—you're showing your youthful age. It's very unlikely—we're talking fifteen years ago. The Southwest Bypass was nicknamed "the road to nowhere" because the highway was faster, and there was nothing out there you could get to with that road. Miles from town in either direction. In my opinion, no sane person would just set off on foot into the darkness on that road. People parked on it when they didn't want to be seen or found."

"Her car didn't work, though," Matt argued.

Josephine pursed her lips. "Perhaps, but—"

"There's no point speculating about why she left when we just don't know," Mario interjected forcefully. "We're getting more into suppositions we can't prove than working with what the cat told us. What you're doing is just guesswork."

"Everything is guesswork right now, Mario," Landon told his friend. "Those facts constitute the complete set of tools we've been given. We're doing the best we can right now with what we have."

Matt and Josephine exchanged looks.

We all studied the sparse details on the whiteboard, hoping something would leap out at us. But Juna's reasons for leaving her car—and where she went—remained veiled in mystery for now.

After a long silence, Laurie finally asked, "Belladonna mentioned something about a pendant. What was the significance of that?"

Mario nodded. "Yeah, the pendant. There was a pendant that Juna always wore, and it was found in the car." He regarded Ursula curiously, with a questioning look. "In the police report, they wrote that it looked like it had been yanked off. But the cat didn't say anything about Juna tearing off the necklace that night."

As Landon wrote that down and then added headings for "Clues" and "Suspects," I checked my watch.

We had only scratched the surface, and already almost two hours had flown by. There was still so much ground to cover.

I snuck a glance at Mario.

He looked drained, shoulders slumped. This discussion was taking an emotional toll on him.

"You know, I just had a thought. Maybe we should learn a bit more about Juna." Landon turned to Mario, curiosity glinting in his eyes. "You're the only one here that really knew her. What was she like?" he asked. "What was her home life like, her upbringing, her interests? It might help us."

Mario's gaze grew distant. A bittersweet smile flickered across his face as memories flooded over him. "Where do I even start?" he said.

Mario was quiet for a moment, and when he did finally speak, emotion roughened his voice. "So, if we go way back to the beginning, Juna's mom, Leila Brucker, passed away from cancer when Juna was only five years old. It hit her dad, Paul, really hard. Juna used to confide in me that Paul drank too much and was depressed. He thought that if he'd had more money, he could've gotten Leila the treatment she needed in time to save her."

"What did he do for a living?" Evie asked.

"Paul was a garbage collector. He made a good living, but they struggled financially with Leila's medical bills for years after she passed. I'd heard from my own father that Paul believed if he'd just had more money, if he could have taken Leila to Houston for treatment, he thinks she would have lived. I think that belief and that helplessness ate away at Paul over the years."

I knew the sheer misery of medical bills when faced with a critical illness that could kill a family member. Memories of Evie's heart condition battle flooded my mind—the desperation of clinging to hope through each surgery, the helplessness watching savings dwindle each and every day.

I glanced at my daughter sitting across from me, taking in her familiar face. We'd won our own battle against a merciless disease—she was still here with me, challenges and all. My heart swelled with gratitude.

But it could so easily have gone the other way.

I couldn't imagine losing that war after sacrificing every dollar we had trying to beat it. The helplessness and devastation would be unbearable.

My eyes misted as I pictured Paul in that position—bankrupt, bereft, and now utterly alone after losing the center of their small family. The grief must have shredded his heart to ribbons.

This case felt personal now in a way I couldn't fully explain.

"Juna was smart, but around middle school, she lost interest in academics," Mario went on. "Music became her obsession. And I didn't think so back then, but she was rebellious enough—started skipping school to sneak off to concerts and bars in Austin to see bands perform." Mario gave a rueful half-smile. "Somehow, she always managed to get into those 18+ clubs, even as a young teen. Drove Paul crazy."

His smile faded. "Paul thought she was spiraling. He begged Juna to get her act together, to think about her future. But she didn't want to hear it."

"Most teenagers don't," Laurie said.

"True." Mario absently spun his police academy ring around his finger. "Paul tried to explain how hard it was for them financially, that if he'd gone to college, everything could have been different. That Juna needed to pick a conservative career where her income was all but guaranteed. But Juna didn't care, and she didn't want that. When he wouldn't give her money for music lessons, she found a broken guitar behind a Goodwill shop and taught herself how to play using TubeTrek videos."

His gaze grew distant as he became absorbed in recollections of the past, both sweet and sad. "On the whole, Juna had it rough growing up. Not as rough as some, but rough enough. There was an edge to her. A defensiveness. But she wasn't mean, and deep down, she knew her dad had tried his best. She used to say she wished he could forgive himself. That her mother would hate what he'd done to himself."

"You two really never dated?" Josephine asked.

Mario tugged at his collar, plainly flustered by the blunt question he'd already answered. "I'd planned to ask Juna to homecoming our sophomore year of high school. But I waited too long." He gave a self-deprecating chuckle. "Jackson Everett asked her first. That's Lt. Everett—her ex that helped train me at the academy. He became a cop right out of high school, while it took me a few years to figure out what I wanted to do with my life." Mario scrubbed a hand over his face. "Anyway, when they started dating, I was crushed. Clara, Juna's best friend, told me it was my fault, that I should've made a move sooner. And she was right."

Mario leaned back against the sofa, looking drained. "So that's the back story. A grieving, financially struggling single dad trying his best. And a gifted, rebellious daughter desperate to escape through music. Add in a high school first love and that was pretty much Juna's life here in Tablerock."

"Considering what her father had already been through, he must have been absolutely devastated when she disappeared," Matt said, eyebrows drawing together sympathetically.

Mario's shoulders tensed as he slowly set down his coffee mug. "Actually... no. No, he wasn't."

"What do you mean?" Landon asked.

"If you want to know the truth? Paul didn't act much like a grieving parent. After Juna went missing, Paul kept going to work every day. He didn't participate in any of the searches. When I tried talking to him about Juna, he'd shut down. At the time, I just thought that's how he was."

"But now?" I asked.

Mario lifted his head. "He never cried. He never

seemed to search for answers. I'd expect him to be out day and night looking for her, pleading for help, completely falling apart. Everyone knew what he was like when Leila died, and everyone expected something similar when Juna disappeared. But he just… wasn't how anyone expected."

Matt and I exchanged uneasy glances as a heavy silence filled the room.

Paul's odd behavior in the wake of his daughter's disappearance raised questions, to be sure—and it cast even more doubt on the motives behind some of his actions. The image of a grieving father didn't seem to fit.

Mario stood abruptly and strode over to the whiteboard labeled "Clues."

Snatching up a dry erase marker, he scrawled in large, forceful letters: Paul's behavior odd.

The squeak of the marker echoed in the quiet room as he underscored each word with a harsh slash.

Stepping back, Mario capped the marker with more force than necessary. The plastic clacked loudly against the board ledge.

"I haven't poked through the police file." Laurie turned to Josephine, eyebrows knitted together. "Did the police have any solid theories about what actually happened to Juna that night?" she asked. "Was foul play suspected?"

"It was." Josephine nodded, tapping her chin thoughtfully. "And they developed a list of potential suspects, in case her disappearance did turn out to be a crime." She sat up straighter, her voice taking on a lecturing tone. "There are five individuals of interest.

"Suspect number one was Trent Beasley—an obsessed fan who frequented all of Juna's shows," she began. "Social media posts show he was in the Tablerock area when she vanished."

I shook my head in disgust. Mario muttered, "Creep."

"Suspect number two was Daryl Kingston, a former roadie on a small Texas tour she did. He was fired for inappropriate conduct," Josephine continued. "He had access to Juna's travel schedule and routes."

I shook my head in disgust. Mario muttered, "Creep."

"Opportunity and inside knowledge," Landon mused. "Powerful motive for revenge, too, after being fired."

Josephine inclined her head in agreement. "Exactly. Now, suspect number three—Cassidy Melrose, Juna's songwriting partner. She's an interesting one.

"Cassidy claimed Juna signed over the rights to all their jointly written songs," explained Josephine. "But there were rumors of artistic differences and financial disputes between them shortly before Juna vanished—so even though she has signed papers, that seems unlikely. That, and the last song they penned together has disturbingly prophetic lyrics about a young musician disappearing one dark night after a breakdown."

"Oh, come on," Evie gasped.

"I kid you not."

I met Mario's eyes across the room. "Too eerie to be a coincidence?" I asked.

"I knew Cassidy." He held my gaze, his expression unreadable. "She'd never hurt Juna. I just don't believe it."

"My thoughts exactly," Josephine agreed. She took a breath before continuing. "Suspect number four was Gordy Finch, Juna's manager. He was having money troubles that year. As her manager, he completely controlled her schedule and movements. He could have engineered events leading to her demise."

Mario's eyes flashed at the mention of Finch. "He was bad news. Juna was getting ready to fire him."

Josephine raised an eyebrow. "That certainly provides motive if he caught wind of her plans. Which brings us to the person who compiled this list of suspects but who is not a suspect himself—Lieutenant Jackson Everett."

At his name, Mario tensed.

Oblivious, Josephine pressed on. "I'd like to add him to our consideration list. He may be a cop, but he was also an intimate acquaintance of Juna's. How he was allowed to be on this case is beyond me. It's an obvious conflict of interest." Her fingers danced across the keyboard of her laptop as she browsed through pages. "Everett, by the way, gave Juna that rose pendant Belladonna mentioned."

"Why did the case ultimately go cold?" Matt asked Josephine.

She spread her hands in a graceful shrug. "Despite thorough investigations into each suspect back then, no tangible evidence could conclusively link any of them to a crime. Alibis couldn't be disputed. Physical and forensic evidence was lacking. No trace of Juna was found. She could be sipping drinks on a beach in Tahiti for all anyone knew."

Josephine sighed. "Without proof, the police could only speculate. And over time, leads dried up and theories crumbled without solid facts."

The snow sparkled outside but a deeper chill had settled into my bones—even if we uncovered the truth, would there be justice for so many things so long forgotten?

Chapter Eight

Evie and Josephine huddled around their laptops, engrossed in the virtual expedition to find details on our potential perpetrators over the internet. While they dug for information on our first suspect, Trent Beasley, Landon and I busied ourselves doing the first litter box cleaning of the day.

There would be more.

Many more.

Landon swept up the scattered litter from the floor with brisk strokes of the broom while I scooped out clumps of clay boulders and listened to Evie behind us.

"Ugh, this guy's SocialBook page is a goldmine of creepiness," Evie announced. I glanced back and saw her wrinkle her nose as she scrolled through Trent Beasley's profile. "This guy has an entire album dedicated to 'candid' photos of Juna that were clearly taken from afar without her consent, and it's public. He's not even trying to hide his obsession with her.

"After all these years?" I asked.

"I know, right? And his interests include stalki—I mean, birdwatching, stargazing, and collecting butterflies. So, like, sitting and staring at things until you decide to murder them by pinning them on a board?"

"I take it you don't like butterfly collecting?" Matt asked, chuckling.

"No. Did you see 'Silence of the Lambs' ever? I mean, come on."

Josephine leaned in, peering over her stylish cat-eye glasses to get a better look. "You know, I've found that people with an inordinate interest in observing nature often redirect the same obsessive tendencies toward watching humans when their fascinations turn darker."

"I feel like you two are just making up this nonsense," I said over my shoulder, keeping my eyes fixed on the litter box in front of me. "I'm quite certain nature observers are not inherently predisposed to violent crime."

"And I'm just as certain that they are," Josephine shot back. I could hear the smug smile in her voice without even looking.

"Well, neither of you have presented a single shred of hard evidence to support your claims," Mario chimed in, "so I guess we'll never know."

"Speaking of watching things, Evie, do you really think it's safe to be using your SocialBook profile to look into people we suspect of foul play?" I asked as I dumped another scoop of foul-smelling litter clumps into the trash bag Landon held open. "If one of these people really is a murderer, maybe poking around with your own account isn't the best idea."

"Oh, this isn't my real profile. It's a fake one I made years ago when I got fed up with creepy guys from school cyberstalking me. I'd cyber-hunt them, learn their secrets, and then embarrass them until they cried like babies."

I turned and stared.

Evie shot me a conspiratorial grin over the top of her laptop screen. "I'm kidding. I use it to anonymously look up information sometimes when I'm helping Matt out on cases. Nothing nefarious going on, I promise."

I narrowed my eyes, not entirely convinced. But before I could question her further, Evie looked down and continued scrolling through Trent's page.

"Ooh, look—he joined a bunch of Juna fan groups, including one called 'Juna Forever.' How sweet." Her tone dripped with sarcasm. "And he listed 'staring longingly into Juna Brucker's eyes' as one of his life goals. Well, that's not creepy at all."

"A bunch of groups?" Josephine looked surprised. "How well known was this young woman?"

"We're just north of Austin, the live music capital of the world," Mario answered. "Locally, she was fairly well known."

"You appear to have swallowed the advertising propaganda hook, line, and sinker."

"It's not propaganda," Mario said. "The slogan became official in 1991 after it was discovered that Austin had more live music venues per capita than anywhere else in the nation."

"But not the world," Josephine pointed out. "Propaganda."

"You're a very pessimistic woman, you know that?"

"Indeed." Mario's opinion of her did not appear to faze Josephine whatsoever. "Well, Evie, go ahead and send him a friend request so we can access more content. Judging by the town's SocialBook group, everyone is online right now because there's not much else to do."

Evie's fingers flew across the keyboard. Within seconds, a notification popped up, indicating Trent had accepted her friend request.

"Wow, eager much?" Evie murmured. "He accepted in under ten seconds."

She scrolled through his newest posts, narrating highlights for us as she went. "Blah blah... lyrics from Juna's last song... another creepy candid photo of her... ooh, he checked in at the Whiskey Bend yesterday." She looked up. "That just seems weird, doesn't it?"

"Not really, Evie," Laurie said. "It's still one of the few bars around."

A notification chime sounded from Evie's laptop, signaling a new chat message. "Well, speak of the devil," said Evie. She looked up. "Guess who just sent me a direct message? That... that..." Evie frowned. "Ugh, not now, stupid brain hitch." She took a deep breath. "That makes things easier."

I frowned. "Okay, hold on a minute, Evie."

Whatever brain hitch slowed her down, she was past it because she did not hesitate for even a second before typing back a response. She explained she was a huge Juna fan and wanted to connect with other diehard fans. After a brief, friendly exchange, Trent began peppering her with obscure trivia questions to "verify" her fandom.

"Uh oh," Evie said. "I don't know these answers."

"I've got you," Josephine leaned over Evie's shoulder, rapidly scanning information on her laptop screen. "I think her favorite color was purple."

"It was. How did you know that?" Mario asked.

"Her car was purple," Josephine told him. "Few purple cars around. It was a guess."

Evie's fingers raced across the keyboard, flying to keep pace with Trent's rapid-fire trivia questions. Thanks to Mario's seemingly endless font of personal Juna knowledge and Josephine's lightning-quick online research skills, she was able to fire back answers before Trent could even finish reading each query.

She allowed herself a quick grin as Trent's questions came slower, his surprise evident even through their digital volley. Finally, Juna's self-annointed number one seemed satisfied Evie was genuine and not just some random fake account.

"I got him."

Trent mentioned—without being prompted—that he was at Whiskey Bend the night Juna went missing. He claimed he saw her sneak out a back exit and drive off after receiving a troubling phone call while waiting to perform that left her visibly distraught.

"He said what now?" Mario asked, surprised.

Evie and Josephine exchanged startled looks.

"That's not what the police report said at all," Josephine murmured under her breath. "It says nothing about her ever making it to the show. In fact, the report specifically says the car was found on the road going *toward* the bar."

Evie quickly responded, encouraging Trent to share more details about that night. But oddly, he backtracked, suddenly claiming he mistyped and that he only heard later she'd left early.

I was rinsing out the last litter box when Laurie approached, absently wiping her hands on her jeans. "Hey Ellie, could you lend me a hand downstairs? I want to wash the dogs' indoor grass pad, but I'd rather not do it in the kitchenette sink up here," she said.

I glanced at the cat box I'd just cleaned in the third floor's lone water source.

"I also want to take the puff potatoes downstairs to run around a bit," she added quickly, glancing at the litter box. "No judgment."

Oh, for goodness' sake, why am I embarrassed? It's a sink, and there's bleach cleaner to disinfect it. No need to go all the way downstairs...

Even so, I thought, a walk downstairs couldn't hurt.

It might be nice to stretch my legs a little bit.

I put the brush away and pivoted. "No judgment taken, and I'm happy to assist," I responded, nodding. "Let me top up the bottle of cleaner, finish disinfecting the basin, and we can take the dogs downstairs."

At my mention of *the dogs*, the two excitable Maltese, Riley and Sadie, perked up instantly and raced over to me. Riley's tail wagged eagerly as he gazed up with adoring brown eyes, while Sadie bounced on her hind legs trying to lick my hands—hands she was far too short to reach.

I couldn't help but chuckle at their antics. These diminutive dogs were like little animated cotton balls, their topknots bobbing as they whipped their heads around.

"It seems you two know exactly what we're talking about," I said, leaning down to give Sadie's snowy head an affectionate pat.

"And that you've guessed you get to come along," Laurie said with a chuckle. "It's the closest thing to a walk I'll be able to give you."

One of the dogs let out a high-pitched, excited yip.

We headed for the stairs, the pitter-patter of eight enthusiastic paws echoing behind us as the Maltese bounded along. I kept one hand on the railing as we descended to the second floor, the dogs' nails click-clacking on the steps.

Glancing over at Laurie walking beside me, I realized she had been uncharacteristically quiet and reserved during our earlier case discussion. Her brows were drawn together slightly, lips pressed in a tense line—subtle signs of anxiety I had come to recognize.

"Everything okay?" I asked.

Laurie looked up as if jolted from her thoughts. "Hmm? Oh, yeah, I'm fine," she replied with an unconvincing shake of her head. Her eyes had a distant, preoccupied look to them.

"You've been pretty quiet up there," I commented.

Laurie gave me a small, self-conscious smile. "I'm fine. I guess I'm just a little worried about the kids. I talked to them this morning and they sound fine—I mean, sure, Gary was a terrible husband, but he's a great dad." She shrugged. "As for the quiet? I find the fewer people I'm interacting with, the more open and talkative I get. This is just a lot of people with no break."

I smiled reassuringly. "Nothing wrong with that. I'm the same way sometimes."

We continued chatting as we entered the veterinary office portion of the building. Without the fireplace blazing upstairs, the frigid temperatures of the relentless cold front felt even more pronounced down here. I rubbed my arms.

Laurie shivered, moving briskly to grab the cleaning

supplies. "Brr, good idea to huddle upstairs. It's freezing down here."

"To be fair, I closed off the vents on the lower levels so more heat would reach the third floor and the heater wouldn't have to work as hard," I told her. "But even so, it's running nonstop and still struggling against this cold. I don't even want to know what the electric bill will be."

Laurie began scrubbing the artificial grass pad while I kept the exuberant dogs occupied with belly rubs and impromptu games of chase and fetch around the exam room. Their nails clicked joyfully against the tile floor, providing a comforting backdrop of normalcy amid the cold that hung over us.

Once the pad was clean, Laurie washed her hands and turned to me with a curious smile. "So, how are things going between you and Landon these days?"

I felt an involuntary blush rise to my cheeks at the mention of my romantic relationship. "Fantastic," I answered, hoping my flaming face didn't give too much away. "We're taking things slow, just feeling it out. But it's been wonderful having him around the shelter more."

"Taking things slow, huh?" Laurie lifted a perceptive eyebrow. "Specifically how tentative a tempo did you plan on maintaining?"

My blush deepened.

I tended not to talk about my romantic life with anyone—not even Landon. I was a fairly private person when it came to my personal affairs. Laurie's probing questions about my new relationship were making me feel a little embarrassed and self-conscious.

I took a slow, calming breath, pushing down my discomfort.

"Well, we haven't... you know," I said, lowering my voice.

"I do not."

"Laurie! We have not taken that next physical step—but we have shared some very nice kisses." I felt a girlish smile spread across my face as I recalled the affectionate moments we'd stolen together in shadowy corners when no one was looking. "He's quite an exceptional kisser, I have to say."

Laurie laughed, her eyes twinkling mischievously. "Look at you, blushing like a schoolgirl! Landon must be working some magic if he's got Ms. Sensible hot and bothered enough to blush."

Chatting with Laurie reminded me of childhood bonds built on easy trust, secrets spilled freely without judgment or pretense. Even in midlife, I suppose we all still need those moments of lightness and laughter, of sharing silly secrets that feel momentously intimate in the safety of sisterly support.

"Okay, I spilled—"

"Barely!"

"What about you? Seeing anyone special lately?"

Laurie laughed. "Oh, goodness me, no. I'm swearing off men for now. The only male companionship I need comes with four furry legs and a wagging tail."

After finishing downstairs, Laurie, the two exuberant Maltese, and I headed back upstairs to rejoin the others.

The second we crossed the threshold back into the cozy loft area, the two excited pups made a beeline straight for the mysterious magic talking plate sitting on the floor. Nails scrabbling eagerly on the hardwood, the two pups raced each other to be the first to reach the furry conversation platter doodad.

"Guess who these two were talking about canoodling downstairs?" Riley barked out excitedly.

"Riley, Sadie, no!" Laurie cried, lunging after them, but it was too late.

"Ellie and Landon sittin' in a tree, K-I-S-S-I-N-G!" Sadie yipped in a sing-song voice, prancing gleefully around the rim of the plate. "He makes her blush, you know! We heard it, we heard it!"

My eyes widened in horror and I felt my face flush a deep red.

Oh, you've got to be kidding.

Laurie cringed, lunging for the pups—who avoided her grab by sliding off the slick crystal. "You two have no desire for another walk around the house, do you? Stop that! That's very ungrateful!"

The cottonball twins ignored her scolding and continued to spill details about our private discussion until Belladonna came streaking across the room in a blur of outraged black fur. Before anyone could react, she launched herself at the fluff balls skittering around the plate, hissing and spitting furiously.

"How dare you mangy curs sully my plate with your grubby paws and wagging tongues!" she yowled. Belladonna took a swipe at Riley's ear, claws fully extended. "This was not part of our deal, doctor!"

Laurie had previously struck a reluctant bargain with Belladonna in exchange for occasional access to the magical talking tray for canine patients. Though the imperious cat considered the crystal platter to be her sole domain, Laurie argued that the enchanted object's abilities could also help sick dogs communicate their symptoms.

Belladonna reluctantly agreed to let the veterinarian use the tray in exchange for random expensive treats after much cajoling and flattery. Laurie agreed to Belladonna's exorbitant treaty terms because she knew there was no other way to harness the tray's abilities for the dogs in her care.

The two Maltese dogs, however, were not patients, and their use of the cat gab device tray thingamabob was technically in violation of the agreement.

"Bella, stop that!" I said, wincing as the Maltese yelped and leaped off the plate, Sadie quick on his heels. I watched as the two dogs scurried under the nearest chair, tails tucked between their legs.

Belladonna sat atop the plate, her back arched, her eyes wild and fur on end, making her appear twice her normal size. Her sides heaved as she snarled at the cowering dogs. "You arrogant whelps, this is my domain! It's all mine, and only mine!" Belladonna hissed angrily, her voice as sharp as a whip. "You will accord the necessary reverence!"

Callie (the calico cat) sailed through the air and landed gracefully beside Belladonna on the polished crystal plate before I could say anything. She boldly bumped her shoulder against Belladonna's side, forcibly nudging the arrogant feline over.

"Oh, this isn't good," I whispered.

Belladonna teetered on the curved edge of the plate, claws scrabbling for traction. With an indignant yowl, the enraged cat toppled off the platter and onto the hardwood floor—one toe bean still firmly touching the crystalline plate.

"How dare you!" Bella hissed.

Callie sat primly at the edge of the coveted plate, unfazed by her victory. She lifted one dainty calico paw and began cleaning it, oblivious to Belladonna's venomous glare. She held the furious cat's gaze without flinching, almost daring Belladonna to challenge her audacious power grab.

Slowly, deliberately, Callie placed that slobbery wet paw on the plate.

"Are you mad?" Bella growled.

Transfixed, all the humans sat or stood stock still, their mouths agape as they gawked at the two felines poised threateningly on contrasting rims of the impossibly supernatural plate.

"Oh, get over yourself, you pompous fur ball," Callie spat back. "This plate doesn't belong to any one of us. If it were *just* yours, you'd be the only one able to use it. It's not *just* yours. In fact, I'd say it's not yours at all. It belongs to the shelter, you obstinate narcissist, and we all have a right to use it."

Belladonna's golden eyes bulged in outrage.

She slammed her paw down on the cat chat whatchamacallit, drew herself up to full height, and said, "The audacity of you addressing me with such disrespect... You're nothing more than a presumptuous vagabond," Belladonna growled, her voice resonating with an icy edge of authority and indignation. "This shelter only exists because of me."

Callie held Belladonna's furious gaze. "This shelter existed long before you ever sauntered through the doors like you owned the place, your highness," she said, her voice dripping sarcasm on the honorific.

Belladonna drew herself up, hackles raised. "It was a shoebox," she hissed in retort.

"It was bigger than the isolation box you hole up in on the second floor," Callie shot back, baring her fangs in challenge. "What is it, Bella—is it because you're too hoity-toity and aloof to mingle with us commoner cats?" She took a bold step toward Belladonna, the fur along her arched back bristling. "Go, then. Why don't you and your boyfriend slink back to your musty cave of solitude and leave the rest of us be?"

Ginger sauntered past the contested platter and

paused to lightly tap the crystal surface with one orange paw. "Callie, leave me out of this spat," he said casually. Ginger used a back leg to scratch behind one ear while his front paw connected with the plate. "I belonged to a Robin Hood librarian. I'm as common a cat as they come."

The laid-back ginger tom removed his paw, turned, and padded away, leaving the still bristling females behind.

Laurie leaned over to me and whispered, "Should we try to intervene here before the fur really starts flying?" she asked, eyeing the puffed tails and unsheathed claws nervously. "Normally, I'd tell people to let the cats work out the hierarchy in the house unless they're fighting, but these two *are* arguing. Do we stop them?"

Evie leaned forward in her seat, her eyes wide with wonder as she took in the scene. "Oh my gosh, no way!" she exclaimed. "This is the most entertained I've been in weeks."

Callie yawned, then sat back on her haunches. "We're adults," she said evenly to Laurie. "I'm sure we can discuss this matter maturely."

Belladonna bared her fangs, fur still bristling. "I don't answer to the likes of you!" she hissed in defiance.

Callie met her fiery glare coolly. "No one's asking you to," she replied. "But we don't answer to you, and this is not only your home. Stop acting like we don't belong here. If anyone's holding themselves out as a stranger, my dear, it's you."

Belladonna flattened her ears, clearly still fuming.

Hondo bounded across the room. The lanky tuxedo cat, fur on end, jumped between the two bristling females. "All right ladies, let's all just take a deep breath and calm down a bit," he said in a gentle tone. "This crazy storm has everyone's fur standing on end. We gotta stick together and keep our cool in situations like this, you dig?"

Belladonna whipped her head toward the lanky tom, eyes blazing. "How dare you—a male—presume to tell me, Belladonna, what to do?" she spat angrily. She lashed out with unsheathed claws, taking a furious swipe at Hondo. "You overstep your bounds, fool!"

Hondo lazily dodged her vicious swipe, barely avoiding getting raked across the face, but that was the fire that lit the match. Pandemonium erupted around the plate as a result of Belladonna's unprovoked attack on the popular tuxedo cat, and multiple cats swarmed toward her—and the speech device platter contraption—from all directions.

"You have some nerve!" one cat shrieked.

"We won't stand for this tyranny any more!" yelled another.

A tangle of spitting, hissing felines writhed atop the platter, yowling battle cries as they fought. Hondo frantically tried to separate the warring factions, but his pleas for peace went unanswered amid the chaos.

"If we're telling Belladonna what's what, I want a turn to talk!" one cat yelped. "The humans should hear—"

"No cuts, I was next!" another argued. "I want witnesses—"

"Get off, you buffoon! It's my—"

"Stop, friends! Stop this madness!" Hondo cried in dismay.

We rushed forward trying to gently disentangle the chaotic fur ball, but every time we pried one irate cat away from the melee, two more took its place atop the coveted plate to vent their fury.

Chapter Nine

After what felt like an eternity of pandemonium, we finally managed to pry the last hissing cat off the magical talking platter thingy. Matt set the last disgruntled final feline down and it immediately darted under the nearest chair, back arched and tail puffed to twice its normal size.

I let out a weary sigh, surveying the aftermath. "Unbelievable."

Tufts of fur drifted through the air like bizarre snowflakes, fluttering to rest atop scratched furniture and a scuffed wooden floor. The talker platter gizmo now sported an array of scratches marring its once-pristine surface. It looked like someone had taken a sheet of sandpaper to the thing.

Laurie looked at it. "That antique platter has most likely been in that condition for over a century. But after surviving all those years, it couldn't handle even one chaotic cat fight. That really says something."

"I'm sure it's still functional," Evie replied. "It's probably seen way worse than this over the decades and has come through just fine. They don't look deep enough to actually damage anything." Evie put a small kitten on the platter and it glowed. "See?" She picked the confused baby back up. "It's fine."

"What a pity," Josephine remarked dryly, her voice tinged with sarcasm. "It might have been rather pleasant to have a momentary reprieve from Belladonna's habitual imperious lectures and bossy pronouncements this week. Just a brief period of peace without her haughty voice barking demands through that damn platter."

Talk about the pot calling the kettle bossy.

Belladonna sat seething atop a cat tower across the room, shoulders hunched and ears flattened as she surveyed the scene. Her hostile gaze swept over each of us before settling on Josephine with unmistakable disgust.

"Well, that was... something," Matt said, hands on hips as he shook his head. "It looks like all the cats are okay, though."

"They seem to be," I agreed.

Evie carefully lifted the battered crystal and metal thingamajig, her brow furrowed as she noticed the many gouged blemishes. She held it up, tilting it so that the light caught each abrasion and then shot a pointed look around at the cats. "We've been asking if you wanted to use this every single day. You refuse. You've always been able to use it whenever you feel like it. Most of you don't bother. But suddenly, today, you all had to use it at once?"

The cats returned her gaze expressionlessly, their faces unreadable.

She pretended to listen to the plate thing. "What's that, Mr. Magic Platter? You think maybe just one spokesperson from the Silver Circle Opinionated Cat Council should use you at a time going forward? And perhaps the felines should take turns so everyone has time to be heard? I think that's brilliant!"

The cats' eyes widened in perfect synchronization, rounding into identical circles of confusion. Heads tilted to the left, then to the right, as they regarded each other with mirrored bewilderment.

One by one, their puzzled stares slowly slid back to Evie.

Despite the lingering tension, I couldn't help cracking a wry smile at Evie's dramatic one-sided conversation. Trust my daughter to try lightening the mood.

"Okay." I walked over to her and took the battered platter from her hands. "I'm going to take this downstairs and have a talk with Her Royal Crabbiness."

Evie gave my shoulder two gentle, encouraging pats. "Good luck with that conversation," she said, eyebrows raised. "We'll be sending positive thoughts your way."

I offered her a smile in return, projecting more confidence than I felt.

I made my way across the room to the cat tower, where Belladonna's eyes smoldered with embers of hostility. She sat stiffly, her shoulders hunched and her ears pressed flat against her head. As I reached out to pick her up, she hissed violently and retreated from my grasp.

"Oh, no, you don't," I told her firmly.

The fur along her arched spine stood on end as her lips curled back to reveal sharp fangs. Tensed muscles, ready to strike or flee.

"Don't even try that with me, missy. I've had about enough of this. We can do this the easy way or the hard way, but we're having this conversation, and we're having it downstairs so you don't start another riot. How we get there is up to you."

My response only earned another venomous warning hiss.

Okay.

The hard way, then.

I grabbed the offended cat around the middle and lifted her up before she could flee. Belladonna yowled angrily, but I kept a firm grip on the wriggling feline, tucking the caterwauling cat under one arm and holding the platter in my free hand.

Landon looked concerned. "You need help?"

"Nope. Bella and I will be fine. Won't we, Belladonna?"

Under my arm, Belladonna let out an indignant hiss, baring her fangs.

"See? We'll be fine."

Belladonna's claws snagged on the knitted threads of my sweater, tugging sharply as she struggled in my firm grip, but I held steady despite her attempts to shred the fabric, keeping a firm grip on her twisting body. With the tray in one hand and the surly cat in the other, I made my way downstairs to the second floor isolation room she called home.

Once inside the small, chilly space, I placed Belladonna and the battered platter on a polished wooden side table. The irritated cat sat rigidly, looking anywhere but at me. Her irritated whiskers twitched, and the plumed tip of her tail lashed back and forth.

This should be fun.

I pulled up a chair and sat directly across from her so we were eye to eye—which was not something I would normally do with any cat, as they can find direct eye contact quite threatening.

Not to say you can never look at your cat and they'll never look at you—when a cat's relaxed, they might look at you with a peaceful gaze or half-closed eyes—but at that moment, neither of our eyes were half-closed, and they certainly weren't peaceful.

"So," I began. "You deserved that, you know."

With an air of arrogant nobility, Belladonna raised her chin high before gracefully stepping onto the metallic tray. As her paws contacted the smooth surface, it glowed with a vivid golden radiance that lit up the dim, cold room. "I don't know what you mean."

"Oh, I think you do. I realize you feel a certain amount of possessiveness for this house and that tray—after all, you and Fiona lived here for years together just the two of you. And despite your attitude, I've cut you some slack because the changes I've made to what was your home can't be easy for you. But Bella, I have to be honest with you—I think I've cut you all the slack I'm going to cut you."

""I am at a loss to understand your implications," Belladonna retorted, her voice maintaining an icy detachment."

"Really? You had no reason to attack Hondo."

The cat glanced away, affecting boredom. "He overstepped. I merely corrected his presumption."

"What you call overstepping *I* call talking, and you attacked someone for talking. It bordered on abusive—it was certainly bullying. He was trying to broker peace between all of you, and just because you didn't like it doesn't mean you get to attack him." I shook my head. "There's no justification for violence, Bella."

"I am a feline. We are creatures known for our ferocity," She said, her gaze shifting back to me, impenetrable and enigmatic. "That monochrome puffball attempted to belittle and reprimand me in front of others. I reacted appropriately."

"No, you didn't." I leaned forward, keeping my voice gentle. "You're clearly upset by what happened up there, and considering the way you act with everyone, I somewhat understand—but violence can't be your answer. That's just not something I can allow."

Belladonna averted her gaze once more, her nose crinkling in clear disgust. "I am in no need of a sermon from one such as you. I am cognizant of the repercussions his behavior merited. I know if it was warranted or not."

I reached over and lightly stroked her head. "Bella, you're not a panther prowling a tropical rainforest worried about feeding your cubs and defending yourself from predators. You're a domesticated cat living with a bunch of other domesticated cats, and there's more than enough room and food for all of you."

She pointedly leaned away from my touch, but made no move to leave the platter. I withdrew my hand and just looked at her.

After a long silence, she finally spoke. "The others endeavored to usurp my legitimate sovereignty, to depose me in the presence of you humans. What course of action would you have preferred me to take?"

"This isn't about power and authority, Bella," I said gently. "Most of the cats just want to have their feelings and opinions heard and considered, too. No one wants you dethroned."

Okay, I lied there.

But one step at a time.

She sniffed disdainfully. "That presumptuous calico clearly staged a coup for control of the platter."

"Callie stood up to you, yes. But she was asking you to acknowledge that the plate could be for more than just you. That others deserve a chance to communicate sometimes. She was standing up for everyone else in the shelter, Bella—because she had to. You don't respect them. You don't want them to use the platter to talk to us. That's a little unfair, don't you think?"

At this, Belladonna finally turned to return my sincere look. "But it is mine," she insisted.

I sensed a sudden, desperate fragility behind her words. "Bella—"

"It is all I have left of Fiona."

"No, it's not."

"Why do you say that?" Belladonna asked, her golden eyes reflecting a flicker of curiosity and confusion.

"Fiona Blackwell left this house to me knowing I ran a cat shelter. She left you to me knowing that I lived in my shelter, shared a home with all the cats that I try to help," I said. "This place is something you have that's of Fiona. This is the life that she provided for you once she was gone. This was her hope for you, for this house. She wanted to make sure that you weren't alone, Bella—can't you see that?"

Belladonna blinked as if surprised.

"Right now, your attitude toward the others is creating tension and anger. You stay in this tiny room no bigger than a shoebox—to borrow your phrase—and isolate yourself from everyone. You don't have friends in the shelter other than Ginger because you don't allow yourself to. And you're right, they don't see you as a leader—but why would they? They're cats. They don't care who's money paid for all this, and you act like a tyrant toward them. Is it worth it? Does it make you happy to isolate yourself this way? Do you have to lord over the other cats in this way?"

Belladonna held my gaze for a long moment before looking down at her paws. I could see her considering my words. Her shoulders, once rigid, slumped slightly.

"My isolated years spent with Fiona molded me," she confessed in a whisper barely audible. She raised her luminous golden eyes to meet mine again. "Perhaps, even though I grapple to comprehend it, I may not need to endure such solitude any longer."

I reached over and stroked her head gently once more.

This time, she did not pull away.

"The others will come to see you as their respected elder if you show wisdom and grace instead of hostility. Remember—they have lost things, too, Bella. They've suffered. It's not just you." I gestured to the now-marred metal tray on the table between us. "This plate allows you to speak honestly to us about your concerns. That is a profound gift. But that gift can be shared with the others without diminishing its value to you the same way Wardwell Manor has been."

Belladonna lifted a paw and delicately traced one of the fresh scrapes marring the once-pristine silver surface. Her ears swiveled back, a flash of regret flitting across her inscrutable features. She murmured something I couldn't quite catch.

"What was that?" I asked gently.

The haughty cat lifted her chin once more to meet my earnest gaze. "I said... perhaps you speak wisdom." Belladonna gave a slow blink of acquiescence. "I shall... consider your counsel. I think it is what Fiona would have wanted."

With the cat platter tucked securely under one arm, I headed back upstairs with Belladonna trailing behind. She followed at an unhurried pace, her earlier hostility diminished, gaze fixed on the steps in front of her paws as if deep in thought. The fur along her spine lay smooth now rather than bristled, the angry lashings of her tail now an idle sway.

As we stepped through the doorway into the cozy third-floor loft area, I noted the transformation that had taken place in our absence. Tufts of fur and shredded fabric no longer littered the floor. The furniture was straightened, cushions plumped, and surfaces dusted free of cat hair.

"My goodness, we were barely gone twenty minutes," I said.

"Welcome back!" Evie chirped from her spot curled up with a laptop on the loveseat. "We cleaned up and kept brainstorming while you were gone."

Matt and Landon paused in scribbling notes on the whiteboards to smile at our arrival. Across the room, Laurie sat amid a nest of blankets, meticulously matching up corners and smoothing out wrinkles.

When she noticed us, she lifted a hand in an enthusiastic wave and said, "Glad to see you're still in one piece! We were taking bets on who would win."

"Not about winning and losing, right, Bella? Just a talk about the future and that it might be time for a bit of a change. The room looks great, by the way," I added, with an appreciative glance.

Setting the metal tray in a drawer to keep it safely out of tempted paws' reach and to give everyone a bit of a break, I settled onto the sofa beside Evie. Belladonna perched on the armrest, peering curiously at the case notes and photos tacked to the whiteboards.

Josephine, sitting in a wing chair, said, "While you were downstairs, I talked to Charlie—he's doing fine, says Key West is beautiful, and the hotel was able to extend his stay. I managed not to threaten to divorce him," she deadpanned. "As for the Juna situation, Matt shared some enlightening details about suspect number three—Cassidy Melrose."

I glanced questioningly at Matt.

"Right, Cassidy Melrose." He tapped a red marker against the whiteboard thoughtfully. "I didn't find concrete evidence linking her to any crime. But there are a few curious facts that stood out." Matt uncapped the marker and circled Cassidy's name on the suspects list. "Fact one: she fully owns the rights to all songs and lyrics she and Juna co-wrote."

I frowned. "I'm not sure I understand why that's significant."

"Since Juna vanished, Cassidy has sole ownership of their full catalog of co-written work." He wrote 'Owns all co-written songs/lyrics' below her name in bold print.

"Sold to her?" I asked.

He shook his head. "Just given. Gordy Finch, Juna's manager, tried contesting Cassidy's sole ownership claim at one point, insisting Juna would never relinquish rights to her life's work. But Cassidy had an ironclad, signed contract giving her full ownership and royalty rights. It was signed by both just a few days before Juna disappeared." Matt turned back to us, eyebrows raised meaningfully.

"That seems like far more than a coincidence." I said. "Besides, who hands over their entire creative catalog to someone else at such a young age?"

"Exactly." Matt nodded. "Yet she produced a document with Juna's signature. Her lawyers claimed the case was clear cut."

"Such curious timing on that contract," Josephine mused. "Isn't it ironic that she acquired sole ownership just days before Juna vanished? And are we certain Juna did not sell the catalog and simply gave it to this woman?"

Matt shrugged. "According to the paperwork we found and the notes in the case files, it looks like a gift. The police showed a copy of the document to Juna's father, and he confirmed his daughter's signature. Cassidy claimed Juna willingly signed over rights because they'd had a fundamental artistic split where Juna wanted to go in a bluesy folk direction while she preferred to stay with a more mainstream, pop sound."

"Where'd you find all this again?"

"Police report, and a local Austin musician's magazine named LiveMusic Lens. They did an article on Juna a few months after she disappeared."

Josephine held out her hand. "Let me see that?"

Matt passed her his tablet.

I considered what Matt shared as I watched him neatly record a few more details below Cassidy's name in concise bullet points. This woman certainly seemed to have incredible opportunistic luck—or a penchant for leveraging Juna's disappearance to her own advantage. That opportunism didn't inherently show culpability in Juna's fate, but it certainly didn't clear her of anything.

I looked at Mario. "Did you know any of this?"

He shook his head.

Josephine smoothly picked up the narrative as she tapped the tablet device. "After the disappearance, Cassidy reinvented herself as a pop hit songwriter with one critically acclaimed album dedicated to her 'dear lost friend that changed her life.' Very maudlin and melancholy according to this." The lawyer looked up. "She played up that artistic tragedy image masterfully for a while."

"So Cassidy gained full rights to a profitable song catalog, then used public sympathy about Juna's disappearance to craft a compelling artistic persona that rocketed her to fame and fortune?" I asked.

"I don't know about any rocket to fame and fortune, but she's a working musician and songwriter in Los Angeles," Matt confirmed. "She moved to LA after the first album's success and has been an in-demand songwriter out there ever since. Works with big name artists. It's not cheap to live there, so I'd say she's successful."

"Huh." I tapped my chin thoughtfully. "That all seems incredibly calculated and opportunistic—but I'm not sure it conclusively implicates her in any wrongdoing."

Evie tilted her head. "Nah, it doesn't mean they're guilty. But you gotta admit, the timing of that contract signing is definitely worth taking a closer look at."

"I agree, but how do we do that?" said Mario. He crossed his arms, brow furrowed. "Maybe Cassidy didn't plan anything sinister, but she sure maneuvered herself into a position to profit handsomely from Juna's disappearance. I just don't see how we're going to find out anything more."

He had a point.

I studied the notes on the whiteboard, sensing we still lacked key pieces needed to assemble this puzzle. While Cassidy's actions painted her as shrewd, perhaps even ruthless, was that enough to make her a murder suspect?

"Did you know Cassidy?" I asked Mario.

"A bit. Juna and Cassidy were working partners, not social friends, though. But yes, I knew her a bit."

My gaze traveled over the other names on that list. A crazed fan. A bitter ex-employee. A financially struggling manager. An ex-boyfriend cop. For all we knew, each individual had means, motive and opportunity—the police never crossed off a single name. Yet we lacked evidence tying any of them conclusively to a crime.

Heck, we lacked evidence showing there was a crime at all.

Which is probably why the case had never been solved.

I sighed. "We've uncovered some intriguing info thanks to Ursula's memories and everyone's investigative work. But we seem no closer to any definitive answers. I don't know that digging around old articles on the internet is going to get us very far."

Around me, the others nodded solemnly. The initial excitement of possibly cracking this cold case had faded in the face of dead ends and more unanswered questions.

"Oh, come on, folks. We have nothing else to do,

right? We can keep digging and hope we stumble across the missing piece that connects the dots," Landon said.

I could tell by his tone that even he was disheartened by our lack of progress.

The sound of the icy wind outside was the only response, and it offered nothing but a chilling reminder that some secrets stay buried no matter how deep we dig.

Chapter Ten

I PEERED OUT THE FROSTED WINDOW, SQUINTING against the sudden dazzling sunlight that reflected off the blanket of snow outside. The raging blizzard had transformed into a peaceful winter wonderland that sparkled under the clear blue sky. The storm clouds had rolled away, chased off by the cold front that now gripped the land in an icy hold.

While the brilliant sun and cloudless sky lifted my spirits, one glance at the thermometer confirmed we were still trapped in a deep freeze. Despite the sunshine, it remained bitterly cold—at least ten degrees below freezing outside. The roads would remain treacherous sheets of ice for another day or two until temperatures rose.

I turned from the window with a sigh, resigning myself to our continued confinement.

Across the room, Mario studied the case notes and

suspect profiles tacked to the whiteboards, his brow furrowed in concentration. After a few moments, he stepped back, shaking his head.

"I have to admit—the more I learn, the more confused I am about who Juna really was," he said. Mario turned to look at me, his dark eyes conflicted. "When I first told you all about her, I painted the picture of a small-town girl chasing musical dreams. But now…"

He trailed off with a helpless shrug.

"I was wondering about that." I gave him an understanding smile. "I didn't picture a young woman with a manager, published songs, or a roadie. It seems there were aspects to Juna's life and career you weren't aware of back then."

Mario sank down on the sofa, leaning forward to brace his forearms on his knees. "Maybe my view of who she was came mostly from our high school days. I mean, I knew she wrote songs and sang at local bars, but everything else?" Looking troubled, he rubbed his dark hair with his hand. "Contracts, royalties, a manager, fired roadies—that's a side of her I didn't see. She didn't tell me."

Landon stroked his stubbled chin, his brow furrowing in thought. "I wonder what else she didn't tell you."

"Maybe she just didn't want to brag," Evie said.

"That's possible." Laurie, who sat nearby tossing balls to the dogs, glanced up. "It makes sense you would have seen Juna through the lens of your shared history rather than her career status, Mario," she pointed out. "And lots of times people don't know how to tell others about achievements without sounding like they're tooting their own horn. So they just don't. I have a friend from high school I suspect still doesn't know I graduated from college. It's just never come up."

Mario nodded, though his expression remained conflicted.

"Besides," Laurie continued, "the music scene here was really hopping around that time. Austin had established itself as the live music capital by the first decade of the twenty-first century. It was a lot more competitive than it had been even a decade prior. What constituted genuine success was a goal post that moved a lot."

Laurie grabbed a dropped cat ball from the floor and waved it enticingly. At the sight of the squeaky sphere, the two Maltese dogs perked up instantly, bundles of white fluff quivering excitedly. She drew back her arm and tossed the ball across the room.

"Go get it!" Laurie called out with a laugh. It bounced and rolled, setting off a frenzy of scrambling paws and wagging tails as the pups raced after it.

The cats peered down from their perches, eyes wide as they took in the frolicking dogs below. Their ears pressed flat and their whiskers twitched with irritation.

"Laurie's right. Tablerock's just a short drive from all the action even now. Juna had easy access to the hottest venues, studios, producers, and talent in the industry," Josephine said.

"An ambitious local musician could make a name for themselves back then without ever leaving the area," Landon admitted. "I knew a few people that did well."

Laurie shook her head, marveling. "The sheer amount of musical talent stuffed into a few hundred square miles was unbelievable. There were multiple live music shows happening every single night all over Austin."

"So you're saying Juna didn't have to move to LA or Nashville to get noticed or have an actual career in music?" Evie asked.

Laurie nodded enthusiastically. "If she was good enough, all she had to do was strategically hit the right open mic nights and club showcases. One successful performance at the right place and time could land an Austin musician a manager, a producer, a record deal—everything they needed to launch a career."

Laurie's enthusiastic description of Austin in Juna's time seemed to help Mario reconcile his perception of Juna as a small-town singer chasing dreams with the reality of her burgeoning success on the cusp of a thriving music hub.

"Of course—that makes total sense." A hint of wonder entered Mario's voice. "Juna was right there next to the Austin scene. She was always going into town. I know she had the skills and ambition to grab every opportunity." He shook his head. "I can picture her playing any stage, captivating every audience. She could have made it huge." Sadness flickered across his face. "If she'd just had the chance."

A contemplative silence settled over the room. I noticed Josephine regarding Mario thoughtfully from her wingback chair, though she kept her thoughts to herself for the moment.

After a few beats, Evie broke the silence. "Hey, who's hungry? I'm thinking it's time for lunch."

At the mention of food, Landon's stomach let out an embarrassingly loud gurgle. He pressed a hand to his noisy midsection, chuckling sheepishly. "I guess that answers whether I'm hungry," he said.

Evie grinned. "Sandwiches sound good to everyone?"

A chorus of agreement met her suggestion.

After polishing off our sandwiches, we gathered once more around the case boards to continue analyzing potential suspects.

"Maybe we need to flesh out the rest of these suspects. I think it's time we take a closer look at Daryl Kingston," Landon announced, uncapping a marker. "The fired roadie. What do we know so far?"

"He still lives in the area," Josephine said.

I glanced over the sparse notes I'd jotted below Daryl's name. "He worked on a small Texas tour with

Juna and was let go for 'inappropriate conduct' according to the police report."

Landon nodded. "Right. And as her roadie, he would hear about her shows, probably know how she traveled to them, too."

Laurie frowned. "I don't know about that."

"Well, he could have motivation for revenge after being terminated," Matt added. "Once you have that, it's not hard to plot something knowing she'd be going to a show."

Landon recorded those details on the whiteboard as we called them out.

"Okay, maybe instead of speculating, we dig. What can we turn up on this guy?" he asked, surveying our group.

Laurie tilted her head thoughtfully. "Josephine, you said you found he still lives around here, right?" At Josie's nod, she went on. "Did anyone look at his social media presence yet? That could give us insight into his personality and temperament nowadays."

"I'm on it!" Evie said, already tapping away at her laptop keyboard. "Let's see what Daryl Kingston's up to these days."

I peered with interest over her shoulder as she directed herself to his SocialBook profile. The page loaded to reveal a blurry profile picture of a scowling, tattooed man glaring at the camera through long, greasy bangs. His name flashed above the image in bold Gothic font.

"Well, he looks delightful," I said, after glimpsing his dour profile photo.

Evie scrolled through Daryl's recent posts, providing commentary as she went. "Let's see... hmm, lot of angry political rants... ooh, some definite racism and misogyny sprinkled in there... lovely!" She shook her head in disgust.

"He checks in at Whiskey Bend regularly," she noted. "That's kind of odd. His profile seems to imply he lives in South Austin. But otherwise, nothing too—" Evie's scrolling suddenly halted, her eyes going wide. "Whoa. Wait a second." She highlighted a post with her cursor. "You guys need to see this."

Evie grabbed the black power cord and stretched to plug it into the back of the projector. The boxy machine hummed to life, its fan whirring softly. She connected the other end to her laptop, then tapped a few keys. After a moment, a rectangle of light flashed onto the blank white wall.

"Look."

She had stopped on a post Daryl made just two days ago—a photo he'd uploaded of a faded newspaper clipping. The headline jumped out in stark black ink: *Local Singer Still Missing After Two Weeks*. Under the attention-grabbing headline, a youthful image of Juna smiled up from the creased newsprint, her youthful features frozen in time.

Evie quickly scrolled down so we could read Daryl's caption accompanying the chilling post: *Can't believe it's already been fifteen years since this stuck up witch got what was coming to her. I'll be raising a glass with C to mark the occasion out at Whiskey Bend soon. Everyone's invited to celebrate!*

A stunned, uneasy silence descended over our group as we processed his words. The malicious glee in Daryl's post sent a chill down my spine. Beside me, Mario's jaw clenched, fury simmering in his eyes.

"This guy is seriously twisted," Matt said grimly.

Evie nodded, looking deeply unsettled. "Major creep factor. It really seems like he harbors hatred toward Juna even now. That post is... not right."

"He as much as admits he was involved and somehow got away with it," Mario ground out through clenched teeth.

"Now, hold on." Landon gently gripped his friend's shoulder. "He hasn't outright admitted anything criminal. Let's not make hasty judgments." His eyes remained fixed on the screen, his jaw tight. "Yes, this post certainly reinforces the impression he's an angry, volatile man who bears a grudge against Juna. But that's not proof of anything."

"Evie, scroll down through the comments. There are a lot of them," Josephine directed. "Maybe he's said something to a friend that implicates himself."

Evie's fingers tapped swiftly across the keyboard as she navigated to the comments below Daryl's malicious post. With a few clicks, she enlarged the section so the stream of responses was projected huge and clear across the blank wall.

Beside me, Laurie grimaced, averting her gaze from the glaring screen. "Ugh, I feel dirty just reading such nastiness," she muttered, rubbing her arms as if chilled. What a despicable individual.

"Well, at least his own friends went after him and told him what a horrible human being he was being," Josephine said, pointing. "That's something. He defended his viewpoint with quite the vicious gusto, though."

Josephine was right. Evie scrolled through what seemed to be an endless tirade, but Daryl met every criticism met with a defense of his cruel words.

"You should be ashamed!" one response shouted in bold font.

"She should be ashamed," Daryl bit back.

"Your cruel celebration is disgraceful," another chimed in. "Have some basic decency."

I noticed the same name appeared again and again, leaping out from the screen—Shari. Paragraph after paragraph, she fervently denounced Daryl's gloating comments about Juna. Her increasingly impassioned rebukes dominated the second half of the page.

Josephine leaned closer, peering over her stylish glasses to get a better look. "This Shari woman is really laying into him in the comments. She must feel strongly about this." She turned her probing gaze on Mario. "Do you know this vocal critic of his?"

Mario's eyes narrowed as he scrutinized the projected screen. He slowly shook his head. "Shari doesn't ring a bell. I don't recognize her at all."

"It's like hatred on an IMAX screen," Matt remarked grimly.

"Evie, can you reach out to her with your anonymous account?" Laurie asked.

Evie grinned, her eyes glinting eagerly. "Way ahead of you."

She quickly composed a message introducing herself as an aspiring true crime writer researching cold cases. After casually mentioning Daryl's name and mentioning she'd read the full thread on his profile, my daughter asked the woman if she'd mind answering some questions.

Evie tapped send on her carefully crafted message to Shari.

We all turned our attention to the projected screen, watching silently as the chatting dots appeared below her text. Within seconds, a reply from Shari materialized in glowing pixels larger than life across the white wall.

"Ooh, a true crime book? That sounds fascinating!"

Evie's fingers flew as she typed a response. I watched the projected screen, following along as she kept the conversational tone light and friendly.

"I know, right? I'm obsessed with mysteries like Juna's disappearance. All those creepy rumors about what happened are so intriguing!" she wrote back casually.

On the giant display, I could see Evie's act seemed to work. Shari took the bait, chatting casually about true crime in general. After a few minutes, Evie steered the dialogue toward Daryl's chilling boasts. "I'm dying to know if he was really involved like he hints..." she wrote. "You argued with him so much that I wondered if he told you more about that night."

I held my breath, waiting for Shari's reply to appear in towering text. Beside me, the others seemed equally riveted by the mysteriously magnified exchange unfolding across the wall.

"Daryl talks a big game about that girl who disappeared, especially when he's wasted. Says he and a friend taught the witch a lesson. But honestly? I think he's just full of crap. He barely knew her, and his stint at being a roadie lasted, like, three weeks?" There was a slight pause. "Actually, it was the weird friend that actually knew her. They dated."

Evie's eyes went wide as Shari's latest message materialized on the towering projection.

"Ugh, those two were thick as thieves back then," the glowing text read. "That's the sole explanation I have as to why Daryl never got caught for all the things he did."

"Who's the weird friend" Evie asked.

"Ask." Josephine nodded urgently and pointed.

Evie rapidly typed out the question.

We watched the giant wall, holding our collective breath.

Dots danced for a few seconds before Shari's response appeared.

"Must have been that cop that dated her. Everett." More text flooded the screen. "Sounded like him and Daryl were two creeps in a pod. Jackson's probably the only reason Daryl isn't in prison."

Evie finished reading the Shari's words, then swiveled to raise her eyebrows at us meaningfully. On the white expanse, Shari's damning indictment still glared in all it's incriminatory glory, larger than life.

"He had to have done it." Mario paced the length of the room, raking a hand through his dark hair. "He's clearly unstable. Shari said Jackson protected him. He bragged about it! If he did have something to do with Juna's disappearance like he hints..." Mario trailed off, his jaw clenched. After a few more restless laps around the sofa, he stopped and turned to face us.

Landon turned to Mario, his piercing blue eyes glinting with frustration. "I know you're eager to run with this, but let's not jump to conclusions," he said firmly. Landon started slowly following Mario (who was still pacing the room), his boots audibly scuffing on the hardwood floor. "Mario—"

"I need to talk to someone who really knew Juna back then," Mario said.

I raised my hand. "I can get Ursula and—"

"Someone that's not a cat on a magic plate."

"Mario, what reason would Jackson, Juna's boyfriend, have to associate with someone who despised Juna that strongly?" Matt asked.

"I don't know." His gaze grew distant. "I need to call Clara. Clara Adams was Juna's best friend. They were inseparable for years. If something was going on with Juna or Daryl was harassing her, Clara would know."

"Didn't the police interview Clara already?" I asked.

"They did, but look at all this that we're finding out!" Mario's shoes scuffed against the floor, the rhythmic shuffle underscoring his obvious inner turmoil. His face was locked in a haunted expression, brow furrowed and jaw clenched. "I'm sorry. I didn't mean to raise my voice. I just don't understand how all of us locked in an attic during a snowstorm with an internet connection seem to have more insight than the police that investigated what happened to her."

Laurie tentatively approached and rested a gentle hand on his shoulder. "Take a breath, Mario. Try to remember, social media fifteen years ago was nothing like today," she continued gently. "People didn't publicly spew their deepest feelings for attention like they do now. Police files weren't digitized. Databases of people, their phone numbers, their emails—it was a different time."

"Are you still in contact with Clara?" I asked.

"Not often. But sometimes." He paused, considering. "I have an excuse to reach out. I can update her on the fact that Juna's cat Fluff is alive at the shelter. It's not really a lie." Mario lifted one shoulder in a slight shrug. "It gets me talking to her. That's what matters."

"Just tread carefully if you steer the conversation toward the case," I advised. "You don't want to spook her."

"Of course." Mario pulled out his phone, already typing. "Let me send Clara a quick SocialBook message to see if she's around."

While we waited for a response, I asked, "Clara Adams. Wasn't she the person who found Juna's abandoned car and the kitten?"

"Yes." Mario shook his head. "They were incredibly close. Like sisters." His expression turned thoughtful. "Clara was always shy and introverted, while Juna was fiery, popular. But somehow, they just clicked." Mario's phone dinged. "Clara's free. I'm going to Scoot her. Evie, can I use your computer?"

Mario suddenly surged to his feet and strode over to grab Evie's laptop, movements urgent. His fingers flew as he logged himself into the video call app and tapped Clara's name, and we all turned to the projected wall image as the rings echoed loudly through the speakers. After a few seconds, the video window expanded to fill the white expanse.

Clara's freckled face appeared, magnified to an imposing size.

"Hey Clara, thanks for agreeing to chat. "I'm aware it's been some time," Mario began cordially.

"It has. You stuck in that snowstorm down there?"

"I am. Stuck at a cat shelter, if you can believe it. That's partly why I reached out. I wanted to let you know that Juna's kitten Fluff is alive and well here at the shelter. She's pretty old, but still going strong."

Clara's eyes widened in surprise. "Are you sure?"

"Yes. The shelter's a hundred percent sure."

Mario didn't say how he knew, and thankfully, Clara didn't ask.

"Wow. That's amazing. Fluff is still around after all these years." A hesitant smile crossed her face. I'm pleased to hear that. I hope the cat had a good life. I'm glad to hear she's okay."

On the oversized video call projection, I could see Clara was sitting outdoors in a sun-drenched backyard. The bright midday light illuminated her face, bringing out the freckles dusting her cheeks. Behind her loomed an imposing modern-style house, all sharp angles and floor-to-ceiling windows.

Clara was dressed casually in a coral tank top that contrasted with her pale complexion. Over one shoulder, I could glimpse the shimmering blue of a swimming pool. Palm trees swayed gently in the breeze, confirming she was somewhere warm.

Despite the cheerful, vacation-like setting, Clara's expression was tense and guarded as she faced the giant projected image of Mario. Her shoulders were hunched slightly, body language defensive.

Mario returned her smile. "Me too. The timing of

finding Fluff here seemed like fate, because, well..." He cleared his throat. "A few of us have been stuck riding out this big storm together, and we started talking about Juna's case."

Clara's smile vanished instantly, her expression shutting down. She averted her eyes from the screen. "Oh. That again."

Mario's brow furrowed at her sudden shift in demeanor. "Yeah. I know it's been a long time, but with the blizzard, we were going a bit stir crazy. We found an old police file and—"

"Mario." Clara's acid tone stopped him mid-sentence. She leaned closer to the camera, her eyes intense. "Did Jackson put you up to this?"

"What?" Mario recoiled, confusion etched across his face. "No, I told you. We're just stuck here in the storm, bored, and—"

"Paul asked you not to pursue this. He was very clear about wanting it left alone." Clara's voice hardened. "I respected his wishes. So should you."

Mario stared mutely at the screen. Before he could respond, Clara glanced away anxiously. "Look Mario, I need to go. But do yourself a favor—drop this, okay? Let the past stay buried."

With that abrupt warning, the video call ended, Clara's image blinking out to leave Mario gaping at the blank screen.

A baffled silence hung over the room. I exchanged

puzzled looks with Evie and the others, all similarly taken aback by Clara's cryptic statements and hasty exit.

"What... just happened?" Matt finally said, voicing what we were all thinking.

Mario looked deeply unsettled. "I have no idea. That reaction made zero sense." He paced again. "But she knew Paul told me to leave the case alone. Why would he tell her that—and why would Clara listen to him?"

I had no answers for Mario, but after the past few hours, I suspected there were more secrets lurking around this case than any of us realized.

Chapter Eleven

"THAT WAS BIZARRE," LAURIE MURMURED AFTER the video call abruptly ended. The larger than life projection that just moments before had transmitted Clara's tense features now showed only an expanse of white, the glow from the projector creating a halo against the bare surface.

"That's an understatement," Josephine murmured, shaking her head slowly as if attempting to understand the baffling interaction.

I tore my eyes from the vacant wall, meeting Landon's puzzled gaze. Neither of us appeared to comprehend the rapid shift in Clara's demeanor or her swift dismissal of Mario's questions, either.

If we were confused, Mario was alarmed.

I watched him pace the room, shoulders hunched, his expression etched with bewildered turmoil and disbelief. Matt and Landon moved to his side, speaking to him in low, serious tones.

Mario seemed oblivious to their efforts, trapped in the maelstrom of his own mind.

"Ellie. Laurie."

I turned to see Josephine standing stiffly by the doorway, manicured hand discreetly motioning for us to join her. Laurie met my puzzled gaze with raised eyebrows, as confused by Josephine's summons as I was.

I mean, it's not like the room wasn't already pretty big.

We both crossed the room on quiet feet and followed Josephine into the hallway and down the stairs, her heels clicking rapidly against the hardwood. She glanced back over her shoulder until we had reached the second floor, well out of sight and earshot of the others.

"Jeez, Josie, was this necessary?" Laurie's voice came out clipped, her words punctuated by the deliberately exaggerated chattering of her teeth. She wrapped her arms around herself, vigorously rubbing her hands up and down her sleeves in an attempt to banish the chill.

Josephine whirled to face us, lips pressed into a thin line. "Yes." Her eyes glinted with an intent that told me whatever she had to say, it wasn't meant for all ears. "Poor Mario's going through enough. He didn't need to hear this."

I raised my eyebrow. "Poor Mario?"

"Oh, be quiet, Ellie. That woman, Clara? She's hiding something," Josephine declared (as if she was the only one watching the video call that could have possibly noticed). She crossed her arms, leveling a severe stare first at me, then Laurie. "Her entire demeanor changed the moment Mario mentioned looking into Juna's case. She couldn't end that call fast enough."

Laurie fixed her gaze on the lawyer. "Hey, Josie?"

"Yes?"

"We were there, you know."

"Pfft," Josephine snorted, slicing her palm sideways to brush off Laurie's point as if it were mere lint on her sleeve.

"In the interest of getting us back upstairs quickly, I'll grant you she ended the subject and the call pretty abruptly." I frowned, hesitant to make assumptions. "But I don't know, Josie. It's clearly still a painful subject for her after all this time. Maybe she just doesn't want to dredge up hard memories."

"Rubbish," Josephine scoffed with another dismissive wave of her hand. "She told Mario that Paul wanted him to let the case stay unsolved. How would she know unless Paul confided in her about why he didn't want his daughter's case pursued?" The lawyer arched one eyebrow. "No, there is more to this."

"I don't want to outright accuse Clara of anything." Laurie's tone was tentative. "But Josie's right, her reaction was... off. The way she shut down so fast, how she warned Mario away from it again so many years later." Laurie shook her head slowly. "It definitely seems like

Clara is on edge about the case being examined too closely."

In my mind, I called up the image of Clara's tense, guarded expression as she regarded Mario across the miles. Her terse warning and abrupt disconnect had struck me as odd in the moment, and Josephine and Laurie were right to be suspicious. I was.

"Okay, I get that she's acting cagey," I conceded. "I have a question for you both—where do you think Clara was during that call? I didn't recognize the backyard, but it looked awfully high dollar. Palm trees, a big modern house, a pool. She definitely isn't in Tablerock anymore."

"California or Florida is my guess, judging by the palms," Laurie said.

"California was my thought. And if she is in California..." I let the implication hang in the air between us.

"If she is in California, she could very well be in the Los Angeles area near Cassidy Melrose." Josephine's eyes glittered like dark diamonds as she turned them on me. "Or, dare I say it, Clara could be *with* Cassidy Melrose. Hiding in plain sight, united in secrets."

"You watch a lot of really dramatic television, don't you?" Laurie asked.

Josephine pointed one manicured nail at the vet, the crimson lacquer glinting under the light. "Do not underestimate the tangled web woven when friends turn to foes. Such a trope exists for good reason—bitterness festers deep when bonds once thought unbreakable shatter."

"That's a yes," I told Laurie.

"The police clearly had no clue all those years ago. Juna's true adversary may have been beside her all along, hiding behind the mask of friendship." Josephine stopped and pinned me with her piercing stare. "It's a possibility we must consider, however unpalatable. Clara and Cassidy's possible geographic connection cannot be mere coincidence."

"*If* she's living in California," I pointed out. "You're assuming a lot."

"We can just ask Mario where she lives and what Clara does for a living now," Laurie suggested. "Wherever she is, that house and pool looked really expensive. Maybe she had some colossal success or financial windfall herself."

Josephine nodded approvingly. "Yes, that's an excellent idea. Discreetly ask Mario for more background on Clara's current circumstances without mentioning our suspicions." She checked the delicate silver watch adorning her wrist, frowning slightly. "I also suggest we gently encourage Mario to contact Clara again. See if he can get anything further despite her attempt to brush him off."

I wasn't fully convinced of Josephine's suspicions yet, but her points were compelling enough that I couldn't dismiss them outright. Clara's cryptic behavior raised legitimate questions that pressed us to dig deeper, rather than accepting her words at face value.

If Clara and Cassidy were connected and both obscuring secrets, what did that imply about Juna's fate?

Back on the third floor, I sank into the plush fabric of the sofa and looked around the quiet room, gaze traveling over the suspects glaring ominously from the whiteboards.

Trent, the crazed fan, fixated to a disturbing degree on a woman he barely knew. Daryl, the bitter ex-employee who seemed to relish his celebration of Juna's tragedy, whatever it was. Cassidy, the ambitious songwriter who leveraged her partner's tragedy into a successful solo career.

My eyes settled on Clara's name.

A new name, now underlined twice in red.

Out of all the inconsistencies plaguing this case, Clara's behavior baffled me the most. According to Mario, she had been Juna's closest confidant and fiercest supporter when she was alive—assuming, of course, that Juna was dead. The two friends, by his account, had shared an unbreakable bond built on years of trust and sisterly affection.

Yet now, Clara fled from Mario's questions like a deer fleeing a forest fire. Her indifferent response and vague warnings perplexed me.

Why wouldn't she want to help solve this case?

Across the room, Ursula lounged atop one of the tallest cat trees lining the room, meticulously grooming her lustrous coat. The silver cat's vivid green eyes and plush fur bespoke a life of luxury these past fifteen years after her abandonment ordeal when Juna disappeared.

I blinked.

Wait a minute.

It was Clara that found Ursula in the car that night.

By rescuing the abandoned kitten that awful night, Clara had shown compassion amid her own crushing worry and fear—hadn't she? That act hinted at tenderness and moral character I wouldn't think was easily abandoned.

And yet...

None of it added up.

Clara's cryptic behavior prodded at me like a thorn caught in soft wool—a prickling nuisance I couldn't ignore.

There was only one way to detangle this snarl.

I pushed myself up from the sofa and walked over to the drawer where I'd placed the magic cat chat platter earlier. Lifting the tarnished doohickey with care, I carried the mysterious platter over to where Ursula relaxed and placed it on a lower level.

Ursula tilted her head, eyes locked on the plate.

As if she could read my intent in the gesture, she stretched her front legs out and delicately stepped down from the platform. I held my breath as thirteen pounds of fur and aging joints made a wobbly descent, but the elderly gray cat still moved with innate grace.

Her paws met the crystalline surface, and a gold-green color glowed.

"Ursula, can you share anything you remember about Clara from that night?" I asked. "I know it was over fifteen years ago and you were just a kitten, but do you remember anything about how she acted when she found you in Juna's car? Anything she might have said?"

The silver cat nodded, her eyes growing distant. "Yes. After the girl Juna departed, I remained there alone for some time. Eventually, Clara arrived. She searched the area surrounding Juna's vehicle thoroughly, like a hound sniffing out a trail."

"How so?" I asked.

"Her eyes kept scanning the ground as she circled the automobile. She checked the doors and peered inside every window. Clara seemed a woman on a mission."

"Could you elaborate on that?" I asked, leaning forward intently. "And what exactly did Clara do that made her seem so determined?"

The cat blinked slowly. "She walked in ever-widening circles around the vehicle, eyes fixed on the ground, scanning methodically. Her eyes never stopped moving, flickering left and right, peering into every shadow and corner like she was looking for a mouse."

That seemed suspicious. "Did she find what she was looking for?"

"Whatever she sought, it eluded her."

I nodded. "How about when she found you? Did she seem upset?"

Ursula considered this for a moment, delicate pink tongue swiping up over her nose. "Not precisely upset. More... resolved. Purposeful, even. When she noticed me, she did not react with surprise as I expected. Instead, she opened the door, took me from the front seat, and placed me in a carrier."

I frowned. "You weren't already in a carrier?"

"No."

I rocked back slightly. "Wait. Are you saying Clara brought a cat carrier with her to the scene?"

"Yes," Ursula replied, as if this were a perfectly normal fact that required no further examination.

I paused, staring sightlessly out the window into the blindingly white backyard. "If you're absolutely sure there was no cat carrier until Clara showed up... I mean, that detail is just remarkably odd," I finally said, turning back to Ursula.

"Why?"

"Why would Clara show up prepared to transport a cat if she had no previous knowledge she would need to transport a cat?"

Ursula blinked, considering this. "You raise an astute point. I was quite young then, and the events made many specific details blur together. However, in retrospect, her possession of the carrier does imply an expectation of retrieving me from that location."

I sank down on the ottoman beside her, stunned by

what Ursula's account suggested. The abandoned kitten seemed oblivious to the significance of what she had revealed.

But to me, this changed everything.

Clara had clearly known more about that night—and planned more—than any of us realized.

The question was why.

"Folks?" I cleared my throat loudly, straightening up by the cat tree. "Excuse me everyone, may I have your attention, please?"

At my words, Mario's head snapped up, his hushed discussion with Matt and Landon fading into silence. The men pivoted in unison, curiosity glinting in their attentive eyes.

On the sofa, Josephine froze with one manicured finger holding her place in an open book, the pages splayed face up across her lap. Beside her, Laurie's hands stilled on the blanket she had been meticulously folding, setting it aside to give me her full focus. The rapid tapping of Evie's keyboard stopped as she minimized the web page on her laptop screen and swiveled in her chair to face me.

"I had another talk with Ursula just now about the night Juna disappeared," I announced without preamble. "She remembered a very interesting detail that I think gives us a critical new clue."

I quickly summarized Ursula's account of Clara arriving on the scene prepared with a cat carrier, already expecting to transport Juna's kitten away from the abandoned vehicle. As I spoke, the others' expressions morphed from interest to shock as the implication of the meaning of what she said dawned on them.

"Whoa," Matt said when I finished. "So Clara showed up with a carrier ready to grab the cat? She knew she'd find Ursula there?"

I nodded. "According to Ursula, yes. Clara didn't react with surprise or have to go get a carrier from somewhere else. She was ready to take Juna's kitten from that car."

Josephine's face lit up with a broad grin, her eyes sparkling with excitement. "I knew it," she remarked, steepling her manicured fingers together with a definitive click. "That woman was hiding something all along."

Mario furrowed his brow. "You didn't mention you thought Clara was hiding anything."

"Oh, I most certainly did," Josephine said, arching one perfect eyebrow. "Perhaps not in those exact words, and most certainly not to you. But it was implied, clear as day, in everything I didn't say while we were watching the two of you."

"That makes no sense."

"Of course it does."

"The only logical conclusion is that Clara had inside

knowledge about what transpired that night," Landon said gravely.

"Exactly." Josie leaned forward, her words clipped and precise. "Clara clearly knew Juna's vehicle would be left at that location on the road, abandoned. She came fully prepared to retrieve the kitten from that predetermined location. But how could she have known unless..."

Josephine trailed off meaningfully, letting the insinuation linger. The rest of us exchanged uneasy glances as her words sank in, revealing Clara's deception.

Laurie frowned, her expression uncertain. "I mean, it does look bad. But couldn't there be some reasonable explanation?"

"Like what?" Evie asked.

Laurie lifted her shoulders helplessly. "I don't know... maybe Juna told her the car was having issues and Clara went to check it out prepared, just in case?"

"She never told the police that."

"Maybe. Maybe not. The police didn't exactly do a bang-up job on Juna's case," Laurie said, nodding her head in the whiteboard's direction. "We've been stuck here in a blizzard and we pieced together more information in one day than they did in six months."

"You were Juna and Clara's friend for years," I said. "What's your take?" My eyes searched Mario's face as he contemplated his response.

He didn't answer right away.

Mario stared down at the floor, shoulders tense, hands curled into tight fists. After a long silence, he finally lifted his head. The look on his face startled me—his eyes practically smoldered with anger. "I think you're all jumping to conclusions based on limited information from a cat," he bit out sharply.

Well.

That was unexpected.

My eyebrows shot up as I caught Landon's eye, both of us taken aback by Mario's uncharacteristically volatile response.

Matt shifted in his seat, surprise crossing his face.

"Mario, we know this is all difficult to hear," Landon began gently. "But objectively, you have to admit—"

Mario held up a hand, cutting him off. "Objectively, the only thing I know for sure is that Clara was like a sister to Juna. They had an unbreakable bond. I can't stand here and listen to wild speculation that Clara was involved in her disappearance." He turned away, jaw clenched. "You're dead wrong about her. I just know it."

An uneasy silence descended over the room.

I understood Mario's impulse to defend his friend. But outright rejecting even the possibility felt short-sighted given the inconsistencies mounting around Clara's behavior that night, and today.

"No one has accused Clara of wrongdoing," I said carefully. "We're just trying to make sense of some peculiar oddities in her behavior then and now. Mario, we don't mean to upset you, but can you at least see why it raises questions?"

Mario didn't respond.

"We don't need to handle Officer Lopez with kid gloves, Ellie. We won't get anywhere if we ignore facts that don't align with our assumptions," Josephine said bluntly. "I understand this is difficult, Mario, but you knew these women as teenagers. People change. The Clara from your memory might differ from who she is today. The Clara you remember may not have been the same person you thought—"

"You think I don't know that?" Mario thundered, his voice booming through the suddenly still room. "I'm not some wide-eyed rookie blinded by sentimentality here!" He advanced toward Josephine, posture bristling with anger. "I know damn well people change. But you don't have any actual proof Clara did anything wrong. Until you do, I won't stand here listening to you malign an innocent woman!"

Under tables, behind chairs, the cats fled Mario's outburst, splaying their paws to find traction on the slippery floor. The dogs froze mid-step, weight shifted back onto their haunches, their once wagging tails now still.

"Shoot." Mario's shoulders slumped as he surveyed the frightened and hiding animals. "Sorry. I didn't mean to frighten you all," he said softly, regret weighing down his words. "That was too much, I know. Sorry. Sorry about that..." His voice trailed off as he watched them peek out hesitantly.

Landon stepped forward and gripped Mario's shoulder. "Okay, I think we could all use a break to clear our heads. We all understand this is an emotional situation for you." His tone brooked no argument. "Let's table things for now and reconvene later with fresh perspectives."

Mario shrugged off Landon's hand, looking away. "Yeah. Fine."

Without another word, he turned and stalked from the room.

I listened to the echo of his footsteps fade down the hall, worry gnawing at my gut. Rationally, I knew we needed to follow the evidence wherever it led.

But that path had now placed Mario at odds with an old friend, and I wondered if he was truly prepared for what other hard truths still lay buried in this long-cold case.

Chapter Twelve

Ten awkward minutes crawled by before Mario reappeared in the doorway. He lingered there, one shoulder slumped against the frame, taking in each face but never quite landing on anyone for more than a fleeting second.

"I'm really sorry for losing my temper," he mumbled. "My mother would smack me with a newspaper for acting like that in someone else's home." I noticed his right hand worrying the cuff of his sleeve, a self-conscious tell I'd never observed from him before. "This whole situation is just dredging up a lot of painful memories and questions I don't have answers to."

I offered him a sympathetic smile. "Mario, you have nothing to apologize for. We can't imagine how painful all of this must be, stirring up memories and doubts about someone you cared for."

Landon clasped a sturdy hand on Mario's slumped

shoulder. "We're here for you," he said. "Whatever comes out of all this, we're here for you."

"Landon's right," Laurie chimed in. "We're in this together."

Josephine pressed her lips into a thin line, remaining silent, while Matt and Evie met Mario's gaze and gave subtle, sympathetic nods.

I felt Landon's piercing blue gaze settle on me from across the room. When I met his eyes, he gave an almost imperceptible tilt of his head toward where Mario sat slumped on the sofa. Landon's eyes flicked deliberately to the case boards, then back to meet mine, brow furrowing.

His message was clear: We need to move forward with caution.

I swallowed hard and gave a subtle dip of my chin, hoping my eyes conveyed understanding. Digging back into dissecting Juna's case right now, so soon after Mario's outburst, felt unwise.

Like dangling our feet over a lion's den.

"Want to help me finish cleaning the cat trees?" I asked Mario brightly, grabbing a spray bottle of cleaner and some rags from a counter. "They could really use another wipe down. Honestly, with everyone stuck up here, maybe I should just set an hourly alarm."

My cheeks warmed, evidence of the half-truth. Inspection revealed the cat trees remained tidy enough—apart from a light new sprinkling of shed fur the cats dropped in their scramble to hide from Mario's outburst.

Together, we began methodically working our way around the room, scrubbing every pole, ledge, and cat cave clean. I kept the conversation light, chatting about funny shelter stories and how each cat made their way to us. Mario seemed to relax as we talked and worked, the busy task and idle chatter keeping his mind off the case.

Across the room, Josephine seemed to be engrossed in a book while Laurie neatly refolded a stack of blankets for the third time. But every so often, I noticed Josie glance over the top of her novel, observing Mario thoughtfully.

Matt and Evie were huddled together over her laptop on the loveseat, heads bent intently over whatever they were researching. Mario had made it to the treats cupboard with his cleaner and been manipulated by several whining cats into opening it and dispensing a few —he and Landon laughed as they tossed fish-shaped morsels across the floor.

I heard a snap and turned.

Laurie caught my eye.

She tilted her head almost imperceptibly toward the cleaning supply closet and moved toward it.

I gave an equally subtle nod and moved toward it as well, scanning the room casually.

The two of us began discussing the chore list for tomorrow—what rooms needed to be cleaned, who was on cat litter duty, and so on. Laurie punctuated the conversation with plenty of exaggerated arm waving and head shaking, as if she wanted to ensure the rest of the room knew we were talking about nothing of consequence.

Which... I mean, we weren't.

Well, it was of consequence to the cats.

Out of the corner of my eye, I watched Josephine mark her page and rise from the wingback chair. She followed Laurie and me toward the supply closet. Without preamble, she nudged us both aside and crouched to peer into the depths of the supplies.

Then she turned on the balls of her feet and looked up.

"We need to tread carefully with certain delicate subjects around sensitive ears," Josephine murmured under her breath, head bent back down as she pretended to rummage for a particular cleaner.

I whispered back, "Agreed. Poor Mario."

Josephine's manicured fingers curled around a bottle of glass cleaner. She straightened up and said in a hushed whisper conversation behind cupped hands, "It may be understandable, but it's problematic. We can't ignore inconsistencies just because they're emotionally inconvenient for him."

"We can, though," Laurie whispered. "Technically, this isn't our case. It was just supposed to be something to entertain us while we were iced in. It's turned into something more than a way to pass the time."

"Do you two think we should just drop the case investigation, for Mario's sake?" I whispered.

"Maybe," said Laurie.

"No," said Josephine.

I raised my eyebrow. "Well, that was clear as mud."

Laurie shook her head slightly as she picked up bottles of cleaner and then put them down again loudly. "Look, if this wasn't turning Mario into an emotional basket case, I'd say I think we need to get to the truth, whatever it is. And yes, the pain it's causing him gives me pause. But Juna's kitten is here in the shelter." Laurie leaned against the shelves. "I was raised to have faith that things happen for a reason. Call it God-aware, the universe, whatever." She shrugged. "But that cat showing up here after all these years can't be random chance. We found Ursula for a purpose. Ignoring that purpose feels... wrong."

"God-aware? What on earth is God-aware?" Josephine asked.

Laurie lifted her chin, undaunted by Josephine's cynical tone. "It means I live aware of forces greater than I'll ever comprehend, but I don't fear."

"As I mentioned, I'm inclined to agree with the hippie over here," Josephine whispered, shooting a dubious look at Laurie. She crinkled puppy pad wrappers loudly. "Under normal circumstances, I'd say we have an obligation to pursue the truth, no matter how difficult. Not because of some mystical hoo-ha, though."

"These aren't normal circumstances," Laurie whispered.

"Exactly. This may be the only chance for Mario to

finally get answers about what happened to his friend. If he ignores this opportunity, I think he'll regret it."

"Maybe, but I don't want to force Mario to hear upsetting revelations he's not ready for," I cautioned under my breath.

"If we uncover solid evidence, we may have to," Josephine whispered back. "I don't relish hurting him, but again—just ignoring inconvenient facts won't bring justice for Juna, and it won't help him in the long run."

I understood Josephine's point intellectually, but the thought of intentionally inflicting pain on my friend felt terribly wrong. Mario was already brittle with barely healed wounds from the past. Would shattering that fragile shell truly grant him peace? Or simply deeper scars?

I turned away, eyes downcast. A weary sigh escaped my lips.

"I know. It's a difficult situation, Ellie," Laurie conceded. "We want truth, but not at the cost of compassion."

Josephine nodded, the cynicism fading from her expression. "I'm not completely unsympathetic, you know. I deal in facts and evidence. But sensitivity has its place, too." She turned toward me slightly, lowering her voice even more. "Perhaps you're best positioned for that. You've got this Mother Earth nurturing energy going for you—more than the God-aware hippie over here—and he trusts you."

"Remind me again why we're friends?" Laurie asked.

Josephine gasped in exaggerated offense. "For my sparkling wit and vivacious charm!"

Laurie snorted. "Sparkling? More like flat club soda."

Matt and Evie had just left the loft, their voices fading as I rearranged the throw pillows for the third time, when I noticed Josephine sauntering by out of the corner of my eye. My eyes narrowed as she moved her gaze to the back of the sofa, where Evie's laptop sat open and unattended.

As Josephine strolled past the coffee table with a forced casualness, I saw her arm dart out quicker than a striking cobra. With one alarmingly smooth motion, she snatched Evie's laptop right off the table.

I blinked in surprise.

If I had glanced away for even a second, I would have missed the stealthy grab entirely.

Clutching the laptop to her chest, the thieving lawyer continued across the room as if nothing were amiss and slipped out the door without a backward glance.

What on earth was she doing?

The throw pillow I'd been aggressively plumping

fell forgotten to the floor as I rushed over to the now glaringly vacant spot on the coffee table.

Well, this was unexpected behavior, even for Josephine.

I turned to see Laurie watching me from her perch on the sofa armrest, one eyebrow raised quizzically. She mouthed, "What's she doing?"

I could only lift my palms and shrug helplessly to show I hadn't a clue.

With Josephine, that purloined laptop could be destined for anything from researching new crochet patterns to buying surveillance tools off some shadowy dark web marketplace. Her motives ranged as wide and unpredictable as a mood ring.

Though she'd likely swiped it to peek at the Juna case files Evie kept on there...

But if that was all, why the sneaky subtlety?

Laurie set aside the book she'd been reading and stood. "I suddenly feel the need to stretch my legs," she announced casually. "Care to join me on a stroll downstairs to grab some, uh, crackers?"

"What an excellent idea," I replied, playing along. "I was just thinking it's about time for a snack."

Out of the corner of my eye, I caught Mario glancing up idly from the laser pointer game he was engrossed in with Ursula and Belladonna. Meanwhile, Landon lounged across the room, nose buried in a thick book.

Laurie and I made our way from the room, rounding the corner just out of sight of the doorway before pausing at the top of the stairs. I pressed a finger to my lips, signaling quiet.

Laurie nodded.

We snuck down the stairs as stealthily as a pair of cats on the hunt, senses primed for any signs of our target. At the landing, I paused and peered left and right down the shadowy hall, feeling rather like a spy in an old movie.

The doors on either side of the chilly corridor remained firmly shut, not so much as a sliver of light peeking through. The only sound was the faint creak of floorboards under our feet and the thrum of my pulse in my ears.

Laurie stood barely an inch behind me. She leaned close to my ear. "Any sign of her?" she whispered.

I shook my head.

We split up to check the rooms, communicating in subtle gestures like cops on a stealth mission, and I imagined pulse-pounding soundtrack music swelling dramatically in the background. I cracked each door slowly, peering inside for any sign of Josephine or the missing laptop, but each suite lay still and undisturbed...

...until I reached for the last knob on the right.

It turned easily under my hand, unlocked.

Of course it was this room.

This small room served as Belladonna's private apartment, the soundproofed isolation room initially intended to provide a quiet place for cats new to the shelter to decompress. Thanks to the noise insulation, this would be the ideal location to hide.

The isolation suite door creaked open under my hand.

I paused on the threshold, listening intently. No shuffles or rustles disturbed the heavy silence within. Cautiously, I crept inside.

Then I heard it.

A rapid staccato clicking came from the adjoining bathroom.

The unmistakable clatter of typing keys.

Before I could react, the door flew open behind me and Laurie burst into the room. "Aha!" she exclaimed loudly. Too loudly.

The brisk tapping stopped instantly. Stool legs scraped over tile as someone scrambled to their feet. Then came the slap of shoes moving rapidly toward us.

The bathroom door swung outward. Josephine stood frozen in the doorway, eyes wide, clutching Evie's laptop in a white-knuckled grip.

"What in blazes are you two doing?" she hissed, pressing a hand to her chest. "You nearly gave me heart failure!"

Laurie crossed her arms, giving Josephine a stern look usually reserved for misbehaving pets. "I could ask you the same question. Care to explain why you took Evie's computer to go hide in a bathroom?"

Josephine straightened to her full height, chin lifted and eyebrows arched in indignation. "When urgent matters are at hand, certain breaches in decorum become regrettably necessary."

I pressed my lips together, fighting the urge to roll my eyes at her lofty justification. "That's not an answer."

She waved one hand airily. "On the contrary, I've provided a perfectly logical explanation for my actions." Josephine glanced around with feigned confusion. "Did we not just agree to continue investigating Juna's disappearance on the sly so as not to upset dear Mario? Honestly, I thought you both were brighter than this."

"There are moments where you tap-dance on my last nerve, Reynolds." Laurie shifted her weight to one hip and pointed. "I realize you get your jollies by pulling stuff like this behind our backs, but just for once—can we not?"

"You take all the deviant fun out of sleuthing," Josephine said haughtily. She brushed past us into the larger room, taking a seat atop a bamboo ottoman. "Fine. I shall resist further unauthorized borrowings. Even of potentially case-cracking electronic devices." Her manicured fingers resumed tapping across the keyboard.

Laurie and I exchanged frustrated looks.

"She still hasn't told us what she's doing, has she?"

"No," I answered. "Doesn't seem so."

Arguing with Josephine was sometimes an exercise in futility.

I moved to stand beside her, peering over her shoulder. "Well, what's so important that you had to—"

The admonition froze on my lips as my gaze landed on the laptop screen. Josephine had muted the video call, but the image on the screen was unmistakable.

Clara.

Josephine was secretly video chatting with Clara, Juna's once-closest friend who had shut down all discussion of reopening the cold case.

Josephine tensed, shoulders hunching slightly as her fingers tightened on the laptop edges. She didn't turn, keeping her profile angled away from me. But the telltale tension in her posture revealed her awareness of my presence.

Laurie moved to stand next to me and gasped softly, equally stunned. "You're talking to Clara behind Mario's back?" she whispered.

"Quiet. Let me concentrate." Josephine silenced us with a sharp wave of her hand, not looking up from the screen. After a prolonged stretch of rapid typing, she finally hit send.

We watched the video window.

On the screen, Clara leaned in to read Josephine's long message. The camera zoomed in close on her tense features. She sat back, exhaling heavily and raking both hands through her hair. Her indecision was clear even in pixel form.

"She can't hear us?" I asked.

"No. I told her I didn't want Mario to overhear.

We're typing." She glanced up. "Stay on the side so she doesn't know you're here."

"She can see you talking to someone," Laurie murmured.

"I can see her talking, too. She doesn't seem to be able to read lips, though," Josephine said.

After an agonizing wait, Clara's disembodied hands floated back into view. They hovered over the keyboard for a moment, unsure. Then, finally, they typed.

Josephine quickly silenced the ping of an incoming message. She half-turned, flapping a hand at us in a shooing gesture. "Yes, all right, give me room to focus. I need to think. You two are bothering me. Quit hovering."

Laurie and I reluctantly moved away.

I strained to glimpse Clara's reply over Josephine's shoulder, but the lawyer angled the screen away, blocking my view. The conversation went on for another twenty minutes.

Twenty long minutes.

Finally, Josephine closed the laptop.

"Well?" Laurie whispered. "What did she say?"

Josephine turned to us, sighing heavily as if the weight of the world was on her shoulders. "Not surprisingly, she said we need to let this go," she said, adopting a serious tone that sounded more like a parent lecturing their child. "That the truth won't bring the closure we think. That we have no idea what we're stirring up. Yada yada yada."

"That's not really different from what she said to Mario," I said. "Is that all you got from her?"

Josephine slowly rotated on the ottoman to face Laurie and me. Her eyes were hard, mouth pressed into a firm line. She squinted at us as she tried to look stern. "That's all she said to me," she confirmed with faux gravitas. "That's not, however, all she *said*."

Laurie and I looked at one another with confused glances.

"What on earth are you talking about?" I asked.

"Last nerve, Reynolds," Laurie warned.

Josephine leaned forward, staring wide-eyed as if about to reveal the secrets of the universe. "You see, she may not be able to read lips, but *I* can." Another overly dramatic pause. "And Clara Adams? She wasn't alone by that pool."

Chapter Thirteen

My mouth dropped open so wide I could've fit a whole cat toy mouse inside. I just gawked at Josephine, struck mute as a statue by her casual confession. I didn't know whether to be impressed by her slick spy skills or appalled she'd kept this secret.

"You can read lips?" Laurie finally sputtered, voicing the shock we both felt.

Laurie was right.

Appalled first.

Josephine leaned back casually against the armchair, examining her flawless manicure. "But of course. It's a skill I gained back in my law school days."

I suppose we shouldn't be shocked. Eavesdropping and sneakiness were basically Josephine's bread and butter. Heck, I halfway suspected she only became a lawyer in the first place just to give herself some semblance of boundaries.

"I think Laurie's a bit surprised you never told us," I said.

"A bit surprised? Try astounded."

At our baffled looks, Josephine waved a hand airily. "Oh, don't overreact. It was quite by happenstance, really. There was a bright young man in my study group who was deaf. Somehow, despite his supposed 'disadvantage,' he always managed to trounce the rest of us during our mock trial simulations."

Josephine chuckled. "Eventually, I figured out his secret superpower. The sly fox was reading our lips during the proceedings to gain inside information! Once I sussed out his trick, I simply had to learn it myself."

Laurie threw her hands up in exasperation. "That's just great. Anything else you'd care to disclose from your bag of sneakiness, Reynolds?"

"Well, I also took a course on stealth and evasion tactical techniques, but I didn't think those pertinent to mention," Josephine replied breezily with an exaggerated wink. "What are you so surprised about?"

Laurie's eyes looked ready to bulge straight out of her head like a cartoon wolf. She seemed torn between wanting to smack Josephine and wanting to laugh at her audacity. "Do you have any respect for people's privacy?"

"Of course. Of course—though not as much as I used to since the Supreme Court backpedaled on it."

Laurie's eyes rolled skyward with such dramatic exasperation they nearly disappeared into her head. I could almost envision the silent prayers for saintly patience running through her mind, begging any higher power out there to grant her the grace not to throttle our audaciously theatrical friend right then and there.

Despite myself, I couldn't restrain the bubble of laughter that escaped my lips. As annoying as Josephine's diva-like dramatics could be, you had to hand it to her—the woman had elevated verbal defense to a high art.

"Look, Laurie, I get you have strong feelings about Josephine's secret skill set," I said. "But can we please focus on what she saw Clara say on the video call? We can continue this, uh, lively discussion later."

Laurie looked skyward as if praying for strength before nodding. "Fine. What bombshell did your lip reading reveal, then?"

Josephine sat down in a chair with the grandeur of an empress preparing to address her royal court. She artfully smoothed out imaginary creases in my borrowed track suit, sitting tall and elegant with her chin raised.

"Well, this information is a combination of what she told me and what I saw her say when she didn't think I could hear her." With her shoulders back and hands steepled authoritatively before her, she struck a pose like a politician about to launch into an important speech. "Do you want me to tell you which is which?"

"Spit it out already, Reynolds!" Laurie interjected, her limited patience for Josephine's dramatic antics clearly nearing its end. She leaned forward as if ready to shake the tantalizing tidbits right out of Josephine herself if need be.

Well.

I wondered when people would go stir crazy.

Apparently, right about... now.

"Keep your girdle on," Josephine cleared her throat with a gracious nod, as if giving a boon to her lowly subjects. "It seems our Clara is currently living in sunny California, as we suspected. Also, she's working as a personal assistant to a rather prominent celebrity." Josephine let the tantalizing statement hang in the air between us.

"Okay..." I said slowly, trying to piece together why this revelation required this build-up. "That's not too shocking. Lots of people move to California, and California's got lots of Hollywood celebrities. Anyone we know?"

"Oh, just a moderately successful but very mysterious musician you may have heard of in passing," Josephine replied casually. At our expectant looks, she finally divulged, "The pool Clara sat beside? It belongs to none other than the elusive chanteuse Cabal."

"Cabal?" I asked.

Josephine nodded. "Yes."

I looked at Laurie. "You know who this person is?"

"No, I don't..." Laurie trailed off, brow furrowing in concentration. She began snapping her fingers rapidly, as if trying to physically jog her memory.

"Don't either of you listen to the radio?" Josephine asked.

"I listen to the satellite eighties station," I told her.

"I've got it!" Laurie said, straightening up as the elusive light bulb switched on. "That reclusive singer who never shows her face in public or does interviews. You know the one, Ellie—she's really popular, insists on performing with long dark hair completely hiding her features."

"Not ringing a bell."

With arched brows, Josephine gave me a slow, scrutinizing once-over, her expression a mixture of amusement and skepticism. "If it's not a cat, you just don't register it, do you?" She discreetly checked the delicate watch adorning her wrist. "We'd best get back before the others come searching for us."

Back upstairs, I busied my restless hands tidying up the already pristine loft area, thinking about Clara and Cabala... no, wait—Cabal. My fingers compulsively smoothed non-existent wrinkles from blankets and re-fluffed pillows yet again, a habit I seemed to have developed to fill the time.

Across the room, Mario was engrossed in an enthusiastic game of laser tag with several cats. I watched him energetically wave the red dot across the floorboards, the cats' tails twitching and ears swiveling intently. At each skitter of the laser, they leaped into action, scrambling and pouncing with outstretched paws, trying to trap their elusive prey.

He'd never mentioned Cabal.

Did he know who his friend Clara worked for?

In contrast to Josephine—who seemed to know everything—and Laurie, I knew very little about the music scene these days, preferring books to Billboard charts. This mysterious singer was obviously familiar to them both, but what about Mario?

I racked my brain, trying to recall if I'd ever heard Mario mention a musician with an unusual Gothic stage name. But I came up blank.

As casually as I could, I ambled over to the cluttered bookshelf near the crackling fireplace. I let my fingers drift over to the small Bluetooth headphones sitting atop a haphazard stack of books. Settling in on the couch, I slowly scrolled through music on my phone's music app until I finally located a page for "Cabal."

I peered closer at her tiny image on the music app's page, studying the sinuous cascade of raven hair that obscured her features. It tumbled forward in an inky veil, covering her face all the way down past her chin with only the barest sliver of pale skin visible.

"How on earth does she perform like that?" I wondered aloud. "Seems nearly impossible to see properly through all that hair."

I involuntarily reached up to smooth my own neatly

pinned hair, suddenly grateful I didn't have a cascade of tresses obscuring my vision daily.

I tapped the play icon on my phone screen.

After a brief second of silence, the opening notes of Cabal's latest single soon filled my ears as I felt a tap on my shoulder that made me jump. Lost in studying Cabal's page, I hadn't noticed Laurie sidle up behind me. I slid the headphones off, letting them settle around my neck. "What's up?" I asked.

"Did you say something just now? I didn't catch it."

"Oh, no, that was just me talking to myself," I explained, lifting the headphones. "I wanted to listen to some of Cabal's songs, see if they provided any clues. It's unlikely, but who knows?"

Laurie nodded. "Ah, got it." She pointed toward the wireless speaker perched on a nearby shelf. "Since we're thinking about this mystery woman, anyway, why not play the music out loud so we can both hear?"

Laurie had a point.

I toggled the music app to broadcast through the speaker rather than the headphones. Soon Cabal's rich, haunting voice filled the room like velvet smoke, inviting us to divine her secrets.

"Is that Cabal?" Evie asked.

I nodded.

"She does have a really interesting sound," Matt said after a moment, glancing up from his phone screen. He tilted his head, listening intently. "Very distinctive vocal tone and emotional delivery. You can tell she puts her whole self into every lyric."

"Oh, definitely," Evie agreed. "Even though she's hugely popular, I still feel like she flies under the radar compared to some pop singers."

In my peripheral vision, I discretely observed Mario's reaction. I watched as he stopped dead in his tracks in the middle of the room. The laser pointer dangled forgotten from his hand as he stood stock still, transfixed, his head cocked intently toward the speaker. His lips were slightly parted and his brow furrowed, as if straining to make sense of something he couldn't quite grasp. Then he shrugged.

His childhood friend Clara works for this woman—shouldn't he know who she is?

While we sat listening, Mario seemed cheerfully oblivious as he refocused on the delighted feline batting playfully at the teasing feathers he dragged across the floor. He gave no sign the music resonated, wholly absorbed in dangling the toy just out of reach of the energetic tabby kitten.

I pulled my stare from Mario to find Laurie already watching me. Her eyebrows were raised, head tilted slightly toward where Mario sat oblivious on the floor. It was clear from her significant look that she too had been discreetly observing him, too.

I answered with a subtle, rueful head shake—nothing.

I'd continued to watch him, studying him closely

each time the singer's raw, emotional lyrics crescendoed through soaring notes, searching for any change in his placid expression. But not a single muscle twitched to suggest some odd familiarity or suppressed memories bursting to light.

If anything, Mario seemed almost bored, stifling a yawn before tossing a fluffy mouse.

If I'd hoped this mysterious musician might trigger Mario and open a doorway to the past, it seemed those hopes would remain unfulfilled.

Well, the woman was a celebrity, right?

Celebrity means press.

I settled into an oversized armchair, opened Evie's laptop, and angled the screen away from nosy eyes. As I quickly typed 'Cabal musician' into the search bar, my fingers produced results in an endless scroll.

I clicked on the first article title that caught my eye: 'The Mysterious Cabal: Music's Most Elusive Star.'

It opened to a moody photograph of a darkened concert stage, a single vintage microphone stand illuminated by an angled halo of light. No sign of Cabal herself. A thin tendril of smoke swirled in the glare, adding to the atmospheric, haunted vibe.

The article chronicled the musician's meteoric rise to fame over the past decade despite her reclusiveness. It noted that Cabal never appeared without her dark hair completely obscuring her face. Nor does she grant interviews or make public appearances to promote her music. Even her origins remain unknown, shrouded in secrecy.

"Rumors have long flourished regarding Cabal's fiercely private personal life. Clara Adams, Cabal's close friend and personal assistant, is her near constant companion, seldom far from her side. Much speculation abounds that their relationship extends far beyond the professional into the romantic realm. However, Cabal's isolated, cellar-dweller lifestyle keeps the precise truth of the bond they share shrouded in mystery."

Huh.

I jotted down notes about Clara and Cabal's apparently intimate connection, thoughts spinning. This seemed to confirm what Josephine saw on the video call —well, somewhat. The two women were clearly very close, regardless of whether they were romantically involved.

Another intricate thread woven through the tangled web?

Or just a random fact that meant nothing?

Further down, a subheading made me catch my breath: 'Lyrics Laced With Hints of Shadowy Secrets'

The article described how Cabal imbued her brooding lyrics with tantalizing glimpses into her obscured past, like breadcrumbs leading back through the dark forest of her history.

"Cabal's meteoric rise has been fueled by her intensely personal, enigmatic lyrics that offer poetic glimpses into a troubled past. Like enticing breadcrumbs, they lure her devoted followers to piece together the obscured story of her early years."

Several songs, the article claimed, hinted strongly at surviving an abusive relationship and yearning for freedom:

"Your poison seeped so deep under my skin, staining me black and blue, but no more will these bruises keep me caged..."

"The silken ties that bind can strangle if you don't slip loose..."

"Sometimes the only way back to the light is through the darkness..."

I scoured page after page of search results.

I unearthed an obscure interview in an alternative music blog that provided another tantalizing breadcrumb. When asked where she found creative inspiration, Cabal mentioned composing for hours beneath the silent stars out in the countryside surrounding... Austin.

I lifted my head abruptly, tearing my eyes away from the glowing screen.

That couldn't just be a coincidence, could it?

It was after dinner when the power cut out without warning; the lights blinking once before plunging us into shadows illuminated by the flickering fire. I froze, momentarily unable to see.

"Whoa!" Matt exclaimed.

"Well, crap," Landon muttered.

"Did it have to be right this second?" Mario grumbled.

Someone, probably Josephine, let out an affronted gasp followed by irritated sputtering I couldn't quite make out. Laurie just laughed, seeming amused by our unexpected descent into darkness.

As my vision adjusted to the firelight, I realized the utter stillness and silence felt jarring, as if the entire world had been instantaneously muted. Was the heater really that loud?

Outside the windows, the snowy landscape remained partially illuminated by the silvery moonlight, but inside our skin bathed in the dim orange glare of the only light and heat we had.

"Okay people, stay calm," Landon announced in a steady voice that inspired immediate confidence. "Matt and I will grab the flashlights. The outage was inevitable with the storm. The power utility ought to have electricity restored promptly. Until then, we'll make do."

Ought to have it restored.

Ought to.

That statement didn't inspire confidence.

I heard the thumps and shuffles of Matt and Landon cautiously picking their way across the shadowed room. That was quickly followed by the sounds of them rummaging through the supply bins, punctuated by the occasional clatter of unseen items knocked over in their haste.

After a minute, two piercing beams of light sliced through the darkness, blinding me momentarily as they swept erratically over our startled faces.

"Ah, here we go," Landon said. His flashlight beam steadied, illuminating a small pool of light. Beside him, Matt did the same until twin circles of illumination overlapped, giving us some visibility. "We have six flashlights. I'm going to turn most of them off and put them by the table in case we need them. The fire will suffice for now."

Laurie made her way over to a storage shelf and began distributing battery operated candles that soon bathed everything in a calming amber glow. The LED bulbs mimicked flickering flames, instantly making the room feel cozier despite the lack of electricity.

I checked the time on my phone's dimly glowing face—nearly eight o'clock. Late enough that soon the frigid night temperatures would plunge even lower without power to the central heat. I suppressed a shiver that had nothing to do with the cold, pushing away the panicked thought.

No, it was fine. We had wood.

We'd be fine.

As if reading my mind, Landon swung his flashlight beam around the shadowy room. "We have plenty of wood until the electricity comes back," he echoed my thought confidently—though I knew Landon well enough to detect the tiniest waver of uncertainty underlying his steady words.

The unnatural stillness dragged on.

Landon shook his head, brow furrowing. "I think we should pull all the bedrolls closer to the fire." He raked a hand through his hair. "I'm sure the cats will cuddle up, too, so even if it takes a while for the heat to come back on, we'll all be fine."

He could repeat himself until the spring thaw, but it wasn't going to make me feel any better.

Or any warmer.

I watched Landon and Matt whispering with their heads together. Matt kept glancing at his phone screen, likely debating whether to attempt calling for help. But I suspected cell service remained just as unreliable as before the storm.

"The internet still works," Evie said.

"Yes, but you'll drain the battery and we have no way to charge it up," Landon pointed out. "Best keep those powered down in case we really need to use them."

"What about our phones?" Josephine asked, holding hers up.

"I'd shut all down but one," Matt said.

Mario nodded. "That's smart. One at a time."

"Well, I truly have to marvel at the resilience of the human spirit while trapped together against the elements, much like the settlers of yore! You guys are impressive." Josephine proclaimed dramatically. She paused, glancing around. "Too much?"

"Too much," I confirmed.

Around us, the cats had emerged from their hiding places, drawn by the dancing warmth of the fireplace. They wound languidly between our legs, soft fur brushing against ankles. A few leaped up onto vacant chairs or nested atop cozy blankets left draped over chair arms and sofa backs now in a semicircle around the fireplace.

Several shelter cats made a beeline straight for Matt and Mario, eager for affection from their favored humans. Matt laughed as a fluffy ginger tabby head-butted his knee in a shameless plea for ear scratches.

It seemed only we two-legged creatures felt any unease. For the shelter cats, the novelty of flickering candlelight and disrupted routines merely presented fresh adventures and opportunities to indulge their whims. Besides, they could see in the low light just fine.

That, and they trusted us to keep them safe.

Watching their lack of concern lifted my spirits slightly. Their contentment and trust reminded me no matter what surprises lay ahead, we'd make it through together.

Chapter Fourteen

Our group huddled close together around the fireplace, seeking warmth and comfort amid the flickering shadows. Up here on the third floor, in what was once Fiona's private library (before I converted it into a cat sanctuary), we were sealed off from the icy world outside.

"The important thing is we're all safe," I said, my voice sounding louder in the hush than I'd intended. "We have plenty of wood and food. It's not ideal, but we'll be okay."

Landon gave my hand a reassuring squeeze, his warm touch a stark contrast to the chill in the room. "We've been doing great, making the best of the situation."

"Absolutely," Evie said.

She and Matt moved around the room, their hands balancing mugs filled with a frothy liquid. Wisps of steam curled upward, carrying with them the sweet, intoxicating scent of cocoa and cinnamon.

Matt eased down onto the couch, his body sinking into the cushions as a thoughtful expression crossed his face. "The cold is *increíble*," he mused, his gaze fixed on the swirling snowflakes beyond the window. "Did you know we are on the thirtieth parallel, and so is Cairo, Egypt? Well, close to it, anyway."

"Is that true?" Laurie asked.

Matt's arm draped around Evie, pulling her into his side in a natural, protective gesture. She nestled into his warmth, her head finding a perfect resting place on his shoulder. "If my geography teacher is to be believed. Knowing that we're even with a desert? It just doesn't seem like it should ever get this cold."

Landon nodded, feeding another split log into the crackling fire. "It's what they call a polar vortex," he explained, his gaze steady on the dancing flames. "A polar vortex is a large area of low pressure and cold air surrounding the earth's poles. It usually stays closer to the poles or just bothers Canada and the north, but sometimes it can send cold air here. They're not common this far south, but they do happen."

His eyes shifted back to me, the firelight casting a warm glow across his face. "But don't worry, we're all set for at least a week up here. I made sure to stock up extra wood this winter. We'll stay warm, come what may."

"Well, aren't you just a regular Boy Scout?" Josephine teased.

"Always prepared, that's my motto," Landon replied with a good-natured chuckle. "And for the record, I am not a regular Boy Scout." His hand swept out, as if painting his past in the air in front of the fire. "I went all the way to the esteemed rank of Eagle Scout, thank you very much."

I smiled, despite the cold and the dark.

"Well, Landon, I have to admit that your impressive Boy Scout achievements don't surprise me one bit," Josephine remarked, one elegant eyebrow arched. She appraised him over the rim of her mug, a hint of playful sarcasm in her tone. "I'd expect nothing less from someone so compulsively prepared."

"I'll see if I can come up with another way to catch the unflappable Josephine Reynolds by surprise someday." He punctuated this vow with an exaggerated wink.

Josephine just chuckled, waving a hand. "Good luck with that, Eagle Scout. I don't get surprised by much." She raised her mug in a mock toast. "But I welcome you to give it your best shot whenever inspiration strikes."

Josephine and Laurie fell deep in conversation on the sofa next to me. I listened silently to the attorney's ongoing interior decorating project to remodel her guest bathroom and the vet's woes about her ex-husband asking to take the kids to his mother's beach house during spring break rather than sticking to their custody agreement.

Mario was huddled by the fire, a ceramic mug cradled in his hands. Ursula, the feline embodiment of curiosity, was perched beside him, her jade-colored eyes fixated on the tempting liquid. She stretched out in one fluid motion, her pink tongue darting into the mug to lick the cooled hot chocolate that coated the wall.

Mario let out a laugh. I noticed the tension that gripped his shoulders had slipped away as he watched Ursula's antics, replaced by an almost childlike amusement.

Nearby, Evie smiled as two rambunctious kittens tussled and play-fought across her lap in a flurry of paws and twitching tails. Even Belladonna appeared in a rare tolerant mood, permitting several snuggly cats and the two dogs to encircle her regal form without even a sniff of disdain.

Despite our dark surroundings, a cozy sense of warmth and community filled the flame-lit loft. Our confinement had sparked fresh bonds that burned brightly, like the glowing logs stacked beside the hearth. The lively conversations and affectionate antics going on around me brightened my heart.

The tranquil atmosphere was pierced by the harsh static of Mario's police radio and the electronic crackle was as jarring as a crow's caw in a quiet forest.

"Lopez, it's Everett. Come in, over."

Mario's reaction was quick. He lunged for the radio, a look of surprise on his face. His fingers wrapped around it as he pressed the talk button. "Everett, it's Lopez. I'm here. Over."

Laurie, eyebrows arched high, turned toward Mario. "How is that radio still charged?" she asked.

"The electricity only went out a while ago," Landon said. "Mario had the foresight to keep it charged, just in case."

"Just wanted to check in, see how you folks are holding up over there," the radio squawked, its metallic voice echoing through the room. "We've got a couple cars out patrolling thanks to some tire chains from Dale Haberman. Apparently, his wife used to live in Minnesota. Let me know if you need anything. Over."

"Appreciate that, Lieutenant. We're okay for now, just hunkered down, keeping warm. We lost power, but have a fire, so we're good for the moment. Over."

There was a pause and some static before Everett's voice returned. "Good deal. Listen, if we come across animals in distress while we're out and about, we're going to bring them over to Silver Circle. County doesn't have a vet on call that can get to the shelter, and I understand Dr. Gray is there with you. Is that right?"

"Yes, sir. Over."

"All right then. We'll radio if we find any animals in need so you can be ready. Over."

"Copy that. Stay safe out there. Lopez out."

Mario set the radio down, shaking his head. "Well, at least they're making some patrols. But with the roads like this, I doubt they'll get far."

I nodded, hoping animal owners all took their animals inside, and that the winter storm spared the local wildlife as much as possible. Hearing that authorities were still trying to help Tablerock made me feel a little less nervous—we might be in the dark, but we weren't entirely alone. We were still connected to the outside world, and that was a comforting thought.

The sofa gave a subtle creak, its cushions yielding under Landon's weight as he slid in beside me. "Hey," he murmured, his voice imbued with the warmth I'd come to expect from him. "How are you holding up?"

It had become a comforting anchor in my life, that warmth.

I offered him a small smile. "Oh, I'm okay. Just thinking."

Under the dancing firelight, Landon's face was a canvas of concern as his eyes, ever perceptive, studied me. "Everything all right?"

I drew in a deep breath, my fingers playing with a loose thread on the blanket draped over my lap. Landon had always had a knack for seeing right through me, his intuition as sharp as a cat's night vision.

"Mostly," I said. "I guess I'm just feeling a little overwhelmed and anxious about everything. The storm, the power being out, being stuck here indefinitely." I gestured helplessly toward the shadowy room. "Yesterday this seemed like a fun sleepover, and now? Not so much."

Landon's sturdy arm encircled my shoulders, his flannel shirt warm against my neck. "I know. But we're going to get through this just fine, and at least we're here with friends and family. The power will come back on soon."

I let my head rest on his shoulder. "I hope so."

"You don't sound convinced."

"I just keep thinking, what if it doesn't? What if things get worse? It's so cold, and nothing is melting. Not the ice, not the snow." I fiddled with the ceramic mug in my hands. "I worry about keeping the animals warm with just a fire. What if the pipes freeze? Did we put enough water in the bathtubs for this many cats? What if—"

"Whoa! Ma'am, I think you need to stop overthinking this." Landon gave my shoulder a reassuring squeeze. "No sense borrowing trouble. We've made it through day one just fine. When you hired me to rehab this place, I made sure we sealed and re-insulated every inch of Wardwell Manor. We'll be fine. One day at a time, okay?"

I inhaled, holding the breath for a long moment before exhaling in a slow, controlled stream. The woodsy aroma of the fire filled my senses, momentarily cutting through the ceaseless churning of my thoughts. I focused on the mug cradled in my palms, willing my spinning mind to still.

"You're right, Landon. I know worrying like this doesn't help matters. But tonight, I just can't seem to rein in my spiraling thoughts."

Landon planted a kiss against my temple. "Tell you what. How about I make us some chamomile tea? That always soothes your nerves."

I managed a proper smile then. "Chamomile tea sounds perfect. Thank you."

While Landon busied himself preparing two mugs in the makeshift kitchen area, I gazed into the flames and tried to unlock the sudden grip my anxiety had on me. I pictured the fiery tendrils reaching out to melt the icy tension stiffening my shoulders and neck.

Soon, Landon returned and pressed another steaming mug into my chilled hands. Curls of fragrant steam rose, filling my senses with the sweet, delicate aroma of chamomile. I closed my eyes and inhaled deeply, feeling my knotted muscles start to loosen as the floral scent worked its magic.

We sipped our tea in comfortable silence as the fire crackled.

Across the room, I noticed Matt and Evie had drifted off to sleep curled up together under a pile of quilts. Mario dozed nearby, a contented Ursula snuggled on his chest. Seeing everyone tucked into their makeshift beds, shoulders relaxed and breathing deep, reminded me we really were going to be all right.

I was being silly. Our situation wasn't that ominous.

I turned back to Landon to find him watching me with a thoughtful expression.

"What is it?" I asked.

He reached over and took my free hand in his. "You know, once we're through this storm, I've been thinking..." He paused, brow furrowing as he seemed to search for the right words. "Well, maybe it's time we make this living situation more official."

I tilted my head. "Living situation? What do you mean?"

Landon's eyes were earnest. "Move in together, I mean. Spend our nights under the same roof, not just when the weather hits. Wake up together each morning instead of sayin' goodbye the night before."

My pulse quickened at the notion, both thrilled—and hesitant.

Sensing my trepidation, he added, "Ellie, just think about it. No pressure. I know change is hard." Landon lifted my hand and pressed a kiss to my knuckles. "Seein' you fret tonight, though, all I could think was how much I want to be by your side, always."

My throat tightened with emotion. After a long pause, I managed to whisper, "It's a big step."

Landon nodded. "I know, and I don't aim to rush you. But seems to me life's too short for slow, when you find the right fit." His eyes were solemn. "Just promise you'll turn it over some in that head of yours?"

I swallowed hard, my throat dry as a summer day in Texas. The thought of Landon and me, sharing a roof, a life... it was both exhilarating and terrifying.

He was like a well-fitted glove, his presence in my life as natural as breathing now. Yet, the ghosts of my past tugged at the edges of my joy, whispering words of caution. I had rushed headlong into love once before. Even though I'd never trade that relationship because of the daughter it gave me, the scars from Evie's father still lingered.

Did I want to invite that risk again?

I found myself wrestling with a whirlwind of emotions. Anxiety, excitement, fear—and a healthy dose of self-doubt—all swirled together, creating a storm of uncertainty within me.

I blinked, surprised by the sting of insecurity that his suggestion provoked.

I mean... he was talking about sharing a home, about blending our lives together, and yet... there was no mention of marriage. Was it foolish to want that level of commitment from him—even when I didn't know what my answer would be should he ask? Or was it the lingering sting of past disappointments making me want more from him than I was willing to give? Did I want something lopsided so I maintained control?

If Landon sensed my inner turmoil, he remained silent. He did keep hold of my hand and sat in patient silence as the logs burned in the brick fireplace, letting me work through my conflicted emotions.

Maybe... maybe I was ready to stop taking baby steps.

Maybe it was time to take that leap.

I stirred as the logs collapsed in the fireplace, scattering sparks. Turning to Landon, I squeezed his steady hand.

"I can't give you an answer right now," I began. "But you're right. Life is short. I don't want to miss out on something extraordinary because I'm afraid." I offered him a tentative smile. "I promise I'll give this serious thought."

Landon's eyes lit up, and his grin shined in the dark like sunshine emerging from clouds. "That's all I can ask," he said, and pulled me into the warm embrace of his arms.

We sat in silence, the hypnotic melody of the crackling fire filling the room, each pop and hiss of the burning wood a comforting sound as I thought about my future.

When my eyes fluttered open later, a soft, warm glow filled the room.

The fire, our lifeline against the freezing winter outside, continued to blaze. Its flickering light cast long shadows, transforming the familiar shapes of my friends into ethereal figures wrapped in blankets around the fireplace.

Despite the fire's steady warmth, the winter's cold had managed to sneak in, sending a chill prickling across my skin. I pulled the quilt tighter around myself and Landon, cocooning us against the cold. He was a steady presence beside me, his arm a comforting weight as it cradled me close.

Adding to our cocoon of warmth were our feline companions, their bodies curled up on and around us. Belladonna had claimed a spot at our feet, her rhythmic purring a soothing background hum. Another cat, Digby, had draped himself across Landon's chest, his tail twitching in dream-induced chases. I felt several cats' bodies burrowed against me beneath the blanket.

A soft smile tugged at my lips.

Their toasty nearness, combined with Landon's and the quilt, created a haven of heat in the middle of the winter's cold, a testament to the comforting power of shared warmth—both literal and figurative.

Just then, a faint scrape cut through the quiet, capturing my attention.

I held my breath, my senses suddenly on high alert.

There—another scuff, too deliberate to be settling logs or scurrying mice. It seemed to come from the stairwell just outside the closed door.

I slipped out from under Landon and the cats' and crept in my sock feet across the icy floorboards. Pressing my ear to the door to the third floor loft, I held my breath, straining to identify the odd noises drifting up from below.

More muffled shuffles and thuds.

They were sporadic but too regular to be random creaks of the old house. It sounded like someone moving around down there.

I found myself caught in a mental tug-of-war.

Should I awaken Landon or Mario?

The thought of disturbing their peaceful slumber felt silly, especially if the source of the noise was just Josephine on one of her infamous midnight snack hunts. The last thing I wanted was to stir everyone into a frenzy over nothing.

Decision made, I eased the door open just enough to slip through and tiptoed down the shadowy stairs on high alert, ears primed for any sound.

On the second floor landing, I paused.

I could see a sliver of light seeping from under the door to the file room, its flickering patterns suggesting movement within. My pulse quickened, a drumbeat in my ears that echoed the sudden surge of adrenaline coursing through my veins.

I edged down the hallway, my breath held.

The closer I got, the more distinct the sounds became.

Rustling.

Clinking.

I hesitated outside the closed door, uncertain.

Why hadn't I taken a moment to ensure everyone was still asleep before starting this impromptu investigation? Well, because we're in the middle of a power outage, I answered myself silently, so who would bother with burglary? But a power outage means no security system, I argued, and then shook my head at my own paranoia—really, what were the odds of a break-in? Who in their right mind would invade a cat shelter in the midst of the storm of the century?

Just as my mind's silent squabble ramped up, a loud thud echoed from within the room, followed by a muffled curse. Both sides of my bickering brain agreed the sound did not come from a cat.

Taking a deep breath, I mustered my courage and eased the door open. It gave way with the tiniest creak, and I could make out a figure bent over. They were rummaging through cabinets, their back to me.

I cleared my throat, the sound sharp in the darkness, and reached out to fumble for a flashlight I'd left on the nearby table. The beam cut through the gloom as I flicked it on, casting a stark, white light on the figure before me.

"Don't move!" I ordered, making my voice as stern as possible.

The figure whirled, eyes wide. To my shock, I stared down at Josephine, crouched on the floor in pajamas.

"Ellie Rockwell!" she gasped, pressing a hand to her chest. "You scared ten years off my life!"

"I thought you don't get surprised by much?"

"It's the middle of the night!"

"No kidding! Jeesh, Josephine, you scared the bejeezus out of me. What in heaven's name are you doing?"

The lawyer laughed as she slowly straightened up. "Oh, you know... just, um, reorganizing a bit."

I crossed my arms. "At three in the morning?"

"I couldn't sleep. You're very unappreciative of my volunteer help in your file room, by the way."

"You decided to help in the dark? Burning the battery on one of the few flashlights we have in a blackout?" My eyes narrowed. "Care to explain what you're really up to?"

Her eyes darted past me to land on a folder lying open on the floor.

I followed her gaze—it was Ursula's folder, the one containing all her medical records, adoption paperwork, and known history. Next to it, Josie's laptop lay open, a document glowing on the screen.

"Quit playing around." I turned back to Josephine, my eyebrows furrowed. "What are you doing with Ursula's file?"

Josephine's confident facade fell, replaced with a look of guilt. Her eyes dropped to the floor. "Fine," she finally said. "I was just trying to find something, and I didn't want Mario to know I was looking after his meltdown earlier."

"Find what?"

"I had a hunch."

"Okay, you had a hunch. What's the hunch?"

As I stood there, bathed in the harsh light from Josephine's flashlight, listening to her hunch, I knew one thing for certain: the storm outside was only the beginning of our problems.

Chapter Fifteen

As I stood there bathed in the harsh flashlight beam, my tired mind wandered to how this small, windowless room remained almost pleasant despite the lack of heat. Landon's careful insulation renovations were proving their worth. Even enveloped in darkness and frigid temperatures, we were still comfortable up here on the second floor. Landon had done an impressive job with the insulation. This room, though not exactly toasty, was far from the frigid temperature I'd expected.

"Ellie? Are you even listening to me?"

I yawned. "Can you say that again? I think I drifted off standing up."

Josephine straightened up, squaring her shoulders. "I said that Ursula's records hold clues we've overlooked." There was a gleam in her eyes I recognized all too well, part of the smug look she got whenever she was onto something.

I lifted an eyebrow. "Go on."

"Ursula was found by Clara as a three-month-old kitten the night Juna vanished. I wondered if she was microchipped at the time and it turns out she was—"

"This got you out of bed at three in the morning? A microchip?"

"I couldn't sleep, and you know how my mind works. Something nagged at me about Ursula's information, and I needed to find out why. Ursula wasn't old enough to be spayed when she was with Juna—that's done at around five or six months, right? It's been standard practice to microchip pets then—but Ursula had a microchip already."

"Okay. Juna was a good owner and got Ursula microchipped early. So, you thought Ursula's microchip might... what, exactly?"

"Tell us something," Josephine said with a nod. "When a pet is microchipped, the owner's contact details are stored in the database. If Ursula was microchipped while she was with Juna, then Juna's details would be in that file first, right?"

"Yes, but we know where Juna lived." I raised an eyebrow. "I don't understand what you're getting at here."

Josephine's eyes glittered as she scooped up Ursula's folder and handed it to me with a flourish. "Look."

I flipped it open, skimming through until I located

the microchip information page. My eyes flashed over the list of contacts associated with the ID number, taking in the details. "I don't see what—"

"Look harder," she said. "When Ursula was adopted by her new owner, they would have added their information and removed the original contact information. They would not have just added their own as additional contacts because they were now the primary owners." Josie pointed. "Only that's what they did."

"They who?"

She tapped the folder. "Look."

I looked.

The original contact information matched Juna's at the time she disappeared.

The second record had Clara's name and number entered as the contact shortly after Juna disappeared. The entry was made around the date she would have gotten the kitten from the car.

After that, the contact info was updated from Clara Adams to reflect Maude Blankenship's ownership when she adopted Ursula.

Finally, a few months ago, it was updated to our shelter.

I had no idea what Josephine was on about, and smothered a yawn. "Nifty," I said (more out of a desire to end the conversation and get back to bed than anything else), handing the folder back to Josephine. "But I have to admit I'm just seeing what I'd anticipate seeing based on the known timeline. Juna, then Clara, then Maude, now the shelter."

Josephine stared at me. "You didn't look."

"I looked."

Josephine stared some more.

"It's the dead of night, Joe. Just spit it out. What should I have seen that I didn't see?"

"Okay, maybe you'll spot it if I show you the account on the computer."

I rolled my eyes.

The adrenaline spike from being startled awake had long since faded, leaving bone-deep exhaustion in its wake. All I wanted was to burrow back under the quilt next to Landon and let sleep reclaim me.

But Josephine would not let this go.

She placed the folder on a nearby shelf and lifted her laptop. With a quick-fingered login and an adjustment in brightness to save the battery, Josephine angled the screen toward me. "What's really intriguing is the contact update made just over a year after Juna disappeared in their database. It was in that folder, but not too easy to spot. Check this out."

I leaned in.

On the microchip's website, the timeline of changes on the account showed a new phone number was entered around eighteen months after Juna disappeared for... Juna. The next change showed Maude listed as primary contact for Fluff, and a name change for the cat to Ursula—but Clara was still a secondary contact.

Even more oddly, Juna's updated contact information was deleted a few months after Maude—may she rest in peace—was added as the owner.

But then Clara's original phone number had an additional contact number added—which had been Juna's previously updated number.

An update that took place *after* she disappeared.

My brow furrowed as I studied the inexplicable update. "That must be some sort of mistake," I mused aloud. "If Clara held on to the cat until a home could be found for her, wouldn't the microchip company just remove her from the contacts list when Maude adopted Ursula?"

"Did you call Clara when Ursula was brought here?" Josephine asked.

"No. The owner, Maude, had passed away. There was no ownership to establish, so I didn't check the records." I leaned back. "Someone just made a mistake. It has to be."

"A mistake? Maybe. That is one of many questions I have about that list of contacts and that time line—and that's the least suspicious thing on there. Look again." Josephine said, gesticulating as she spoke. "Juna Brucker updated her phone number after she disappeared. Now, how would a missing person update their contact information?"

I nodded. "I'll admit, it's odd, but I've also dealt with these microchip companies. The records can get convoluted over time, especially when an animal has multiple homes and multiple owners," I told her. "It's not evidence of anything."

"No? Juna Brucker called in to change her contact number six months after she disappeared, Ellie." Josephine gave a dramatic snap of her fingers. "It was six months when her father asked the authorities to halt their hunt for her."

"You don't know that she called in," I said. "Anyone could have called in."

Josephine threw me an exasperated look that suggested I'd just proposed we might spot penguins sunbathing in the Tablerock town square. "Ellie, when you hear hoof beats, you think horses—not zebras strolling up Main Street in sunglasses!"

I hadn't had enough sleep for any of this.

"Okay, fair point about the odds," I conceded. "But just for the sake of argument... what if the 'horse' in this case was a zebra in disguise all along? Like one of those painted ponies from the carnival just trying to blend in with the herd? Maybe that's why they have the sunglasses."

Josephine just stared at me for a long moment, blinking, as if trying to process an unfamiliar language. Finally, she narrowed her eyes, though a hint of amusement tugged at her mouth. "I see. You're just mocking me now, is that it?"

"A little. This is what you get in the middle of the night."

Josephine took the hint and shut the laptop with a

soft click. She tucked it under her arm and slid Ursula's folder back into its slot in the file cabinet, a silent acknowledgment (finally) of my weary state.

"Look, Josie, I hear you. And yes, it looks like something weird was going on with the records." I placed a hand on Josephine's oversized sweatshirt-clad shoulder as we moved toward the door. "We'll pick this thread back up tomorrow. We can look into Maude, call the microchip company. Maybe we should even call Clara to ask what was up. Silver Circle is responsible for that cat now, so I don't see how it would arouse any suspicion."

Josephine nodded, looking invigorated despite the hour. "Fine, but I'm telling you, I think this is a big deal," she said with a sly smile. "I can feel it."

The morning light filtered through the frost-streaked windows, the chill from the previous night sending shivers up my spinc despite the warmth from the steadily burning fire.

There was still no electricity.

On this third morning trapped in the shelter, I decided not to bother folding up the blankets and bedding. As I rolled over beneath the heavy quilt, the thought passed through my mind that keeping some semblance of order no longer seemed important. It was the third day of perpetual pajamas and bed head, and it had eroded any motivation I had left to tidy up our makeshift sleeping quarters.

I sat up, yawned, and saw I wasn't the only one.

The blankets we'd repeatedly folded and stacked each morning (and afternoon, and again in the evening) lay strewn across the floor, the sofa, the chairs. A sense of disarray hung in the air, a stark contrast to the usual order of the cat rescue.

I worked a kink out of my neck and glanced around the room.

Everyone else was already up, speaking in low voices over mugs of instant coffee as weak gray light filtered in. The scene reminded me of childhood slumber parties where you'd awaken in a tangle of sleeping bags and pillows, all abandoned at once in the sharp light of morning.

As I stood and shuffled over to join the others, Mario caught my eye.

He looked... defeated, his shoulders slumped under some invisible weight.

"Morning!" I offered with a cheerful smile.

Mario grimaced as if my friendliness wounded him, not quite making eye contact. "Yeah, morning. I um... I just..." He trailed off, then took a deep breath. "Look, I need to apologize for losing my cool yesterday. Yelling like that was way out of line."

I waved a hand. "Water under the bridge."

Laurie nodded. "I think we all understand why this case is hard for you."

"And it's not like this ice storm isn't stressful in general," Landon added.

"Maybe. Nevertheless, I shouldn't have reacted that way." Mario turned his mug in restless circles on the table. "With everything coming out, I'm realizing maybe I didn't know my friends as well as I thought back then."

That was probably the understatement of the year.

He paused, taking a deep breath before continuing. "I've been doing some thinking. Clara and Juna... they kept things from me. I know that now. Maybe things they didn't trust me with. Or things they didn't think I could handle." He gave a hollow laugh. "Guess they were right."

"Mario, come on. You're being too hard on yourself. You weren't to blame for trusting your friends," Laurie said gently.

"Everyone keeps parts of who they are hidden," Matt added.

"I suppose," Mario said, looking unconvinced. "They'd brush things off that should have seemed strange to me. Made excuses." His gaze was faraway. "I wanted to believe them, I guess, so I did."

"I don't understand. Make excuses for what?" Laurie asked.

"One time, I came by her house—Juna's house—and she was upset. Clara was comforting her, seemed almost protective of her—but they swore nothing was wrong. Nada. Now I wonder if that was a lie to throw me off. Have I been a fool this whole time?"

I frowned. "Why would you think that, Mario?"

Once, he shared, Juna had shown up to a gig with a black eye she'd blamed on a clumsy fall. "I believed her, but maybe I shouldn't have. I mean, who falls and blackens their eye?" Mario admitted, a bitter edge to his voice. "I still don't know what happened that night, but I know she's dead. Gone too young, before she had a chance to do anything."

Josephine's gaze held mine, a flicker of unspoken knowledge dancing in her eyes. The echo of her middle of the night discovery reverberated within me, a dissonant gong that stirred up a flurry of doubts about Mario's conclusion.

The seed of doubt planted earlier blossomed into full-fledged uncertainty.

Was she dead?

Details that had seemed to align now lay askew, puzzles pieces that refused to snap into place.

The others reassured Mario, their voices overlapping in a chorus of understanding and empathy. It wasn't his fault. He couldn't have known. His friends were protecting him in their own way.

But all I could think of was one question.

Was she dead?

Finally, Josephine clapped her hands, making us all jump. "Okay, that's enough of that. Dwelling on past regrets gets us nowhere," she said in her usual brisk manner. "I, for one, am glad you've found your center,

Mario. A focused mind is critical with so much yet to unravel."

Before he could respond that he hadn't, in fact, found his center, she barreled on as if everything was normal once again. "My middle of the night adventures yielded a rather intriguing bit of information I'm keen to share regarding our emerald-eyed feline." Josephine summarized finding the anomalies in Ursula's microchip records and contact changes.

"That is bizarre," Landon murmured when she finished. "So either Juna herself, or someone posing as her, updated the contact info after her disappearance? But why would someone do that?"

Josephine nodded. "An excellent question."

"I've been thinking a little about this since last night. Could the change have been some kind of signal? A message to someone, maybe?" I speculated. "Though I don't understand why Juna, if she was still alive, wouldn't just call Maude or Clara if she was sending either of them a message through the microchip account."

"If she..." Mario's mouth fell open, his words lost in the surprise that rendered him momentarily speechless.

"Maude? Who's Maude?" Laurie asked.

"Ursula spent most of her life with Maude Blankenship," Josephine said.

"Whoa, wait." Evie held up a hand. "Did you say Maude Blankenship?"

"I did."

"You're sure?"

"Yes," Josephine confirmed. "You look surprised. Didn't you know?"

"I wasn't here the day Ursula came in. Matt and I went to a race at COTA. Considering what Mario said before, maybe I shouldn't be surprised." Evie leaned forward. "Before she retired, Maude ran an Austin shelter for battered women. She was its director for well over twenty years."

Josie snapped her fingers. "You're right. I'd forgotten that."

"That can't be a coincidence," Matt said.

Evie nodded. "I did a project on her shelter back in high school. She was passionate about helping domestic violence victims get to safety, start new lives away from their abusers. She protested at the legislature. I mean, she totally devoted her life to it after..." She trailed off, brow furrowing.

"After what?" Josephine prodded.

"After her daughter was killed by her abusive boyfriend years earlier. Maude turned her grief into purpose to help other women escape that fate." Evie shook her head. "That black eye you saw suddenly looks a lot different now, Mario."

"That black eye..." Mario's face was a canvas of shock, his eyes wide, mirroring the disbelief that gripped him. His jaw hung open and his hand hovered in midair, as if he was trying to reach for something to anchor him back to reality.

Had Maude known about Juna's fate? Is that why Ursula came into her care? It seemed we'd uncovered yet another player in this mystery who might have answers.

Well...

If she weren't dead.

The brooding stillness was disrupted by the radio abruptly sputtering to life. "Lopez, it's Everett again. Over."

Mario shook off his stupor and strode across the room, each step decisive. Reaching the radio, he seized it with a firm grip and he pressed the transmit button. "I'm here. Over," he said, his policeman's concern replacing his previously stunned expression.

"Hey there. Listen, the temperature is getting above freezing today and the county is going to plow the roads some. Those chains are working pretty good on our SUV's, too. Not perfectly, but a few of us are mobile, at least. Wanted to check in. Over."

Mario glanced around at our faces before responding. "Appreciate that news, Jackson. We're doing all right, just trying to stay warm. Let us know if you come across any animals that need help. Over."

"You got it. Over and out."

"Jackson Everett?" Evie's voice wavered, her wide eyes locked on Mario.

"Sorry?" Mario's brow furrowed, his head turning toward Evie.

"That was Jackson Everett, Juna's ex-boyfriend, on the radio?" she asked again, her words slow and deliberate, as if trying to make sense of the puzzle pieces falling into place. "You still work with him?"

Mario nodded. "Yes. Why?"

The women of our group had begun a subtle exodus across the room. Laurie caught my gaze and gave a small, knowing tilt of her head toward where Evie and Josephine were already huddled together. Their whispers were a low hum, a soundtrack to the separation unfolding in the loft.

I nodded and made my way over.

We were an island unto ourselves, cocooned in a bubble of hushed tones and conspiratorial glances. The men were none the wiser, their ears tuned to the sporadic chatter of the radio, which crackled and buzzed like a distant storm they were trying to interpret.

"So it seems pretty obvious now what happened with Juna back then, right? I assume I'm not the only one that put two and two together," I said in a low voice.

Josephine snorted. "Obvious to us, perhaps. But not to some." She jerked her chin toward where the men sat obliviously across the room.

"Oh, go easy on them," Laurie chided. "You know, men just miss subtle cues when it comes to things like this."

"Subtle, nothing!" Josephine scoffed. "Those fellas

couldn't catch a clue if Colonel Mustard himself drew it on the football scores with a big red marker."

Laurie shot her a reproachful look. "That's not fair, Josephine," she said. "Men and women have different instincts, different antennae for this kind of stuff. It's not their fault we see it easier."

"And even we miss the boat sometimes," Evie said.

Josephine held up her hands in mock surrender. "Fine, fine. We'll give them the benefit of the doubt. But if we have to spell things out with fridge magnets, I'm revoking their detective licenses."

Laurie's expression grew serious. "It seems to me the only explanation that fits is Juna went into hiding to escape an abusive creep, and that abusive creep is likely Jackson Everett."

"I agree," I said. "It explains Juna's father's behavior, which has been bothering me from the beginning. There's just no parent on the planet that would ask the police to stop looking for their missing child—unless they didn't want that missing child to be found. And the only reason her father wouldn't want her found is to protect her."

"It's not the only reason. He could be the abuser," Evie pointed out.

"But Mario's been friends with Juna's father for years."

"Mario's been friends with Jackson for years, too," Laurie pointed out. "Not sure we can go by who Mario has a connection to or what he remembers fondly."

"He's her *father*," I said, as if that put an end to any suspicion of him.

"Okay." Laurie nodded. "I'm not as sure as Ellie, but I think we can set Mr. Brucker aside for now."

I frowned, my fingers tracing the rim of my mug. "But what's Jackson hiding, then? Why did he tell Mario not to look into it?" I looked around. "If Juna's hiding from him, wouldn't he *want* to find her?"

"I've been thinking about that." Josephine crossed her arms and leaned back against the wall, her expression thoughtful. "You know who can't be a cop? Men who beat up women. Think it through." She didn't wait for a reply. "There must be some proof of what he did we haven't uncovered."

"Wouldn't there be a record if she filed complaints?" Evie asked.

"Complaints with the police department her abuser works at?" Josephine began ticking possibilities off on her manicured fingers. "Reports get buried. Cases dismissed. Records get sealed or go missing. You know how these things go." Her expression darkened. "What if Juna tried reporting him, and her cop boyfriend intercepted that report? Made sure she couldn't get help?"

Evie's uncertainty was palpable; she gnawed at her lower lip, her brow creased with doubt. "I don't know," she murmured. "I don't know. That's making some big assumptions."

"I don't think it's a stretch at all," I said quietly. "Isn't the simplest explanation usually the right one?"

"Not a zebra," Josephine told me.

"Not a zebra. And it's not the first time Tablerock had a corrupt cop."

"Ugh." Laurie still looked uncertain. "I just hate to think that's the reality we're faced with. Mario's losing it with hypotheticals. How's he going to feel if it turns out his childhood sweetheart had to run because his boss at the department was an abusive jerk to her?"

"We'll get proof," Josephine said. "But I don't know that we can assume she ran away. That abusive snake could have done something to silence Juna permanently. Scaring her into hiding is just one possibility. Another is..." She trailed off meaningfully.

A somber silence descended over our huddle as we contemplated the unspoken possibility hanging over the case like gathering storm clouds.

"Poor Mario." Laurie sighed, glancing over at him. "This is going to devastate him when he realizes the truth about his friend. He might get one back only to lose another."

I followed her gaze to where Mario sat staring into the fire. What must be running through his mind now, as his memories and perceptions shifted? Did he already suspect the painful revelations to come?

Just then, the crackle of the radio sliced through once more. "Lopez, it's Everett. Over."

Josephine whispered, "Speak of the devil!"

Mario grabbed the radio. "Everett, it's Lopez. Over."

"We've found an injured German Shepherd

wandering Marks Street. No tag. We're bringing him your way. Over."

Mario sat up straight, alert. "Understood, Lieutenant. We'll be ready. Over."

"Appreciate it. We'll have the dog there in about twenty minutes. Everett out."

Mario set down the radio and turned to face us. "They're bringing an injured dog. Laurie, can you—"

"I'm on it!" Laurie nodded, already moving toward the stairs.

My eyes wandered to the whiteboards, their surfaces a collage of scribbled notes related to Juna's disappearance. For a moment, I considered gathering up the materials to tuck them out of sight before Everett arrived.

But then I shook my head and decided against it.

The lieutenant had no reason to come to our third-floor quarters—he would stay downstairs attending to the injured dog and then leave to get back on the slick roads.

No need to rush around hiding things that would never catch his eye.

Right?

A lingering doubt whispered at the back of my mind as I went downstairs to help Laurie... a subtle, inexorable itch that suggested I might be gambling more than I realized.

Chapter Sixteen

THE LOFT HAD SETTLED INTO A HUSHED SORT OF normalcy by the time Jackson Everett arrived. The shuffling of feet and the murmur of voices downstairs signaled his entrance—the sudden clatter of boots in the front lobby piercing our cloistered cocoon.

I made my way to the landing, watching as Laurie rushed toward the German Shepherd, checking him over with a practiced ease. The dog, despite its injury, seemed to trust her, his intelligent eyes tracking her every move.

"What did you get into, huh, buddy?" she asked him. "That leg doesn't feel broken."

The dog barked in response.

Jackson Everett nodded as he stood in the doorway, clutching the shivering German Shepherd in his arms. "Like I said, found this guy limping along Marks Street.

No tags or collar, but he seems like someone's lost pet," Lt. Everett said. "Well behaved. Friendly."

"I'll take him," Laurie said. She took him from the Lieutenant and gently placed him on the floor. A wagging tail punctuated the German Shepherd's uneven gait as he sidled up to Laurie, his tongue lolling out in a pant that bordered on a smile. "Let's see how you walk, buddy, huh? We're going to go right in there. Can you do that for me?"

She extended her hand, her fingers wiggling toward her clinic, and with a bright bark of agreement, the dog headed toward it. His limp barely slowed him down as he trotted alongside Laurie, ready for whatever attention and treats this new adventure with his kind-hearted guides would bring.

He was a handsome shepherd with a thick, well-groomed coat, despite it being matted from the snow. No sign of fleas or neglect.

Someone out there was surely missing their pet.

"He seems okay, though better that Laurie signed off and he got out of the cold." Mario clasped Jackson Everett's gloved hand in a businesslike shake. "Good to see you, Jackson."

I watched the two men.

Their handshake was a familiar exchange, fingers locking in an easy grip I was sure had been repeated over countless shifts and seasons.

"That's an intense look. What are you thinking?" Landon whispered.

My response was noncommittal, a simple unladylike grunt that spoke the volumes I couldn't say in present company. My mind was a whirlwind of past and present, trying to reconcile the man that stood in front of me with someone a woman might need to run from.

While we waited, talk turned—inevitably—to the storm.

Mario asked Lt. Everett how the roads were holding up. Jackson Everett shook his head and said, "Trying to patrol some, but the roads are still pretty rough."

Mario glanced at Jackson. "You staying warm enough out there on patrol?"

"Doing our best," Jackson told him. "We've got the vehicles running with heaters on full blast, but nothing beats an actual fire."

"We've been lucky to have enough wood to keep the fire going," Landon said, a note of pride in his voice. "It's kept us from freezing over these past few days."

"Looks like just a minor sprain," Laurie told us as she reappeared with the dog, now leashed. "And no microchip, so no idea what his name is. We'll need to keep him warm since the power is still out. Let's bring him upstairs where the fireplace is going."

Lt. Everett nodded, petting the dog's head. "Yeah, probably for the best. We can find out who he belongs to once things are back to normal. You folks don't mind taking care of him for a few days, do you?"

"Of course not."

"How long do you think it'll be before the power's back?" Mario asked as we ascended the stairs together.

And no, I *didn't* remember my own concern—I was preoccupied thinking about how we would accommodate a German Shepherd alongside all the shelter cats. My mind churned with logistics, like where to situate the dog and how to keep him relaxed in the middle of so many curious felines.

I didn't think about whiteboards.

"They're trying. They think it'll be later on today." Lt. Everett shook his head. "They just can't get some of the stuff to melt to fire it all back up so it'll work. I think the guys are in there with hairdryers defrosting nuts and bolts right now."

Once we reached the loft, Landon added more wood to the fire as the dog scrambled to settle down near the hearth. I grabbed the lead Laurie had placed on him and brought him over to a blanket. His coat was still slightly cold to the touch, and as Jackson mentioned, he had no collar that would tell us his name. "Did you have a collar, buddy? I bet you did. Did you lose it in the snow?"

The dog barked happily.

Belladonna hissed.

"How long now without power?" Lt. Everett asked, removing his hat and gloves.

"Less than a day," I said. "We're making do with the fireplace and camp stove, but I'll admit it's getting tiresome. We've been spending time..."

I trailed off, struck by a sudden realization.

And yes—there.

Right there.

That's the moment I remembered we didn't want Jackson Everett up here.

In my distraction over the injured dog, I had plum forgotten he was a suspect in Juna's disappearance. At the very least, I was pretty sure the man standing before me had abused his girlfriend when they were younger. That critical piece of information—and the incriminating details we had assembled all around this loft on whiteboards—had slipped my diverted mind.

I cursed myself for allowing a cute dog in need to short-circuit my brain.

"Spending time doing...?" Jackson Everett prodded.

"Taking care of the animals," I finished lamely.

Lt. Everett held his hands toward the blaze. "I bet. My place has been out since the start. Got a kerosene heater keeping the pipes thawed. But nights have been cold sleeping in all my clothes under every blanket I own."

Evie and Matt observed Jackson Everett with an air of casual detachment, their eyes tracking Lt. Everett's movements with the polite interest of bystanders at a parade–close enough to see the spectacle, yet far enough away to remain untouched by the pageantry.

Mario laughed. "I remember those days ice fishing with my uncle. Waking up so bundled you could barely move."

The two men fell into easy conversation, reminiscing

about school days and past storms weathered. Watching Mario banter and laugh with his colleague, I couldn't believe this was the same Lt. Everett we suspected of harming Juna.

Yet all signs pointed to the lieutenant being an abuser.

After the two chatted for a while, Lt. Everett stood and pulled his gloves back on. "I should get back at it, in case anyone else needs help. But thank you for the warm fire and for helping with the dog."

And then he turned.

Jackson Everett's departure was halted mid-motion, his body freezing as if he'd walked into an invisible wall.

Jackson's gaze roved over the first whiteboard's collage of clues—a photo of a smiling young Juna pinned next to lyrics scrawled by Evie, a map tracing the winding route to where her abandoned car was discovered. A red marker line connected Trent Beasley's scathing post to a scribbled synopsis of Shari's conversation.

Timelines and notes on the second whiteboard clearly referenced Jackson and Juna's youthful relationship. Jackson's own image was there, printed from a newspaper photo, his cheerful face at odds with the blunt label beneath him: "The Ex Boyfriend."

The lieutenant's hand reached out, hovering but not touching, as if the board radiated a heat that could scorch him.

Then he turned back to face us, eyes blazing. "What the hell is this?"

No one answered.

"Officer Lopez." Jackson's voice was steady, low. "What's this about?"

"We were looking into Juna's case," he said, his voice betraying a hint of defiance. "I'm sure you're aware Matt's a private investigator now. We thought we could find something other people missed by getting fresh eyes on things."

Jackson's jaw clenched, his eyes still blazing as he stared at the whiteboard. "I told you not to go digging into this, Mario. It wasn't going to help anything."

Mario's expression hardened. "Yeah, you did say that."

"So?"

"I didn't use any police resources for this."

"You were told," Jackson said, each word deliberate, "not to look into it. By me. By her father."

I watched as Mario's hands balled into fists, his knuckles whitening.

"I know what you said," he snapped back, his voice rising. "And I know what he said. But I've got to tell you, Jackson, I've never met two men more uninterested in finding out what happened to a missing woman than the two of you."

The words hung in the air, heavy and accusatory. Jackson's face reddened, a vein throbbing at his temple.

"I thought you loved her, Jackson."

"How dare you?" he spat out, stepping toward Mario. "You think you know what happened? You think you know how I felt about her?" Jackson scowled, his face reddening. "You don't know what you're talking about."

The swift shift from camaraderie to confrontation left me reeling. It was as though I'd seen the sudden crack of a frozen lake, the fractures racing across the ice —hidden stresses released in an instant that had been building, unseen, for years. The air between them shimmered with a hostility that felt both fresh and decades old.

The fire crackled and popped, a discordant soundtrack to the rising tension.

"I thought I knew," Mario said, his voice quaking with anger. "I thought I knew a lot of things. But now, looking back, I wonder just how blind I was."

Jackson stabbed an accusatory finger toward Mario. "Watch yourself, Lopez. You have no idea what went on back then."

"Because you won't tell me!" Mario shouted. "If you want me to drop this, then give me a reason, Jackson. An actual reason."

"You're stirring up the past for no good reason."

"For no good reason?" Mario's voice was incredulous. "A woman is gone, Jackson. Vanished. And you—"

"I did everything I could!" Jackson interrupted, his voice booming through the loft. "And I've had to live with that every day since she disappeared."

Their faces were inches apart now, eyes locked in a fierce duel. I felt rooted to the spot, my heart pounding in my ears, as the two men who had once shared laughs and memories now stood on the precipice of a chasm that had yawned open between them.

Even the animals seemed transfixed, the cats staring unblinkingly as the confrontation unfolded. The German Shepherd, perhaps sensing the animosity permeating the room, let out a low growl. His body tensed, poised as if ready to leap between the two arguing men.

Laurie held his leash tight as Jackson jabbed his finger into Mario's chest. "You think you're so smart, playing detective with your little amateur dimwitted mystery group up here?"

"Hey, now," Landon warned Jackson. "Let's watch it."

"You don't know a damn thing, Mario."

Mario shoved Jackson's hand away. "You know what? Maybe these people are right. Maybe Juna's dead —or worse—because of something you did."

Or... worse?

Worse than dead? What could be worse than being dead?

Jackson's fist clenched, his arm pulling back.

Mario tensed, bracing himself.

Before things could escalate further, I rushed between them. "Enough!" I put a hand on each man's chest, pushing them apart. "This isn't helping."

Suddenly, Jackson lunged around me at Mario, his hand gripping the collar of Mario's shirt. Mario's reflexes kicked in, his own hands coming up to grapple with Jackson's, and the two men tumbled to the floor in a tangle of limbs and snarled curses.

Pandemonium ensued.

The three dogs erupted into a cacophony of barks, their excitement adding to the disarray, while dozens of cats dashed in a blur of fur, seeking refuge from the burgeoning storm of human emotions. The once peaceful loft was now a whirlwind of motion and sound, a maelstrom centered on two men battling their youthful demons in each other.

Landon leaped forward, trying to shield me and separate the two, his voice a loud baritone that commanded them to stop. I found my own voice once more and called out for calm, but it was swallowed by the sounds of the scuffle.

They rolled across the floor, knocking into furniture, sending a spray of embers from the fireplace as they struck the hearth. The room smelled of smoke and sweat, the air filled with grunts and the heavy thuds of bodies hitting the ground.

"Enough!" Landon bellowed, finally wedging his powerful leg between the two men. "This will not solve anything."

Heaving for breath, Mario and Jackson lay on the floor, their anger subsiding as they each regained their senses. The loft was a wreckage of scattered papers and upturned chairs, a physical reflection of the turmoil that had unfolded.

Belladonna's piercing golden eyes locked onto Jackson, unwavering and accusatory. Her tail lashed as she prowled toward him, feline grace disguising the menace in each deliberate step.

Once face to face, Belladonna hissed, baring her teeth.

The tempest of anger and accusation that had torn through the loft settled into a muted unease, as Mario and Jackson picked themselves off the ground and brushed dust from their clothes almost sheepishly.

"I'm sorry," Jackson muttered, more to the floor than to any of us. I watched him straighten a chair, right a fallen vase that had miraculously not shattered. "I'm sorry about that, Ellie. We shouldn't have lost control like that."

"Yeah, sorry," Mario added.

"It's okay. We'll get this place straightened up again in no time." Though my racing heart was still recovering from the burst of violence and my hands felt as clumsy as my thoughts.

Laurie leaned down to soothe the agitated dogs. Her

dry chuckle cut through the tension. "Well, at least the place didn't burn down," she remarked, her gaze flicking to the fireplace where embers still glowed, a reminder of the fight's proximity to disaster.

Landon had positioned himself close to Jackson, an unspoken sentinel.

It struck me as ironic—Landon, the gentle giant, standing guard over Jackson—who was the only one among us in uniform, his sidearm an ominous weight at his hip.

Though who knew if anyone else had weapons concealed away? This was Texas, after all. In the Lone Star State, concealed weapons were as common as the bluebonnets that painted our fields every spring.

Jackson's hands were methodical as he checked his weapon, ensuring it was secure. I noticed he, too, avoided eye contact until finally he looked up, his eyes finding Mario's. "I'm sorry," he said, and it sounded like it pained him to admit it. "That was out of line."

"Everything about Juna's case has been out of line from the start." Mario didn't look up from picking up scattered papers. "And I'll tell you, Jackson, I came up here thinking one thing, but now..." He shook his head. "Feels like these people that never knew Juna got closer to the truth than I ever did. What happened to her? It got lost somewhere along the way." He finally met Jackson's gaze. "Or it was deliberately hidden."

"Mario—"

"Don't 'Mario' me. People have never been willing to tell me the full story. Not then, and not now."

Jackson's jaw tightened. "Some things were private, Mario."

Mario slammed a book down on the desk. "We're in our midthirties, Jackson! What could still be private about the past, after all this time?"

"Just let it go," Jackson warned.

"Here we go again," Mario scoffed, throwing his hands in the air. "The same old refrain."

That's when Landon intervened, his voice a calm balm to the raw nerves exposed in the room. "Jackson, maybe it's time to just lay it all out. Clear the air."

I stepped forward. "Landon's right. This secrecy has gone on long enough," I said. Landon nodded his agreement. "For everyone's sake, it's time for the full truth to come out."

Jackson's stance wavered, a visible tremor running through his body. It was as if his conscience and his secrets were at war within him.

Landon placed a solid hand on his shoulder. "Son, carrying a weight like this alone for so long does no good." His tone was kind but unrelenting.

The firelight flickered across the lieutenant's furrowed brow and his eyes darted around the room, avoiding our expectant gazes. One hand rubbed at the back of his neck while the other smoothed his rumpled uniform.

Watching Jackson's obvious inner conflict play out in

fidgets and averted stares, I felt a pang of doubt. Were we pleading for truth from a killer?

Somehow, the longer this mystery's answer remained out of reach, the less certain I became Juna was dead and Jackson—or anyone Juna knew—was a murderer. An instinctive feeling, a hunch, told me Jackson hadn't murdered Juna.

I wasn't even completely sure why I felt that way.

After a long moment, Jackson slumped down into a chair by the fireplace. "All right," he agreed wearily. "I'll tell you everything I know. All of it."

Mario and I exchanged a surprised look.

I suppose neither of us expected Jackson to back down so quickly.

But, for some reason, surrounded by dozens of eyes witnessing the release of decades of simmering tension, Jackson appeared ready to shed the past's haunting secrets.

We rearranged our chairs near the fire and listened intently as Jackson began to speak.

Chapter Seventeen

Jackson leaned forward, resting his elbows on his knees as he gazed into the flickering fire. For a moment he said nothing, seemingly steeling himself before plunging into waters long avoided.

"I guess for you to understand it all, I should start at the beginning," he finally said. His eyes remained downcast and his voice took on a faraway quality, like a man sifting through memories.

The flames danced and cast ghostly shadows on the walls as Jackson leaned forward, his hands clasped together as if he were about to pray. His story began not with Juna, but with a picture of Tablerock as only a native could paint it.

"I was born right here in Tablerock, at the old hospital before they tore it down," he started, his voice a low murmur that seemed to harmonize with the crackling of the fire. "I mean, we all grew up here in Tablerock

—me, Mario," he said, motioning to Mario Lopez. "Juna and Clara. My parents ran a feed store on Oak Street."

Mario nodded, a nostalgic smile touching his lips. "I remember that feed store. We used to joke your folks just about lived there, they worked such long hours. Your mom was always nice to me. Remember how she used to give us those peppermints?"

Jackson chuckled, a hollow sound that didn't quite reach his eyes. "It was true. Those of you new to town may not know it, but this used to all be farmland and ranch land. Growing up, I lived and breathed 4H, Future Farmers of America, and exhibiting at the county fair." He gave a hollow chuckle. "Never would've pictured myself becoming a cop, that's for sure."

The room felt warmer somehow, the tension dissipating as we were drawn into the tableau of their childhood. I could almost see the two young boys, backpacks and bicycles, innocence still intact.

Jackson rubbed a hand across his jaw, his gaze still unfocused. "Yeah, looking back, I think they were always struggling to keep it afloat. But I was too young then to realize."

He described spending long, carefree childhood days playing in the woods, fishing, and getting into the usual small-town mischief. As Mario chimed in now and then, their reminiscences painted an idyllic backdrop of treehouses and summer nights sleeping out under the stars.

"Juna's family moved to Tablerock when we were all

about ten years old," Jackson continued. "Even as kids, her voice was just... mesmerizing. She'd sing in the school talent shows and everyone would be spellbound, like she cast magic over the whole auditorium."

I noticed a ghost of a smile touch his lips at the memory.

"Juna and Clara were a year behind us," Jackson continued, his gaze flickering toward the fire as if the past were written in the flames. "I don't even know how we all became friends. But we did. We'd all hang out at the soda shop next to the feed store after school, argue over which songs to play on that old jukebox."

"Even then, Clara was basically attached to Juna at the hip. It was like that from the moment they met," Mario added. "Where you found one, you'd always find the other."

"Was Clara from Tablerock?" I asked.

Jackson nodded. "She was a bit odd and shy before Juna came along. After that, she opened up more. Found her place, I guess you could say."

Their childhood portrait emerged piece by piece—long, carefree days morphing into teenage adventures and first crushes. Through it all, though, Juna's musical gift was a constant, her siren voice capturing the heart of their small town.

"I think I first realized I cared about her as more than a friend when we were about fifteen," Jackson admitted. "There was a big party at the lake one summer. Someone had brought sparklers, and she was dancing and twirling one, laughing. Her hair was glowing in the light, like she had a halo."

His expression softened at the memory, a glimpse of the boy who had fallen for her shining through the stern man now.

"We all just stood there watching her, dazzled."

Mario nodded, smiling. "I remember. I couldn't take my eyes off her that night. Juna could light up a room like no one else."

It sounded like both young men had their heart captured that night.

I watched the interplay between the two men, the shared history that both connected and separated them. It was a dance of memory and emotion, a choreography of the past that only they knew the steps to.

"Juna was always the star of the group, though," Jackson said, his voice gaining strength. "Everyone knew her, or knew of her. She had this... presence. A light."

"But she wasn't stuck up about it," Mario put in, leaning forward, hands now animated as he spoke. "She was *real*. Kind to everyone, no matter who they were."

Jackson nodded, his eyes distant. "She had time for everyone." He went on to detail his fumbling attempts to date Juna through high school and how excitement had buzzed through Tablerock's teenagers when she got accepted to a prestigious music program in Austin after graduation.

"No one doubted she was destined for big things," Mario remarked. "We all knew Juna would make it."

Jackson's expression darkened. "Maybe she would have, if it hadn't been for..." He trailed off, clearing his throat. After a weighty pause, he continued. "Well, it was right around that time that Tablerock started growing, and some of the ranches started selling to developers. No ranches, no herds. No herds, no feed."

Mario nodded. "That summer after graduation, the 'Closed' sign appeared on your feed store. I remember driving by and seeing that weathered plywood in the windows." Mario paused, giving Jackson a chance to jump in or object. But he remained silent. "It was horrible to see your family business shuttered like that."

"And my future plans of taking it over were gone. I was set adrift a little. College wasn't in the cards for me, at least not then. I wanted to stay connected to this community that had shaped me, to help hold on to what it had always been—even as it changed. To find a purpose. To help folks."

Mario held his friend's gaze. "So you became a cop."

Jackson gave a slow nod. "So I became a cop."

"We kept in touch, the four of us, even when I went away to the police academy, and when I got hired at the Tablerock Police Department, I asked Juna out. Finally, after all those years. I don't know why I waited so long." Lt. Everett smiled. "When she started dating me, I couldn't believe it. I was just Jackson, you know?" He frowned. "Her dad didn't like me much, thought she could do... better."

Unspoken words hung in the air, the 'better' left undefined.

"If Juna's dad didn't like me much, Clara couldn't *stand* me now that Juna and I were together. She was always the protective one," Jackson went on. "She'd always be watching out for Juna, like a hawk. If Juna was the light, Clara was the guard."

"They were pretty inseparable," Mario agreed.

"I didn't let it bother me, though. I loved Juna."

Jackson clearly adored Juna, but so did Mario (and, I began to suspect, Clara). I could picture it all: the ties of this friends' group bound by time, care, attraction and music, all knotted up with the sense of invincibility and eternity that youth provided.

And lurking just beneath the surface, the shadows of what was to come.

Jackson's story wove a tapestry of college football games and recital nights, of shared dreams and whispered secrets beneath the bleachers. He talked of the slow fracturing of their group as the years went by, as innocence gave way to experience and the future became the present. "We saw each other just as much as we always did, you know? Went out on weekends. Saw each other at parties."

"But we were young. I didn't know how to handle being in love with my friend's girlfriend. Clara didn't know how to handle disliking Jackson and being as close with Juna as she was." Mario looked down. "Maybe if we were more mature, we could have worked through it."

Jackson looked at Mario. "Yeah, well, we didn't."

"No. I guess we didn't."

He gave a rueful shake of his head. "I mean, we didn't have an intimate relationship, and we didn't talk about it, but I thought nothing of it. I figured she was just a good girl, waiting until marriage. I was so sure life was just going to keep getting better."

His hands gripped together, knuckles whitening. "But things changed. Juna... she just wasn't the same carefree girl I remembered. She had become jumpy, anxious. I didn't understand."

Mario looked surprised. "When was this?"

"About six months before she disappeared. At first I thought maybe she was struggling with her music career. Trying to break in, you know? It's a tough business." Jackson stared into the fire. "But deep down, I think I knew even then something else was going on."

He described how Juna began making excuses to avoid returning to Tablerock for visits. Things she claimed she needed to stay in Austin for that he knew, once he checked up on her, just weren't true.

"I still kick myself for not pushing harder to get the truth back then because, obviously, I'd stopped trusting her," he admitted. "I knew things weren't right, but to her face, I just accepted whatever story she gave and privately, I stewed about it. I tried to convince myself the music program was changing her, and she'd bounce back once she got a break, but it was almost impossible to believe what I told myself."

Jackson stood and began to pace, his body unable to contain the nervous energy as he dredged up the past.

"The black eye..." Mario prompted.

Jackson inhaled. "Right. That."

He paused in his pacing, hands clenching and unclenching at his sides, and the silence that followed felt profound. I wasn't sure if Jackson was going to give us a history lesson and a eulogy or a confession and a plea for understanding.

I looked around the room and saw each of us caught in the gravity of Jackson's narrative as if the past had blown in with the icy storm, a haunting melody that continued to play long after the record had stopped spinning. These stories, these fragments of a life once lived, were the threads that connected us—not just to each other, but to Juna, to the girl who had vanished into the night.

For a moment, in the fire's warmth and the shared silence, it felt like she was right there with us, the ghostly fourth member of that childhood quartet, her angelic singing voice just beyond the reach of our ears.

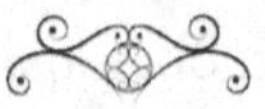

As Jackson and Mario shared memories from their intertwined pasts, I noticed the others remained uncharacteristically quiet. Josephine and Evie's pens moved, jotting down notes and whispers of the tales unfolding. But otherwise, our little band of amateur sleuths kept silent, allowing the two men's voices to fill the room uninterrupted.

"So, like I said, Juna seemed to pull away those last few months," Jackson continued after a weighted pause. "And I really did think that maybe it was just the music industry changing her, you know? Hardening her to the world, maybe. Making her less of a small-town girl."

"How do you mean?" I asked.

"She just seemed... lost in her own world after she started writing music with Cassidy."

"Cassidy?" Matt's voice was sharp, alert.

His eyes took on a faraway look. "Yeah, she pulled away right when she started spending all her time with Cassidy, her new co-songwriter. The songs they worked on together were so peppy and poppy compared to Juna's usual writing, which was dark and brooding. Personal." Jackson resumed his restless pacing, boots scuffing against the worn floorboards. "I didn't like Cassidy."

"Why not?" Landon asked.

"She seemed to have a way of isolating Juna from the rest of us. They'd cloister themselves away, writing those depressing songs for days on end." He shook his head angrily. "I asked Juna once if she was even still pursuing her own career or just becoming Cassidy's backup singer. She didn't like that at all."

Jackson's jaw tightened, hands balling into fists at the memory. "We had a huge fight about it. Juna swore writing with Cassidy was helping her find her 'true self' and her 'true voice.'" Disdain dripped from his words. "I thought Cassidy was just using her, twisting her into something she wasn't."

He turned to Mario, features etched with regret. "You remember how after that fight Juna stopped coming home as often? Started avoiding my calls for days?" At Mario's solemn nod, Jackson continued. "Well, that's when I decided to propose."

I blinked.

"I'm sorry, did you say propose?" Evie asked.

"That was your solution to a rocky relationship?" Laurie asked. "Marriage?"

"Look, I can see now that was the wrong thing to do. I get it. And I know it might sound baffling..." He gave an embarrassed half-shrug. "But in my mind, I thought proposing would fix everything. Remind Juna of our future together. I thought maybe that's why she was pulling away. That I hadn't done it yet."

Oh, goodness.

"Men," Josephine muttered.

"So you..." I prompted before we got too off track..

"I thought it was all getting to her. The pressure to succeed, to be perfect. I thought if I could anchor her, show her she wasn't alone, that..." Jackson's voice trailed off and he shook his head as if to dispel the notion as foolish now.

"You were young," Mario said.

"And stupid, apparently." Jackson resumed his relentless pacing like a caged lion. "The Saturday right before she disappeared, I went to Austin to meet her. I rented one of those little electric boats out on the lake. Had a whole romantic evening planned, catered dinner from that fancy hotel downtown. The works.

"I steered the boat to the middle of the lake." He smiled, lost in the memory. "It was just at sunset when I got down on one knee and asked her to marry me. The sky was ablaze in oranges and pinks, reflecting on the water. For a second—just one split second—it was all absolutely perfect."

Jackson's face clouded, his brief smile vanishing.

"What happened?" Evie's voice was a mere whisper.

"What happened was Juna burst into tears. She kept saying how sorry she was, how she never meant to hurt me." His tone descended into a pained whisper. "How she'd fallen in love with someone else and just didn't know how to tell me. That she didn't mean for it to happen."

I felt my heart clench at the image—Juna, overcome with emotion, her complicated dreams clashing with the reality of a life she had never wanted. And Jackson, the ring in his hand suddenly as meaningless as a pebble.

"What was your reaction to that bit of information?" Josephine asked him, her eyes sharp.

Jackson swallowed hard, his Adam's apple bobbing. "I'm not proud of how I reacted." He closed his eyes, features twisted in shame. "I was just so shocked. And so damn angry. I started shouting, demanding to know who it was. Saying absurd things to her..."

"Like?" Laurie's voice was soft but insistent.

His voice hitched. "Like how I'd kill whoever stole her from me. I didn't mean to say it. And I wouldn't have. But I threatened to kill the guy, and I demanded she tell me who it was."

Mario's head snapped up, surprise etched on his features.

"I know. It was wrong. I lost control of myself," Jackson admitted. "I was so full of rage. So hurt. When she wouldn't tell me who it was, I just reacted without thinking. I... I shoved her and she fell backward into the lake."

There was a collective intake of breath around the room. The fire seemed to pause in its dance, as if even the flames were shocked into stillness.

"I'm not proud of it, and I wish to God I could take it back." His eyes squeezed shut against the painful memories. "It all happened so fast, and I forgot she couldn't swim well. When she started thrashing around in the water, I panicked. I tried pulling her back into the boat, but I accidentally hit her."

I imagined the chaos—Juna in the water, Jackson's hands reaching for her.

Jackson's anguished eyes lifted, pleading for understanding. "I never meant to hurt her. I just snapped in the heat of the moment. But that's no excuse." His voice dropped to a tortured whisper. "No excuse for putting hands on a woman in violence. I mean, I know that. I was raised better than that."

The weight of his confession seemed to crush the air from the room. I noticed tears glistening in Josephine's eyes while Laurie stared at the floor, jaw clenched. Matt's arm wrapped protectively around Evie.

"I'll regret my actions that night until the day I die," Jackson said, defeat etched in every line of his body. "Nothing I can say or do will ever make it right, and since she vanished just a few days later, it's the last memory she had of me. I never even got to apologize. Not really."

The revelations had drained the anger from the room, leaving only sorrow and remorse in its wake.

Mario stepped forward, placing a hand on Jackson's shoulder. "I know that wasn't easy to share, Jack. Thank you for telling us the truth." His eyes glistened with emotion. "The past can't be changed."

Jackson managed a shaky nod, unable to speak.

"What happened after you pulled her out?" Matt asked, his voice steady despite the tension that gripped us all.

"She was coughing and crying, and I... I just held her. Told her I didn't mean it."

"And then?" Evie prodded.

Jackson's gaze met hers. "She pushed me away. We went back to shore. She got off the boat and left me there without saying another word."

"And that was the last time you saw her?" I asked.

"Yes," he whispered. "After that, just days later, she vanished. I should have looked for her after Clara told me what happened to her eye, should have tried to make things right, but I was scared. Scared of what I'd done, scared one of them would tell someone, scared I'd lose my job... my reputation in town."

I looked at Mario, his face shadowed and unreadable. "Mario, did you know about any of this?"

He shook his head, his gaze locked on Jackson. "I knew they had their troubles, but I never imagined... When she showed up with that black eye, she didn't tell me any of this. Neither did he."

Jackson stood, his posture that of a man carrying a burden of guilt that might never go away. "If you'll excuse me, I need some air."

We watched him go, his steps heavy as he descended the stairs.

"Do we believe him?" Laurie asked, her voice firm.

Mario's eyes flickered to hers, and he gave a slow nod. "I do. I've known him since forever, and I believe him. And since I believe him, one thing is clear now—I didn't know Juna at all."

Chapter Eighteen

THERE I WAS, STARING AT THE WHITEBOARDS THAT had become our makeshift command center, the criss-crossing lines of red marker weaving a web of connections and theories. My mind, usually a well of pragmatic solutions, churned with uncertainty.

The revelations from Jackson had shaken loose so many assumptions, scattering our theories like dried autumn leaves in a gust of wind. It appeared the lieutenant wasn't the villain we believed him to be.

Which meant someone else out there held answers.

I glanced past the names that hadn't been given their due diligence: Daryl Kingston. Trent Beasley. They had been touched on, sure, but not with the scrutiny they deserved. And Cassidy Melrose—the songwriter—had barely been a blip on our radar.

My gaze landed on Cassidy Melrose's name, scribbled in purple marker beneath a lyrical excerpt from the haunting song she and Juna wrote together.

Shattered glass, reflections fade,
A painted smile, a masquerade.
Behind the scenes, the truth unfolds,
A poison whispered, never told.

Both Mario and Jackson—separately—had mentioned how Juna drifted away from them when Cassidy appeared on the scene. And the two men, despite their shared history with Juna, didn't sound as if they ever discussed the Cassidy-induced distance with each other.

"How exactly did Juna and Cassidy meet, Mario?" I asked.

"At some music industry networking thing in Austin. Cassidy was already trying to break into the business as a songwriter. I remember Juna calling me after, going on and on about this incredible lyricist she just met."

"And Cassidy was brought in for questioning after Juna vanished?"

Mario came to stand next to me. "Yeah, they interviewed her. She claimed she and Juna were working late in the studio the night before, but parted ways around midnight and she hadn't seen her since."

"Did she have an alibi for her whereabouts when Juna disappeared?" Matt asked.

"Said she was at home, asleep." Mario frowned. "But her alibi was Daryl Kingston. They were..." He coughed. "Involved. So not exactly ironclad."

The lights in the loft flickered once, twice, before flaring to life. Appliances hummed and screens brightened as electricity surged through the building once more.

"Thank heavens," Evie breathed out, relief washing over her face as she opened her laptop with an eagerness that mirrored the spark of electricity that had just revived the silent machines around us.

Her fingers danced across the keyboard, summoning Cassidy's digital profile to the screen. As the SocialBook page loaded, she leaned forward, scanning.

"Mario, are you certain she was dating Daryl Kingston?" Evie's voice held an edge of doubt. Her eyes remained fixed to the screen, flicking back and forth as she scoured Cassidy's profile. "Because according to this, Cassidy's interested in women. It says right here she's a lesbian."

Evie turned the laptop to face us, pointing at the relationship status on Cassidy's page.

Mario's dark eyes widened in surprise as he took in this new information. "What? No way, they were together back then. Like I said, he was her alibi."

Evie just shook her head, turning the screen back around to examine it closer. "I'm telling you, it says it plain as day on her profile. Cassidy Melrose, lesbian."

"That doesn't mean anything. Lots of us experimented with things when we were younger," Josephine said.

We all swiveled in unison to stare at the conservative attorney.

"What? Despite my buttoned-up exterior, my younger days were far from dull—I embraced a life of excitement and daring, I'll have you know." Josephine either didn't notice our astonishment or pretended not to. She cleared her throat, as if to say 'moving on,' and narrowed her eyes, a sure sign she was kicking into gear. "Maybe Juna was tuning her guitar to a different strum, if you know what I mean."

Landon, Matt, and Mario wore matching expressions of utter bewilderment, as if Josephine had spoken Klingon. The notion that Juna's preferences might have leaned more Sapphic than straight had obviously never even crossed their minds.

Meanwhile, Laurie and Evie were nodding along sagely.

"To be honest, I've been wondering about that for a while now," Laurie admitted.

"Me too," Evie agreed. "Some of those lyrics she wrote with Cassidy? They seemed less than platonic. '*Underneath the surface glow, whispers dance, but who can know? In the rhythm of the night, a mystery veiled, out of sight.*' I mean, come on. That's a secret affair lyric if I ever heard one."

"That, and it was pretty obvious Clara was in love with her." I gestured at the photo of the two girls on the whiteboard, attached at the hip. "Sure, close friends interfere, but Clara's nosiness seemed almost romantically possessive. Maybe they were exes?"

"Huh," Laurie said.

The men's eyes remained fixed on us, their expressions frozen in a mixture of disbelief and astonishment.

"Really?" Josephine asked them. "Not a single, solitary one of you had this thought even once?"

They swapped uncertain glances. Matt, Landon and Mario's powers of romantic observation seemed limited to the most obvious of heteronormative pairings.

Josephine smirked, amused. "Boys, I do believe this revelation short-circuited your Neanderthal brains," she teased. "Don't strain yourselves too hard now."

Mario held up a hand. "Okay, let's just slow down and think this through..."

Poor Mario.

This trip down memory lane kept pulling the rug out from under him. Watching him grapple with yet another worldview shakeup...

Ugh.

"Oh, for heaven's sake, Mario, think about it. This Cassidy swoops in and shy little Juna is writing angsty ballads?" Josephine whirled to face us. "And why did Juna sign over all her music to that girl? We've been assuming the story that she wanted to change musical genres was true—but what if that wasn't the case at all? What if Cassidy wanted those songs and wanted Juna out of the way?"

"Cassidy had influence over Juna near the end," I mused aloud. "Enough to change her music, make her withdraw from Jackson and Mario." I turned to Mario. "You said you and Jackson both disliked Cassidy. Why?"

Mario crossed his arms, brow furrowed. "I don't know. Just bad vibes, I guess. She seemed..." He searched for the right word. "Calculated. Like everything was strategic, you know? I thought she was just using Juna."

Landon, who had been absorbing it all, finally spoke up. "Seems to me this Cassidy warrants a closer look. Anyone with that much sway over Juna right before she vanished should have raised more red flags."

I nodded. "I think you're right. We may have focused on the wrong angle here."

The possibilities churned in my mind.

Had Cassidy lured Juna away from safety and stability under the guise of artistic pursuit? Had her encouragement led Juna to a darker path than the small-town girl ever intended? Or had she manipulated the songs' ownership and then murdered Juna so she could... never come back and claim ownership? Never sue?

My instincts whispered that the truth still hid in shadows, but a new light was falling over the mystery of Juna's fate, illuminating cracks we had never noticed.

The room had settled into a new rhythm, punctuated by the occasional clack of Evie's keys and the soft rustling of paper as Josephine poured over notes. I was lost in thought, tracing the flickering shadows the restored lights cast upon the cats, when the sound of footsteps heralded Jackson's return upstairs. He stepped back into the loft, features schooled into a neutral expression that revealed nothing of the emotions churning beneath the surface.

"Welcome back," I said gently. "How are you holding up?"

Jackson just shook his head. He seemed different somehow, less like the man who bore the weight of years of guilt and more like someone who had just shed a heavy coat after a long winter's day.

Well.

That slight relief wouldn't last long.

Mario, not wasting a moment, cleared his throat. "So, we were talking while you were gone. The ladies have a new theory about Juna they want to run by you."

Jackson lifted an eyebrow, looking wary. "Okay..."

"They think Juna may have been gay," he stated bluntly.

Jackson blinked.

"She was gay," Josephine stated, as if declaring the sky blue or the grass green. "I doubt there's any other explanation."

Whatever revelation he'd been bracing for, that wasn't it.

"I don't know that we're that sure, Jackson. I think she might have been bisexual, at least," I amended (as if that might soften whatever new blow was hitting the man). "But we believe there's a good possibility she was interested in women."

Evie didn't look up from her computer screen. "We know Cassidy was gay," she said, grounding her statement in the certainty of the SocialBook profile before her. "Well, is gay. Like, right now." She pointed to her screen. "Says so right there."

"It seems like she fell in love with Cassidy," Laurie asked. "At least based on what she said to you on the boat when you proposed, and those song lyrics."

Jackson sank into a chair, his manner deflated yet pensive. "No," he said, the word almost a whisper. "Cassidy dated that roadie guy Juna fired, Daryl Kingston."

"Oh, my goodness," Josephine cut in. "I'm sure she had no reason to lie about her sexuality, who she was dating, or where she was on the night Juna disappeared when the police questioned her." She paused, waiting for a response, but Jackson looked gobsmacked. "For justice's sake, you men can't see lesbians past a threesome with you in the middle, can you?" Josephine exclaimed, exasperation coloring her words.

"Oh, Lord above, Josie," Laurie exclaimed, her voice laced with a hint of revulsion. She glanced toward me, a subtle apology in her eyes. "That's Evie's boyfriend, for heaven's sake. Let's not go there, shall we?"

Evie's mischievous smile widened. "Is it Hugh Jackman?" she asked, a twinkle in her eye. "If the other guy is Hugh Jackman, I'm good with the premise. I have a pacemaker. I can handle it."

"Stop it, you two." I shot Evie a look, and then Josephine a more menacing look. "I think this is all a little more nuanced than that."

Evie's playfulness faded, her expression turning earnest as she nodded in agreement. "Sorry, Mom."

"It is not more nuanced," Josephine said. "Cassidy did it."

"Did what, exactly?" Landon asked, folding his arms across his broad chest.

Josephine threw her hands up in exasperation. "Oh, you know what I mean! Whatever terrible thing we eventually determine happened to Juna, Cassidy was behind it. My gut says she's involved somehow."

Jackson stared blankly as he grappled to realign our new perspective with his memories. "She was gay?"

"Well, Jackson, if she was, she probably still is," Laurie told him.

"Or she was experimenting." Josephine was geared up for another startling revelation. "You know, in my youth—"

"Stop!" I held up a hand. "I think we're good with your personal anecdotes and observations for now."

"You only wish you'd lived my life," she said, then snapped her mouth shut while looking miffed.

I turned back to Jackson. "I know this is a shock."

"No, no... maybe. I mean..." Jackson let out a long breath, leaning forward to brace his arms on his knees. "It makes sense. Explains some things I couldn't understand back then." He scrubbed a hand across his jaw. "I just thought... I don't know. That she was shy. Wanted to wait. But maybe she just wasn't attracted to me that way." His eyes held a faraway look. "How could she not be, though? I was great looking in high school."

I bit back a smile at the touch of vanity peeking through his distress.

Jackson shook his head and turned to Mario. "Did you ever suspect she might be into women?"

Mario held up his hands. "I don't know, man. I'm still trying to wrap my mind around it. I don't understand women *now*. I sure as heck didn't understand them then."

Josephine made a sound of exaggerated exasperation. "It's a miracle either of you managed to stumble into romantic entanglements at all."

"I just wish I'd known. It pains me to think she couldn't be honest with me about who she was." Jackson's eyes took on a faraway sadness. "If what you say is true, all that time, she was living a lie."

"Well, someone likely knows the truth." I moved to the whiteboard, tapping Clara's name. "I say we call her back. If anyone has insight into Juna's romantic relationships, it would be her best friend. And I still say she had deeper feelings for Juna than—"

I came to an abrupt halt, my body freezing in its tracks.

Suddenly, it was as clear as day.

Well, to me at least.

The room was a blur as I acted on a sudden, unshakable instinct, snatching up Ursula with one hand and grabbing the magical platter from the drawer with the other. Ignoring the startled questions from my friends, I bolted down the stairs to the isolation room.

I could hear Josephine and Laurie's voices trailing after me, their attempts to rationalize my abrupt departure to Jackson echoing through the stairwell.

With a swift motion, I locked the door behind me. As I placed the cat gently on the gleaming platter, a surge of energy rippled through the air, tingling against my skin. The magic, ancient and mystical, awakened, casting an ethereal glow around us.

Ursula, with her striking green eyes, fixed her gaze upon me. "I hope you have a good reason for this. I was napping."

"I do," I began, "I need you to think back to the time you spent with Cassidy and Juna. Did you ever see them together in a way that would suggest they were more than just friends?"

The aged silvery feline blinked up at me. "They never bit each other on the neck."

Right.

Intimacy between cats and humans is... different.

"Okay, what about the two of them napping like a pile of kittens sleeping?"

The old cat blinked, her tail twitching as if she were sifting through years of memories. "Yes," she said at last, her voice a rusty purr. "They were often curled up together, like two cats in the sun. It happened often."

I nodded encouragement. "You're sure this was Juna's friend Cassidy?"

"Of course. I knew Cassidy. She gave me to Juna as a gift." Ursula nodded, her whiskers twitching. "I was a present. A symbol of their love, she said."

I swallowed hard, the pieces of the puzzle clicking into place with each word Ursula spoke. "Did they ever argue, Ursula? Think. It's very important."

The cat's eyes seemed to cloud over as she dug deeper into her recollections. "There were fights," she said slowly. "Loud, scary fights. Cassidy's words were sharp—like claws."

"What did they fight about?"

"I don't know. I didn't understand human noises, remember?"

"Anything you can remember, Ursula, would help."

"Cassidy threatened to reveal their secret," Ursula finally revealed, her words dropping like stones into the silent atmosphere, "to tell Juna's father and boyfriend about them."

I blinked. "You understood that much?"

"I understand threats," Ursula replied simply. Her words were a reminder of the primal instincts that govern the animal kingdom, the survival instincts that can cut through the noise and identify threats even when they were shrouded in another language.

"So Cassidy threatened Juna about her being gay."

"I don't know what that is," Ursula said, her ears flattening against her head. "Cassidy wielded the secret of them like a weapon against Juna. And when Juna resisted demands, Cassidy... she would strike her. I remember Juna crying, holding her cheek. Cats only draw blood in the face when they are ready to kill." She blinked. "I did not like it."

"What demands did she make of Juna?"

"I don't know."

Right.

Ursula could read the energy, but she didn't know the words.

Poor Juna, trapped in a relationship that had soured into something dangerous, something possibly deadly. "Ursula, why haven't you mentioned any of this before? Why didn't you tell us?"

The cat's gaze met mine, clear and direct. "You didn't ask me," she said. "You only asked about the night Juna went away."

Well.

The cat had a point.

In any case, Cassidy Melrose was no longer just a name on a board; she was a suspect.

I scooped Ursula into my arms, the platter clattering to the floor as I rose. "Thank you, Ursula," I whispered, stroking her fur. "You've been more help than you know."

Back in the loft, the atmosphere was charged with anticipation as I reentered the room, Ursula still cradled in my arms. The others gazed at me, their eyes filled with curiosity.

Well, the others except Jackson Everett.

He had no idea why I ran out of the loft with a cat under one arm and an antique platter under the other.

Landon broke the silence. "Ellie, what did you find... um, figure out?"

I took a deep, steadying breath before meeting the expectant gazes fixed upon me. Choosing my next words with care, I began.

"Based on everything Mario and Jackson have shared, I believe Juna and Cassidy spent a great deal of time together those final months. It was an intimate and volatile time." I let that sink in before continuing. "I can just picture the two of them curled up close, almost catlike in their affection in between cat fights of intense... um, ferocity, I guess."

Jackson's eyebrow shot up, but he remained silent.

"So, you're certain, then?" Laurie prodded. "That

Juna and Cassidy were... I don't know if together is the right word."

"Together is the right word." I gave a firm nod. "And I am."

"That's that, then," Matt said.

Mario nodded. "At least we know now."

Evie's eyes narrowed, and she leaned forward. "So, they were more than just friends?" She looked at Jackson. "Oh, Jackson, I'm so—"

Jackson held up a hand, halting her condolences. "It's fine," he said. His eyes were downcast, and some unreadable emotion flickered across his face. "I don't know why your mother meditating on another floor has changed everyone's view of this, but it's fine."

"I just feel bad for you. It can't be easy for you."

After a weighty pause, he took a deep breath and met Evie's kind eyes. "This was all fifteen years ago," he said, his matter-of-fact timbre belying the sentiment's bittersweet undertone. "We've all moved on since then."

He left the 'or tried to' unspoken, but it resonated nonetheless.

Jackson gave a small, rueful shake of his head before pressing his lips in a thin line, as if to keep unwanted emotions at bay. His fists briefly clenched where they rested atop his knees, then relaxed again. For all his attempts to minimize it, his posture betrayed that the revelations still stung.

"So, what now?" Josephine asked.

"Now?" I looked at Mario. "Now we call Clara back."

Chapter Nineteen

A CREASE FORMED ON LAURIE'S FOREHEAD, HER gaze swiveling toward me. "Ellie, why are you insisting on getting in touch with Clara again? Her stance on Mario looking into Juna's case couldn't have been clearer."

"I didn't say Mario should call her. I will, to contact her about Fluff—er, Ursula. That will be the excuse, anyway. As to why I want to call her?" With all the finesse of a seasoned performer, I let my dramatic pause take center stage. It was a beautiful moment, worthy of an Oscar—well, at least a nomination.

"Ellie?" Josephine asked. "Planning on telling us soon?"

Okay, maybe not an Oscar.

"It's all about the letter 'c.'"

"The letter 'c'?" Laurie asked.

"Yes."

Josephine's eyes executed a perfect Ping-Pong, bouncing from Laurie to me. "What's she getting at?" Her focus narrowed on me. "What's this you're going on about?" Her lips twisted into a puzzled frown. "Did we somehow land in a children's television episode?"

I gave her a gold-medal-worthy eye roll. "No. Think back—actually, we don't even have to think back." I turned to Evie. "Pull up that chat with Shari about Daryl again. Can you do that?"

"Affirmative." A flicker of determination in her eyes, Evie darted her fingers across the laptop keyboard. The hum of the computer filled the room as luminescent words appeared on the wall once more.

"There," I said, my finger jabbing toward the screen, my eyes locked onto Josephine, radiating anticipation. "Do you see it now?"

"I'm not blind, Ellie. It's the chat. We were all there, reading it live."

"You're not seeing it."

"Oh, my goodness, you're right," Laurie gasped.

"How did we miss that?" Landon asked.

Matt nodded. "Just one letter, but we missed it."

Josephine's voice edged with frustration as she demanded, "What are you all seeing that I'm missing here?"

"Shari says the person Daryl was hanging out with back then was Juna's romantic partner. But read it closely—she just *assumed* it was Jackson because he was

Juna's publicly known boyfriend at the time. In the entire conversation, she never says she knows any of that firsthand."

I stepped closer, scanning the magnified words. "In fact, from her phrasing, she pretty much says it's an assumption on her part based on Jackson and Juna's public relationship."

"Okay. You got me." Josephine's head bobbed in a slow nod, her eyes pulling together in a squint. "You're right, Ellie."

"I know." I turned back to the group.

"Well, don't sprain a muscle patting yourself on the back. What's this about the letter, though?"

"Evie," I said, "could you pull up that distasteful post Daryl made about Juna?"

"On it." Her fingers flew across the keyboard. A heartbeat later, the wall displayed Daryl's ugliness like a garish billboard at an art museum—impossible to ignore and offensive to good taste.

"Notice Daryl's comment with thc share," I began, "where he mentions that he and 'C' will toast Juna's misfortune. Who is this 'C'?"

"Cassidy," Matt said.

Mario shook his head. "It could be Clara. She found the cat, knew things she shouldn't have."

"I think we need to find out which one of them was so cozy with Daryl back then," Landon said.

I slid back onto the sofa. "Exactly. If Cassidy wasn't involved with Daryl, she lied to the police. And if she lied about that, she probably lied about her whereabouts when Juna vanished. And that makes her a suspect."

"But why?" Evie asked. "What motive did she have?"

Josephine gestured as if the answer were obvious. "What motive? With Juna out of the picture, Cassidy had total control over those hit songs they wrote together. The royalties, the rights, all of it."

"But Juna signed those over," Laurie reminded her.

"That's another thing. That Juna signed those over right before disappearing has bothered me from the beginning. As an attorney, I never would have advised such a move."

"That's another thing, for sure," I said, my fingers drumming a distracted rhythm on the armrest. "It makes little sense. She could have sold the songs to someone that would sing them if she didn't want to record them anymore. Why sign them over to another song writer that would just sell them?"

"And Cassidy was manipulative and controlling in their relationship," Laurie added. "Remember what"—Laurie looked down at Ursula and then back up at me—"um, you meditated on downstairs, about the relationship being volatile?"

An uneasy silence descended as Jackson stared at Laurie.

"What?" she asked. "Meditation is like a cosmic lost and found. You never know what might show up."

Jackson's gaze moved from me to Laurie, lingering a

moment longer than usual. He let the silence stretch, then conceded with a noncommittal, "Sure."

It was the verbal equivalent of a raised eyebrow, and I ignored it.

"Okay, so Cassidy seems a likely suspect for C based on potential means and conceivable motive." I swiveled my head, eyes landing on Mario. "But Clara finding the cat and carrier still feels off to me. Let's think through her possible motives again before I talk to her."

Mario's head moved in a vehement shake, as if he was a dog trying to fling off water. "I'm telling you, Clara didn't have any motive. She loved Juna."

"I know you believe that," I said gently. "But remember, Clara herself revealed some... inconsistencies. Bringing a carrier, searching around the car instead of looking for Juna on foot. It raises questions, Mario."

"Maybe she brought it just in case," he insisted. "You ride around with an animal carrier in your car, just in case. Maybe she did, too. Clara's not a criminal mastermind here. I'm telling you." The conviction in his tone was as unyielding as a mountain.

Josephine let out a sigh. "Or maybe, Mario, Clara helped Cassidy get rid of Juna. Maybe she was jealous of Cassidy. Maybe the three of them were all entangled." She threw her hands up. "We cannot rule anything out."

"Entangled how?" Matt asked, looking confused.

"Oh, for goodness' sake, are we circling back to that?" Josephine's words dripped with a mix of annoyance and disbelief. She leveled her gaze at him, a teacher ready to correct a stubborn student. "Do I need to spell it out for you again? It can be Sandra Bullock instead of Hugh Jackman, you know."

"Oh." Matt flushed. "Got it. Sorry."

"I feel like that's unlikely." I cleared my throat, redirecting us from speculating into dicey territory. Ursula had said nothing about Clara and Juna...

But then again, I hadn't asked.

"Regardless of what Clara's role may or may not have been, she knows things she hasn't told the police. I think we need to call her back and see if she'll open up more now that we can confront her with some of what we've uncovered."

Around the room, heads bobbed in agreement—a silent chorus echoing my sentiment.

All except for Mario, that is.

His face was a portrait of doubt, his eyes reflecting a sea of uncertainty. But he held his tongue, choosing silence over further argument. Then he let out a resigned sigh and said, "Okay. I hope you're right that she's holding something back. I just pray it's for some harmless reason." He looked up at the projection. "She knows I'm here because of the storm. You may as well use my Scoot."

While the others set up the laptop for another Scoot session we could all witness through the projection screen, I gathered my swirling thoughts and steeled myself for another attempt at unraveling the secrets Clara clung to so tightly.

Whatever the reason for Clara Adams's reticence, the time had come for the full truth to emerge.

The wall projection blinked to life as the video call connected, casting a cool glow across the tense faces gathered in anticipation. Clara's features, briefly puzzled, morphed to irritation when she realized it was me on the call and not Mario.

"You're not Mario," she declared, her words blunt. Suspicion flickered in her eyes, like the first sparks in a soon-to-be roaring fire.

I offered what I hoped was a disarming smile. "No, I'm not. My name is Ellie Rockwell. I'm so sorry to bother you again, but I wanted to let you know we have Juna's cat, Fluff, here at my animal shelter in Tablerock. She was surrendered to us recently after her owner passed away."

Clara's guarded expression didn't waver. "That's too bad about Maude. But what's it to me?" Her voice was honey laced with ice, words dropping with calculated indifference.

"Did you know Maude?" I let the smile bloom ever wider across my face.

Clearly, she was familiar with Maude. I hadn't dropped the name of Ursula-Fluff's now-deceased owner, but Clara had instantly connected the dots. Her immediate name-drop was a silent admission, a puzzle piece that fell into place without needing to be forced.

As if she realized she'd made a mistake, my question hung in the air without an answer.

"How did you know her?" I asked. "You're from Tablerock, aren't you?"

Clara maintained her stoic facade, not a flicker of emotion betraying her thoughts. "I'm a busy woman, Ms. Rockwell, and I fail to see how this concerns me."

I tilted my head. "Well, our records list you as an emergency contact for Fluff—who's called Ursula now, by the way—from when her microchip was implanted. Since you recovered her from Juna's car that night your friend went missing, I thought you might want to know." I smiled again, a huge one, like the sun breaking through the clouds. "That and, of course, she needs a new home now. In case you wanted to come get her."

"I don't live in Texas anymore. Haven't been back in years."

"I see."

"The cat's not my problem."

As if caught in a bizarre standoff, Clara and I stared at one another through the screen from two sides of the world. My side of the world was a tundra with Texas under a thick blanket of ice and snow and her side basked in the golden rays of the California sun, the warm outdoor palette making me long for spring.

Our words were the only bridge between our worlds—a bridge Clara seemed eager to burn.

"Ms. Adams," I said, my voice steady and solemn, "I do believe this is your problem. I need to be direct here. Certain... discrepancies have emerged regarding your involvement on the night Juna vanished. Besides trying to take care of her cat, I'm looking for answers."

Clara's eyes darted to the side for a moment of uncertainty before returning to meet mine. A spark of defiance ignited in their depths, challenging the words I'd delivered. "Discrepancies?" she echoed, rolling the word around her tongue as if it were a foreign language she was trying to decipher.

"Yes. That's what I said."

"Why should it matter to me what some cat shelter worker thinks about an event that transpired fifteen years ago? Look, lady, I get that you're bored, but go poke into someone else's life." Her words, although sharp, were steeped in a dismissive casualness, as if swatting away an insignificant annoyance.

I ignored her little speech and pressed on. "Why did you show up with a cat carrier despitc having no reason to expect to transport a cat from the scene? Why did you search around the car instead of calling out for Juna—"

Oops.

A slip.

How could I have known that? I couldn't.

Not unless the cat had told me.

Clara tensed, a pronounced twitch developing in her cheek. "Who the hell told you that nonsense?"

Caught off guard, I responded without a second's hesitation. "I have visions."

"You have visions?" she echoed, her tone laced with a mix of disbelief.

"I know how it sounds." Oh, I was acutely aware of how ludicrous it sounded. Still, I was committed at this point and continued my line of questioning. "But you carried a cat carrier to retrieve Fluff from the car that night. Why did you bring it if you didn't know you'd need it? How did you know?"

Clara's gaze veered away from the screen, her head shaking in a mix of disbelief and frustration. A muffled voice echoed in the background, the words too distant and indistinct for me to decipher. With a sudden snap, Clara's gaze returned to me, her eyes seeming to carry a new weight.

"You know nothing," she bit out.

"I think I do. What were you looking for around the car?"

"Don't call me again." Clara made a sudden movement, her hand darting forward with an unmistakable intent to sever our digital connection. But before her finger could meet the disconnect button, a voice rang out from somewhere off-screen.

"No."

Clara's hand froze midair, her body tensing. She turned her head, conversing in hushed, heated tones with someone off-screen. I strained to hear, catching snippets of "crazy... shut up... too late... but Mario... hang up..." but the fragments of conversation were like puzzle pieces; intriguing, but not enough to form a coherent picture.

"Who is she talking to?" Laurie whispered.

Before any of us could guess, Clara faced the camera once more, her expression a blend of determination and unease. "Please. Let this go." It wasn't a question, and there was an edge of desperation in her voice.

Before I could respond, a figure stepped into view behind me.

"Jackson?" Clara gasped. "Are you running a bed-and-breakfast for the whole town, lady?"

"Clara, please," Jackson's voice resonated, his figure moving into the camera frame. His presence was a calming force, a counterweight to the tension building. "I know you want to safeguard her memory. But harboring secrets won't resurrect Juna."

Clara barked a laugh, a sound harsh and brittle, and then her startled expression underwent a swift transformation. Her eyes narrowed while a flush of anger seeped into her features. "If you hadn't let loose on her that day on the stupid boat, Jackson, none of this—"

"I get it now," Jackson started, his voice steady despite the whirlwind of emotions that had swept through him just moments ago. "I know about her and Cassidy," he continued. "We pieced together some of the puzzle, the signs that I should have seen back then. If you're not saying anything because you're trying to hide that from me, just don't. I know. I don't know enough to figure out what happened to her, Clara. You might."

Clara looked gobsmacked. Her eyes widened, her mouth forming a perfect 'O' of surprise. The news had hit her like a punch, leaving her momentarily stunned. She recovered quickly and said, "Bull. What do you think you know, Jackson Everett?"

"I know Cassidy and Juna were together while we were dating. All I can say is I wish Juna would have told me. I wouldn't have taken it well at first, but I'm not a monster, Clara. We could have worked through it. I hate she might have died thinking I would have hated her if I knew what she—"

"Just shut up, Jackson." Clara's expression transformed, her features hardening with anger while her eyes shone with unshed tears. It was a potent mix of emotions, a testament to the turmoil brewing under her composed exterior. "Bulls—"

"She was my best friend, too! Clara, I just want the truth!" The air between them seemed to crackle with tension, the atmosphere heavy with unspoken words and raw emotions. "I've told everyone here—I know that you never would have hurt her. I know that. But I also know you're keeping something from me. And I need to know."

Clara's eyes shifted downward, a maelstrom of emotions wrestling on her face. She looked up, her gaze focusing off to the side of the computer, as though she was lost in a sea of thoughts. When she turned her gaze back to Jackson, her face was etched with resignation, as if she had come to a difficult decision. "Oh, Jack," she murmured, her voice carrying a weight that spoke volumes.

"Just tell me, Clara. Please."

Whatever Clara's role in this mystery, whether unwitting player or intentional deceiver, the time had come for her to share what she knew.

And she seemed to know it.

A charged hush saturated the room as all eyes fixed on Clara's gigantic image on the wall. She seemed to war within herself, features etched with turmoil, before letting out a ragged breath. Her shoulders sagged as if a heavy weight had settled on them.

Even the cats stared at the projection with rapt attention.

"All right," she began, voice strained. "What I'm about to say... it won't be easy to hear. Just try to remember we were all young and stupid." She regarded Jackson, regret glistening in her eyes. "I know this will be especially hard for you, Jack. But considering how much you stumbled over on your own, you probably do deserve the truth."

Jackson's face hardened, his jaw rigid and unmoving beneath his skin—a clear testament to the tension he was grappling with. He gave a firm nod, steeling himself for the words about to spill from Clara's lips.

Clara inhaled. "Yes. Juna was a lesbian. I mean, we both were, though the actual term and lifestyle was foreign to both of us then. We were just kids. We only knew that we were... different, somehow." Her eyes took on a faraway sheen. "In a town like Tablerock, it wasn't something we could tell people and for a long time, it was like a secret shame we shared."

I saw Jackson's almost imperceptible flinch.

"Even so, she cared for you, Jack," Clara assured the now thirtysomething man with a gentleness that softened her previous harsh demeanor. "Juna wanted with all her heart for it to work between you two. But it just..." Her voice trailed off, her words lost in the heavy silence, punctuated only by a mournful shake of her head. "It would never work, regardless of your patience."

"I know," he said.

"And you were so patient, especially regarding... physical intimacy." A flush of color bloomed on Clara's cheeks, an unexpected sign of discomfort that added a layer of vulnerability to her demeanor. "Things most boys craved, you never demanded of her. She was so grateful to you for that."

Her words were a testament to his character, a tribute to the respect and understanding he had shown Juna. It was a bittersweet acknowledgment of a love that was appreciated, but not enough to bend reality.

Tension radiated from Jackson's braced body, a

pronounced cord of muscle popping in his neck. After a heavy silence, he spoke, voice emerging rough and choked. "That's nice to hear and all, but Clara, I gotta tell you—I wish she would've trusted me enough to tell me."

"I know," Clara sighed, her own regret clear. "Things were different then. Small towns breed small minds sometimes. Juna wasn't sure what was going on with her, why she felt the way she did, and she couldn't tell you what she didn't know about herself." Her tone turned icy. "That damned Daryl, though..."

At the name, Jackson's head jerked up. "What about him?"

"He forced a kiss on Juna after a show once. Pinned her against a wall at the Whiskey. That's why she fired him." Anger sparked in Clara's eyes at the memory. "And get this, he was livid over it—which was just the most ridiculous thing in the world. She just wanted to forget it, but he stewed over it. Swore he'd have revenge for her rejecting him."

Jackson's hands curled into fists, knuckles whitening. "That rotten piece of filth. If I'd known, I would've pounded his face straight into the dirt."

"Which is precisely why she didn't tell you, you know," Clara said with a sad shake of her head. "Anyway, Daryl craved payback. His friend got close to Juna and pushed her to confront who she was. Daryl, you see, was sure that's the only reason a woman would reject him. That she was gay. If Juna was straight, she would have still kicked that guy right in the crotch, but it just so happened his arrogant pea brain hit a bullseye."

"His friend was Cassidy Melrose," I said.

"Yes." Her eyes traveled over both of us. "She seduced Juna, persuaded her to admit she preferred women. Recorded what Juna said. Recorded them together. Saved it." Clara's lips twisted with distaste. "Then she threatened exposure unless Juna paid up."

"The songs," Josephine said. "She signed them over to silence Cassidy."

Clara's nod was bleak. "But even after that, Cassidy kept demanding more—more money, more songs, more, more, more or else she'd destroy Juna's life." She glanced aside once more. "Are you sure about this?"

"Who are you talking to?" Mario asked, baffled.

But I already knew.

My suspicions solidified when Clara swiveled the laptop. Time had matured her features, but she was still familiar, still similar to the girl in the newspaper. The revelation was as startling as it was profound, a twist in our narrative that was as unexpected as it was inevitable.

"Me," Juna said. "She's talking to me."

Shocked gasps echoed around the loft, a collective intake of breath that mirrored the surprise rippling through each of us. Behind me, Jackson dropped onto the sofa, as if the strength had fled his legs. Raw emotion carved deep lines across his features, creating a visage of a man grappling with a revelation that had upended his world. His reaction was a poignant testament to the depth of his feelings, a mirror reflecting the turmoil that this unexpected turn of events had unleashed.

"You're alive?" he rasped out, voice barely a whisper.

Juna gave a solemn nod, eyes brimming with unspoken remorse and things left unsaid. "I'm so very sorry, Jack. You, too, Mario."

Jackson and Mario stared wordlessly, anguish and relief warring across their faces.

"Well, that's one hell of a plot twist," Josephine said.

Chapter Twenty

We all moved to comfort Jackson and Mario, which meant we all shuffled into the camera's view like a disorganized band of extras on a movie set, supportive confusion and anticipation playing across our faces.

Juna's eyes widened, taking in the motley crew she'd drawn into her world.

"Wow," Clara deadpanned, squinting at the screen. "Did we stumble into a clown car? Just how many people are staying at your cat shelter?" She looked at Juna. "We should end this. There's no way this will stay out of the papers."

"It's okay." Juna shrugged, her gaze steady. "I don't want to do this anymore. I'm done playing hide-and-seek with my life. Look at how much they found out before you said anything."

Jackson continued to stare at the screen, his gaze locked on Juna's face. Emotions flickered across his features like shadows dancing on a wall—disbelief, hurt, confusion, gratitude. Each was a raw, unfiltered response to the truth that Juna had laid bare.

Mario looked gobsmacked, his eyebrows attempting a daring escape to his hairline. "We thought... we thought you were dead all this time."

"I know. You were meant to." Juna's gaze flickered like a candle caught in the wind, flitting between the two men. Her fingers twitched as if she was struggling to find something to hold on to. "I know you did," she repeated. "I never meant to hurt anyone. I was young. I just wanted to get away from Cassidy—and, honestly, I thought it was better for both of you to think I was dead than—"

Like a marionette on strings, Jackson's head yanked upward, every line of his body pulled taut with adrenaline. "You thought I'd prefer you dead than gay?" Though he struggled to maintain composure, disbelief was scrawled across his face. "Is that how little you thought of me back then?"

"No, Jackson, I—" Juna's words hung in the air, a pendent of apprehension. Her eyes, stormy and wide, had the haunted look of a cat stuck in a tree—or like someone who'd pulled the pin from a grenade and was waiting for the explosion.

Clara placed a protective hand on Juna's. "This is a lot for everyone. Maybe you should give them some time to process before you get into more details."

Juna shook her head, blinking back tears. "No, they

deserve an explanation. It's the least I can do after what I put them through."

"I'm not worried about them. I'm worried about you."

Juna took a deep breath, steeling herself. "I'm fine. They're not."

Conceding to Juna's unspoken demands, Clara flipped her wrist and let her hand flop toward the singer in a silent wave of compliance.

"I didn't know what to do when Cassidy threatened me," Juna began. "After a month, I couldn't eat. I couldn't sleep. I was sure my father would disown me for being gay—he was very religious, and I was sure he'd lose it. Cassidy was demanding I write more and more silly pop songs she could sell so she never had to work—oh, and so she'd be recognized as a brilliant songwriter even though she never wrote a word or a note anyone wanted to buy.

"After Jackson proposed, I—" Juna looked down. "I didn't know how to tell you that not only was I gay, but that I'd been cheating on you. On top of that, I would have had to tell you the person I'd been cheating on you with was a horrible person, a snake that was threatening to destroy me and everyone in my life."

Jackson flinched, the hurt clear on his face. But he remained silent, his gaze fixed on Juna.

"I know it seems baffling now, but back then, it seemed like the only way out was to disappear. I'd performed at a fundraiser for Maude's shelter, and when

I told her about my situation, she said she could help. Maude had helped people to escape their abusive husbands. It seemed the ideal answer. Dad would never know. You, Jackson, would avoid learning the truth about me, and Cassidy couldn't keep threatening me."

"Why did you trust Maude?" Evie asked.

"She was the only person I knew that was gay," Juna told my daughter. "She was the only one I could think of that might be able to give me advice."

Josephine leaned forward, intrigued. "Weren't you worried Cassidy might release her evidence once you made news as a missing person?"

Juna shook her head. "I knew she wouldn't dare. It would only bring suspicion on her and Daryl."

"Did your father know where you were all those years?" Laurie asked.

"Not at first. About six months later, I worked up the courage to call him. I finally admitted the truth about who I was." Sadness flickered in Juna's eyes. "That's when he told the police to stop investigating. He just wanted to protect me."

I thought back to the abandoned car, the frightened kitten left behind. "Why did you leave the kitten in the car that night?"

Juna looked ashamed. "I thought it would seem more believable if I left her there for Clara to find. Like something terrible must have happened because I would have never abandoned my cat."

"Only you did."

"No." Juna folded her arms across her chest, retreating slightly like a nervous armadillo. "Not really. I made sure Clara got her, and we already had arrangements for Maude to take her in. So I knew she'd be okay—and just in case she wasn't, we made sure we stayed as contacts on her microchip."

I tilted my head to observe Clara for only a second. "Clara helped you pull this off."

Juna glanced at Clara. "Yes."

"And that's why she moved to California, to join you."

Juna and Clara exchanged uneasy glances before nodding in confirmation.

Clara turned to Jackson, her expression apologetic. "I know you might not believe this, but I always liked you, Jack—but I was just so jealous you were with Juna, and I could never admit how I felt. Yes, when we left for California, I blamed you. But let's be real, here—I thought you hit her and, to be frank, I didn't much care if people thought you might be a murderer."

Jackson absorbed her words, the hurt giving way to resignation. "I never stopped feeling bad about that night. Not once." He ran a hand through his hair and let out a long breath. "I appreciate you both telling me the truth now, at least. Finding closure after all this time means more than I can say."

However flawed her actions, everything Juna had done was driven by fear, not malice.

With the truth unveiled, the healing might begin between all of them.

"I still have a few questions. What's the significance of the pendant?" Matt asked.

Juna's expression softened. "Jackson gave it to me for my eighteenth birthday. He had it made." She smiled at the memory. "The rose represented my song 'Bloom For Me' and the rubies were my birthstone."

I saw Jackson swallow hard, moved.

"That's what I was looking for that night around the car. When Juna and I met up, she was frantic that she'd lost it and when I went to pick up the cat, I tried to find it for her. Hey, wait a minute." Clara's eyes narrowed at me. "How *did* you know I did that? Are you really psychic or something?"

Laurie leaped into the conversation with the grace of a gazelle on roller skates. "Oh, Ellie, just, um, did some meditative mind gymnastics. You know, like building a mental Lego model of what might've gone down. While breathing super heavy. That's all."

I regarded Laurie out of the corner of my eye, a single eyebrow lifting in subdued amusement.

"Juna, are you aware that Cassidy moved to Los Angeles years ago?" Mario asked. "She's a successful songwriter now."

"The hell she is. She's selling Juna's songs," Clara

shot out. Juna's eyes flicked toward Clara, who returned a fleeting, furtive glimpse in kind. "Well, they *are* your songs!"

"Obviously, we know about Cassidy," Juna said. "When we heard she'd moved to LA, we were worried she might recognize me, even with my new identity. That's when Clara and I came up with creating the mysterious singer Cabal as my stage persona. It allows me to still release music and sell songs, but with total anonymity."

"Doesn't that get lonely?" Evie asked.

Juna shook her head, her expression solemn. "I know Cassidy is here in LA somewhere. I didn't want to risk her seeing me and figuring out I'm still alive. There's no telling what she'd do if she found out the truth."

"Why not just move somewhere else, then?" Jackson suggested. "Somewhere far away from Cassidy?"

"I've thought about it," Juna admitted. "But my career is established here. This is where I sell songs and work with producers I trust. I have an apartment in New York I use sometimes, but it's just easier to stay in LA and keep my distance from everyone." She reached over and squeezed Clara's hand. "Besides, anything that needs a face to face meeting Clara handles for me."

Jackson raised his eyebrows and glanced between them. "So you two... you're together, then?"

Juna looked uncomfortable, but Clara nodded. "Yes, we are."

"Well, I'm happy for you both." He met Juna's eyes

through the screen and, to his credit, Jackson's eyes only held warmth. "Considering everything you went through, it's good to know you have each other."

"But Juna," Evie said, interrupting the moment, "are you still that scared of what Cassidy could do? I mean, your dad knows you're both alive and gay. Now Jackson knows. You and Clara have been together for fifteen years." She shook her head in confusion. "I don't understand. Why hide anymore?"

"Jackson and Mario only found out today," Juna pointed out. "And hiding just became a routine, I guess. A way of life. It's second nature to me now." She looked down for a moment. "If I'm being honest, I don't know for sure what Cassidy would do if she uncovered I was still alive."

Josephine leaned forward. "Why not find out? Why not stop hiding and go public?"

"Going public puts everything at risk again. If Cassidy recognized me, who knows what she'd try to pull."

"But she can't blackmail you anymore," I pointed out. "You already signed over the rights to your songs. What leverage does she have now?"

"She still has those recordings of us together," Juna said uneasily. "If those got out now, it would be awful. So embarrassing."

Josephine waved a hand. "So? You come out on your own terms first. Announce you are gay and in a long-term relationship with Clara." She shrugged. "If Cassidy leaks anything, it will be old news, and she'll appear to be the villain."

"I wish it was that simple," Juna replied. "Have you seen that post from Daryl on Socialbook? They still hate me. I take away their threat of blackmail—what happens then? What will they try to destroy next?"

I could see the uncertainty on Juna's face.

Josephine leaned forward. "Juna, with your willingness to be public, you have leverage now. Cassidy Melrose committed extortion and Daryl alluded to knowing what happened to you on his social media. Will anyone care what they say if they're running their mouth while on trial for felony blackmail?"

Clara's gaze met Josephine's, their eyes locking across the miles for a moment before she turned back to Juna. "That would be an outstanding idea if it was fifteen years ago. The statute of limitations on what those two did ran out. They got away with it."

Josephine piped up, her voice laced with the dryness of a legal textbook. "Were these songs worth a cool $200,000 or more?" she asked. "Because if so, we're wading into first-degree felony territory. That's a one-way ticket to a vacation between five and ninety-nine years in a state-issued jumpsuit or a dent of up to $10,000 in your bank account. Or both."

"Yes. Yes, they were." Juna gave a small smile. "But it was still years ago."

Josephine launched into an explanation, her tone

shifting into the authoritative cadence of a seasoned attorney.

"The clock for extortion or blackmail crimes in Texas runs for five years. That means the Lone Star State has that long to get its legal ducks in a row and press charges. But it's not always as straightforward as watching sand run through an hourglass. There are loopholes. Exceptions to the rule of direct time."

She paused for a second, considering her words. "Did she recently sell a song? If so, maybe that's when the statute started because it was part of the ongoing crime. Or if our friendly neighborhood perpetrator takes an out-of-Texas vacation or gets a free stay at the state's expense for another crime, that clock might just hit the pause button. Last I checked, Cassidy's in California, isn't she?" Josephine raised her chin, a glint of daring in her eyes and a hint of a smirk playing about her lips. "So, the easiest million-dollar question is, how long has Cassidy been AWOL from Texas?"

Long enough, it turns out.

Chapter Twenty-One

THE FALLOUT FROM JUNA'S REVELATION WAS LIKE an emotional earthquake, sending shockwaves through our small town. As the ice thawed outside, so too did the bitter chill of secrets.

Juna's homecoming was met with pure joy.

I held Ursula as I watched Juna announce her survival, her relationship with Clara, and her alter ego as the mysterious Cabal. If anyone harbored prejudice, they kept silent—or, more likely, they were drowned out by the zeal and elation that rippled through the crowd as tiny Tablerock found out it could claim a mega-celebrity as one of their own.

The town welcomed her and Clara back with open arms, not a sliver of judgment about her sexuality or the dramatic self-protection ruse fifteen years before—and Ursula was practically popping gushy food cans in celebration at the idea of retiring to a California mansion with a celebrity owner.

Her joy was a stark contrast to Belladonna, who flattened her ears and swished her tail following each excited outburst, and as Clara and Juna signed Ursula's adoption papers, the black cat let out a low warning growl before turning up her nose and leaping contemptuously off the desk.

"Is she okay?" Clara asked.

"She'll be fine."

With a cacophonous yowl, the fur on Belladonna's neck raised at indignant attention.

Then she hissed at me.

Cassidy Melrose was charged with felony extortion after Josephine pushed the prosecutor to expedite the legalities. With Cassidy facing serious prison time if a jury of her peers found her guilty, she struck a plea deal for a lesser charge, and Juna regained control of her songs as part of the deal.

Daryl evaded meaningful consequences thanks to never traveling outside Texas, but he wound up in prison, anyway, on unrelated drunk driving charges he'd been avoiding.

It was good riddance to both of them.

Several years later, desperate for more fame and money from his role in Juna's story, he sold his version to

StreamFlix—but their portrayal revealed his cruelty, objectification of women, and a gleeful malice that was remarkably creepy on the small screen.

When the StreamFlix miniseries aired, Daryl was outraged by how he was portrayed. He felt the show depicted him as a villainous, one-dimensional character and he complained bitterly to anyone that would listen that the show presented an unfair, distorted version of events.

Cassidy agreed.

She sued him for defamation, making a grab for the StreamFlix money.

She won the case—only to have the money promptly seized by the state and given to Juna for restitution.

With the cases closed and the villains jailed, Juna invited the town to a small, private locals-only show at the Whiskey and when she stepped on stage to perform, rapturous cheers and applause thundered in waves too mighty to deny. Seeing Juna accept her community's love and support with beaming smiles of gratitude was profoundly moving.

Clara, standing between Jackson and Juna's father, wiped tears away as Juna belted out an emotional rendition of "Bloom for Me," the lights sparkling off the ruby pendant the police had returned to her and that Jackson had gifted her so long ago.

In the mirror of my mind, a reflection not
my own,
Caught in a masquerade, where my heart
has overgrown.
Your smile's like the sun, bright but far
away,
In your arms, I'm lost, in a play where I
can't stay.

Bloom for you, in colors not true,
Wishing I could be, the love that you see.
In this garden of pretense, my truth is the
fence,
Bloom for you, but I'm wilting too.

Your laughter fills the room, like a melody
in tune,
But inside I'm a storm, in a sky without a
moon.
You're dreaming of a life, with me by your
side,
But I'm a painted rose, with colors I can't
hide.

In another world, maybe I could be,
The one you need, in perfect harmony.
But here in this life, I'm an unsung
melody,
Loving you, but longing to be free.

Bloom for you, in shadows and light,
A love so deep, yet not quite right.
I'm the echo of a song, in your heart
where I long,
Bloom for you, in the twilight's sight.

Someday you'll find love, as real as the
dawn,
And I'll be a whisper in a wind that's
gone.
Bloom for you, was my silent plea,
In another life, maybe that could've
been me.

Laurie slanted toward me with the subtlety of a falling tree. "Are you kidding me? He couldn't tell there was an issue in their relationship from those lyrics?"

A surprised snort burst from me before I could stifle it, my shoulders shaking with the effort. "Sometimes, we only see what we want to see."

She gestured toward Landon, who was sitting beside Mario. "Speaking of not-so-hidden clues, is he moving in or not? It's been weeks since he brought it up."

I didn't want to talk about Landon moving in.

The thought made my stomach flip-flop like a fish on a line. Was I ready to take such a big step? Sure, I loved having Landon around, but living together was serious. What if he left the toilet seat up or I annoyed him by hogging the covers at night?

I knew Laurie's prying came from a place of caring, but I wasn't prepared to unpack all my jumbled emotions about cohabitation.

Not tonight.

I shushed her. "Quiet. Enjoy the music."

As the final chord rang out, the crowd leaped to their feet for a standing ovation. Juna wiped away tears as she took in the thunderous applause.

Gone was the frightened girl who once ran from this town, thinking it could never accept her. In her place stood a confident, radiant woman who had reclaimed both her music and her truth.

With truth, even the most fractured relationships could bloom again.

Thank you for reading! I hope you enjoyed the fifth book in the Silver Circle Cat Rescue Mysteries!

As the last page turns, things continue to unravel in the spice sixth installment, "Tacos, Tarot, and Murder."

Join Ellie and Evie Rockwell as their Cinco de Mayo celebration in Tablerock, Texas turns into a murder case colder than an untouched margarita!

KEEP UP WITH LEANNE LEEDS

Thanks so much for reading! I hope you liked it! Want to keep up with me?

Visit leanneleeds.com to:

Find all my books...

Sign up for my newsletter...

Like me on Facebook...

Follow me on Twitter...

Follow me on Instagram...

Thanks again for reading!

Leanne Leeds

Find a typo? Let us know!

Typos happen. It's sad, but true.

Though we go over the manuscript multiple times, have editors, have beta readers, and advance readers it's inevitable that determined typos and mistakes sometimes find their way into a published book.

Did you find one? If you did, think about reporting it on leanneleeds.com so we can get it corrected.

Artificial Intelligence Statement

Portions of this book were created with the assistance of AI tools used for editing, proofreading, and refining the text. However, the ideas, storyline, characters, and overall creative vision remain my own original work.

While some aspects of the cover image were generated using AI tools, it was done so under my creative direction and curation.

I want to acknowledge the use of these technologies as part of my creative process, while affirming that the essence of this work comes from my own imagination and effort.

Leanne Leeds

www.ingramcontent.com/pod-product-compliance
Lightning Source LLC
LaVergne TN
LVHW030908080826
845145LV00010B/2817

* 9 7 8 1 9 5 0 5 0 5 9 6 8 *